PENGUIN BOOKS

THE PENGUIN BOOK OF INDIAN GHOST STORIES

Ruskin Bond was born in Kasauli, Himachal Pradesh, in 1934, and grew up in Jamnagar (Gujarat), Dehradun and Shimla. His first novel, *The Room on the Roof*, written when he was seventeen, received the John Llewellyn Rhys Memorial Prize in 1957. In the course of a writing career spanning thirty-five years, he has written over a hundred short stories, essays, novels and more than thirty books for children. Three collections of the short stories, *The Night Train at Deoli, Time Stops at Shamli* and *Our Trees Still Grow in Dehra* have been published by Penguin India.

Although a prolific writer, this will be the first anthology Ruskin Bond will have edited.

THE PENGUIN BOOK OF INDIAN GHOST STORIES

Edited by
RUSKIN BOND

PENGUIN BOOKS

PENGUIN BOOKS
Published by the Penguin Group
Penguin Books India Pvt Ltd, 11 Community Centre, Panchsheel Park, New Delhi 110 017, India
Penguin Group (USA) Inc., 375 Hudson Street, New York, New York 10014, USA
Penguin Group (Canada), 10 Alcorn Avenue, Toronto, Ontario, Canada M4V 3B2 (a division of Pearson Penguin Canada Inc.)
Penguin Books Ltd, 80 Strand, London WC2R 0RL, England
Penguin, Ireland, 25 St Stephen's Green, Dublin 2, Ireland (a division of Penguin Books Ltd)
Penguin Group (Australia), 250 Camberwell Road, Camberwell, Victoria 3124, Australia (a division of Pearson Australia Group Pty Ltd)
Penguin Group (NZ), cnr Airborne and Rosedale Road, Albany, Auckland 1310, New Zealand (a division of Pearson New Zealand Ltd)
Penguin Group (South Africa) (Pty) Ltd, 24 Sturdee Avenue, Rosebank, Johannesburg 2196, South Africa

Penguin Books Ltd, Registered Offices: 80 Strand, London WC2R 0RL, England

First published by Penguin Books India 1993

All rights reserved

10 9 8

Typeset in Palatino by Digital Technologies and Printing Solutions, New Delhi

The editor and publishers would like to thank the following copyright holders for granting permission to use their stories in this volume : Sandip Roy for Satyajit Ray's 'Fritz' and 'Anath Babu's Terror', R. V. Smith for 'Ghost of Korya Khan', Sudhir Thapliyal for 'The Yellow-Legged Man', R. K. Narayan for 'Around a Temple', Jug Suraiya for 'A Shade Too Soon', Victor Banerjee for 'Red Hydrangeas', Ravi Shankar for 'Mixed Blood', O.V. Vijayan for 'The Little Ones', and Jaishankar Kala for 'The Loving Soul-Atmah'.

While every effort has been made to ensure that permission to reproduce copyright material included in the book was obtained, in the event of any inadvertent omission, the publishers should be notified and formal acknowledgements will be included in all future editions of this book.

Made and Printed in India by Swapna Printing Works Pvt. Ltd.

This book is sold subject to the condition that it shall not, by way of trade or otherwise, be lent, hired out, or otherwise circulated without the publisher's prior written consent in any form of binding or cover other than that in which it is published and without a similar condition including this condition being imposed on the subsequent purchaser and without limiting the rights under copyright reserved above, no part of this publication may be reproduced, stored in or introduced into a retrieval system, or transmitted in any form or by any means (electronic, mechanical, photocopying, recording or otherwise), without the prior written permission of both the copyright owner and the above mentioned publisher of this book.

Dedicated to the memory of my uncle,
James Bond,
Who was a dentist by profession and not,
As some believe, a secret agent . . . .
His epitaph reads:
Stranger! Approach this spot with gravity,
James Bond is filling his last cavity.

Contents

Introduction

When I was ten or eleven, my stepfather took me along on one of his shikar trips into the forests near Dehra. I dreaded these excursions. The slaughter of wild animals never did appeal to me. To see cheetal being potted from the back of an elephant, or a tigress being shot while it was drinking at a water-hole, did not strike me as being particularly noble or exciting.

But during one such week in the forest, I discovered that the forest rest-house in which we were staying had a shelf full of books concealed in a dark corner of the little sitting-room. In order to avoid the next monotonous 'beat' in the jungle, I feigned a headache and stayed back while the adults fanned out into the forest with their weapons. One of the first books I discovered was a tome called *Ghost stories of an Antiquary* by M.R. James. I was hooked. The shikaris came and went with their plunder, while I remained shut in my room, convinced that the supernatural world had more to offer than the man-made excitement of the beat. Masterpieces such as 'Oh, Whistle and I'll Come to You, My Lad', 'The Mezzotint' and 'A Warning to the Curious' influenced me in more ways than I can tell and made me an addict of this genre of writing. Over the years, I have read and collected ghost stories from many lands, not only as literature, but as an important aspect of this earth's folklore.

But have I ever experienced the supernatural? Have I ever seen a ghost? These are questions that I am often asked.

In my childhood and youth I did not see any ghosts. But as I grew older, I found myself becoming more 'receptive' to the spirits of those who have left this world and may be living on another plane.

Lafcadio Hearn (1850-1904) accounts for this in his essay, 'A Ghost', when he speaks of 'the knowledge that a strange silence is ever deepening and expanding about one's life'—an expansion of consciousness that can only grow within us as we grow older.

'Meantime,' he writes, 'in the course of wanderings more or less aimless, there has slowly grown upon you a suspicion of being haunted, so frequently does a certain hazy presence intrude itself upon the visual memory. This, however, appears to gain rather than to lose in definiteness: with each return its visibility seems to increase . . . . And the suspicion that you may be haunted gradually develops into a certainty.'

Hearn was a traveller in the East, who spent most of his life in Japan; his essay does not strictly belong to a collection of Indian ghost stories. But his wanderlust gives his writing an international character, and his thoughts on the supernatural are very close to my own thinking on the subject. His little collection, *Karma and other stories and essays* (first published in 1921, many years after his death) is only one of many neglected but beautiful prose-poems by a writer who sought to break through the barriers between the quick and the dead.

Ghosts do not recognize our impermanent, man-made frontiers. Still, for the purposes of this anthology we have adopted the geographical approach and confined ourselves largely to ghosts and hauntings on the Indian subcontinent.

Who was John Lang, and how did he get into this book? Most of you will not have heard of him because his works lie forgotten in the archives of the British Museum and are not easily found elsewhere.

I became interested in John Lang when I came to live in Mussoorie in 1964, and learnt (from a friend in Australia) that he had died in Mussoorie exactly one hundred years earlier. Another coincidence lay in the fact that a year after his death, in 1865, Rudyard Kipling was born in Bombay. But I'll come to that later.

John Lang was, in fact, the first Australian-born novelist (*The Forger's Wife*, 1855). A barrister who fell out with the Sydney establishment, he sought his fortune in India and did well at the Calcutta bar, representing the Rani of Jhansi in her litigation against the East India Company. Later he edited *The Mofussilite*, an up-country newspaper, and became a regular contributor to Charles Dickens' magazine, *Household Words*, spending his last years in Landour, Mussoorie. When I discovered that he had died here, I went in search of his grave, and after several fruitless but fascinating visits to the Camel's Back cemetery, discovered it hidden by a layer of moss, ferns and periwinkle. Years later, when I found his story about the Meerut cemetery, in 'Wanderings in India', published in *Household Words*, 23 January 1858, I was struck by the similarity between his own experience and mine. There is no tangible ghost in his story and yet it is full of the ghosts of long-dead soldiers, and their wives and children, and the reader is left feeling quite haunted by their proximity.

Kipling's early writing, especially in *Plain Tales from the Hills* (which headed the bestseller lists in 1890), is not dissimilar to Lang's. Both were young men who took a rather satirical look at English society in India. Both saw everything larger than life, brighter than life. Lang poked fun at the British and became unpopular with them, one reason why his novels on India (*The Wetherbys*, etc.) fell into neglect. He died at the age of forty-seven. Kipling, as he grew older, became a champion of Empire, and met with the approval of his countrymen.

Did Lang's spirit transmigrate into the infant Kipling? There is much similarity of style, spirit and gusto in Lang's writing and that of Kipling as a young man. Do the spirits of dead writers sometimes enter the living, using them as mediums for the continuing expression of their personalities? Kipling himself was conscious of a 'daemon' at work within his subconscious, an influence over which he had little or no control:

> My Daemon was with me in the *Jungle Books*, *Kim*, and both Puck books, and good care I took to walk delicately, lest he should withdraw. I know that he did not, because when those books were finished they said so themselves with, almost, the watch-hammer click of a tap turned off. One of the clauses in our contract was that I should never follow up a 'success', for by this sin fell Napoleon and a few others. *Note here.* When your Daemon is in charge, do not try to think consciously. Drift, wait and obey. *(Something of Myself)*

This is a theory that requires further exploration.

Rudyard Kipling was a pioneer of the ghost story in India, and he is represented here by two of his best tales of the supernatural: 'The Strange Ride of Morrowbie Jukes' and 'The Mark of the Beast'. There were many others.

His friend Arthur Conan Doyle was deeply interested in all aspects of the occult and would have spent more time on the subject but for the success of his Sherlock Holmes stories. He did not visit India, but in 'The Brown Hand' taken from Doyle's collected *Tales of Twilight and the Unseen* he has a ghost from India visiting foggy London on a strange but compelling search.

As I have said, Kipling set the trend for the ghost story in India, and the genre became very popular in the early years of this century. *The Fourth Man,* by Hilton Brown, is a classic of its kind. It appeared in the Madras Mail Annual of 1930. Hilton Brown spent many years in India and wrote an excellent biographical appreciation of Kipling in 1945.

Over the years I have collected, among other things, old magazines, and I have a complete run of the *Indian State Railways Magazine* from 1927 to 1933. There is hardly an issue which does not carry a story of the supernatural. Among the contributors were A.C. Renny (a district collector), C.A. Kincaid (a civil servant of some distinction) and F.R. Corson, who must have served on the Railways in its pioneering days.

Nor has the ghost story been neglected by Indian writers after independence. Satyajit Ray loved writing ghost stories and mysteries. They come over very effectively in his simple, unadorned style. Although a deodar growing in Bundi is more unlikely than a ghost, we must allow him a little cinematic or supernatural license.

R.V. Smith, who writes a column for the *Statesman* called 'Quaint Corners', attributes his story to the 'old shikari', Cyril Thomas, a larger than life character who died last year, lying on a broken cot under a neem tree in the compound of St. Paul's church at Agra. This old familiar of the U.P. jungles had been struck down by a vehicle, for the sixth time in five years! As a young man he had lived a carefree life in the jungle, often going without food for days. Once he was taken for a ghost by dacoits when found cooking a meal in a cremation ground around midnight. Until a few years before his death he lived in an abandoned hut on the outskirts of Bainpur village, often walking the five or six kilometres into Agra to meet old friends. He did not write himself but he was a genuine teller of tales, and could keep an audience enthralled for hours.

Other contributors include writers like Jug Suraiya, O.V. Vijayan and Ravi Shankar who have made their mark in recent years; and the actor Victor Banerjee, who has chosen to live right next to the Landour cemetery, where he may sometimes be found rehearsing the gravedigger's scene from Hamlet. The collected short stories of Jug Suraiya and O.V. Vijayan have been published by Penguin India, as have selections from R.K. Narayan's gently ironical saga of Malgudi. Sudhir Thapliyal was for many years a *Statesman* correspondent. Both he and Jaishankar Kala belong to the Garhwal Himalayas, where the spirit world is still very much a part of the experience of people living in remote areas. Jaishankar Kala, an artist, now lives in Paris.

F.W. Bain was a 19th century English writer whose somewhat romanticsed translations from the Hindu epics gained great popularity in the West. Titles such as *Bubbles of the Foam, A Digit of the Moon, The Descent of the Sun,* and *In the Great God's Hair,* were all bestsellers in their time.

As for me, my contacts with the spirit world have been limited to the more ephemeral of ghosts; like that of great-aunt Lilian who, fifty years after leaving her earthly abode, returns at times to tuck me into bed late at night. I have never actually seen her at my bedside. I am a restless sleeper and my blankets often end up on the floor. Then an unseen hand recovers them and places them gently over me. I know it's great-aunt Lilian, because she used to do this for me when I was a boy.

And then there was the occasion at the Penguin, or rather, Puffin launching party, at a five-star hotel in New Delhi, just over a year ago. Before I could even sip the evening's first cocktail I saw, standing at the other end of the room, the outline of Mr Rudyard Kipling. Having seen so many portraits of him, I could hardly mistake him for anyone else. And I could see right through him: David Davidar of Penguin Books was approaching with two of his guests, and they walked right through Kipling's spectral form. For the first time in my life I fainted away completely.

Later, I found myself in the East-West Medical Centre, where I spent a peaceful night. The doctors could find nothing wrong with me. And I could hardly tell them that I had seen the ghost of Rudyard Kipling, for then they would have sent me to a different kind of hospital.

Why, I wonder, did Kipling visit me that evening. Was he annoyed because of something I had said or written about him? Or had he arrived simply to share in the success of Penguin India? Whatever the reason, it has prompted me to include *two* of his stories in this collection. I don't want him turning up again in the middle of another cocktail party, or at my birthday party, this evening.

19 May 1992 *Ruskin Bond*
Landour, Mussoorie

Out of the Dark

Ruskin Bond

At a ruin upon a hill outside the town,
I found some shelter from a summer storm.
An alcove in a wall, moss-green and redolent of bats,
But refuge from the wind and rain; and entrance once
To what had been a home, a mansion large and spacious;
Now dream-wrecked, desolate.
And as I stood there, pondering
Upon the mutability of stone, I thought I heard
A haunting cry, insistent on the wind—
'Oh son, please let me in,
Oh son, please let me in . . . .'

Just the soughing of the wind
In the bending, keening pines;
Just the rain sibilant on old stones;
Or was it something more, a voice
Trapped in the woof of time, imploring still,
And lingering at some door which stood
Where now I sheltered on a barren hill.

At home, that night, I settled down
To read, the bedlamp on. The night was warm,
The storm had passed and all was still outside,
When something, someone, moved about, came tapping on the door.

'Who's there?' I called.
The tapping stopped. And then,
Entreating, came that voice again:

Out of the Dark

'Oh son, please let me in!'
'Who's there, who's there?' I cried,
And crossed the cold stone floor,
Paused for a moment, hand on catch,
Then opened wide the door.
Bright moonlight streamed across the sill
And crept along the stair;
I peered outside, to right and left:
Bright road returned my stare.

But long before the dawn, I heard
That tapping once again;
Not on the door this time, but nearer still—
Now rapping quickly on the window-pane.
I lay quite still and held my breath
And thought—surely it's the old oak tree,
Leaves gently tapping on the glass,
Or a moth, or some great beetle winging past.
But through the darkness, pressing in,
As though in me it sought its will,
As though in me it yet would dwell—
'Oh son, please let me in . . . .
Oh son, please let me in!'

Underdone, overdone, undone!

F.W. Bain

There was once a Brahman named Kritákrita[1] who neglected the study of the Wédas, and walked in the black path, abandoning all his duties,[2] and associating with gamblers, harlots, and outcasts. And he frequented the cemeteries at night, and became familiar with ghosts and vampires and dead bodies, and impure and unholy rites and incantations. And one night, amid the flaming of funeral pyres and the reek of burning corpses, a certain vampire[3] of his acquaintance said to him: 'I am hungry: bring me fresh meat to devour, or I will tear you in pieces.' Then Kritákrita said: 'I will bring it, but not for nothing. What will you give me for it?' The vampire replied: 'Bring me a newly slain Brahman, and I will teach you a spell for raising the dead.' But Kritákrita said: 'That is not enough.' And they haggled in the cemetery about the price. At last that abandoned Brahman said: 'Throw in a pair of dice that will enable me always to win at play, and I will bring you the flesh you require.' So the vampire said: 'Be it so.' Then Kritákrita went away, and knowing no other resource secretly murdered his own brother, and brought him to the cemetery at midnight. And the vampire kept his word, giving him the dice, and teaching him the spell.

Then some time afterwards, Kritákrita said to himself: 'I will try the efficacy of this spell that the vampire has taught me.' So he

---

1 'Done and not done.'

2 *Achárabhrashta,* an apostate or decasted person. See *Manu,* p., 108.

3 *Wétála,* an uncanny being, generally possessing magic powers, given to occupying empty corpses and devouring human flesh.

procured the body of a dead Chándála,[4] and taking it at the dead of night to the cemetery, placed it on the ground, and began to recite the spell. But when he had got halfway through, he looked at the corpse, and saw its left arm, and leg, and eye moving horribly with life, the other half being still dead. And he was so terrified at the sight, that he utterly forgot the rest of the spell, and leaped up and ran away. But the corpse jumped up also, and a vampire entered its dead half, and it rushed rapidly after him, shuffling on one leg, and rolling its one eye, and yelling indistinctly: *'Underdone, overdone, undone!'*[5] But Kritákrita fled at full speed to his house, and getting into bed lay there trembling. And after a while he fell asleep. And then suddenly he awoke, hearing a noise, and he looked and saw the door open, and the corpse of that dead Chándála came in, and shuffled swiftly towards him on its left leg, rolling its left eye, with its dead half hanging down beside it, and crying in a terrible voice: *'Underdone, overdone, undone.'* And Kritákrita sprang out of bed, and ran out by another door, and mounting a horse, fled as fast as he could to another city a great way off.

And there he thought: 'Here I am safe.' So he went day after day to the gambling hall, and playing with his dice, won great sums of money, and lived at his ease, feasting himself and others. But one night, when he was sitting among the gamblers in the gambling hall, throwing the dice, he heard behind him a noise of shuffling. And he looked round, and saw, coming swiftly towards him on one leg, the corpse of that dead Chándála, with its dead half rotting and hanging down, and its left eye rolling in anger, and calling out in a voice of thunder: *'Underdone, overdone, undone.'* And he rose up with a shriek, and leaped over the table, and fled away by an opposite door and left that city, and ran as fast as he could, constantly looking behind him through the forest for many days and nights, never daring to stop even to take breath, till he reached

4 The lowest caste, whose very proximity was pollution to a Brahman.

5 This is all one word in the original, *únádhikákritamkritam*, 'what has been done is too little, too much, and not done at all.'

another city a long way off. And there he remained, disguised and concealed, as it were, in a hole. But all the gamblers in that gambling saloon died of fear.

And after some time he again accumulated wealth by gambling in that city, and lived in extravagance at his ease. But one night, when he was sitting with a courtesan whom he loved, in the inner room of her house, he heard the noise of shuffling. And he looked round, and saw once more the corpse of that dead Chándála coming swiftly towards him on one leg, with its dead half, from whose bones the flesh had rotted away, hanging down, and its left eye blazing with flames of rage, calling out with a voice like the scream of Ráwana: *'Underdone, overdone, undone!'* Then that woman then and there abandoned the body in her terror. And Kritákrita rose up, and ran out by a door, which led out upon the balcony, while the Chándála hastened after him. And finding no other outlet, Kritákrita flung himself down into the street, and was dashed to pieces, and died.

(Translated from the Sanskrit by F.W. Bain (1901), in *A Digit of the Moon*.)

The Meerut Graveyard

John Lang

I cannot leave Meerut without taking the reader to the churchyard of that station.

An Indian churchyard presents a very different aspect to a churchyard in England, or elsewhere. The tombs, for the most part, are very much larger. When first erected, or newly done up, they are generally, of *chunam* (plaster), which somewhat resembles Roman cement; but after exposure to only one rainy season, and one hot weather they become begrimed and almost black. The birds, flying from structure to structure, carry with them the seeds of various plants and herbs, and these if not speedily removed, take root and grow apace. A stranger wandering in the churchyard of Meerut might fancy that he is amidst ruins of stupendous antiquity, if he were not aware of the fact that fifty years have scarcely elapsed since the first Christian corpse was deposited within those walls which now encircle some five acres of ground, literally covered with tombs, in every stage of preservation and decay. I was conducted in my ramble through the Meerut churchyard by an old and very intelligent pensioner, who had originally been a private in a regiment of Light Dragoons. This old man lived by the churchyard, that is to say, he derived a very comfortable income from looking after and keeping in repair the tombs of those whose friends are now far away; but whose thoughts, nevertheless, still turn occasionally to that Christian enclosure.

'I get, sir, for this business,' said the old man, pointing with his stick to a very magnificent edifice, 'two pounds a year. It is not much, but it is what I asked, and it pays me very well, sir. And if you should go back to England, and ever come across any of her family, I hope, sir, you will tell them that I do my duty by the grave;

not that I think they have any doubt of it, for they must know—or, leastways, they have been told by them they can believe—that if I never received a farthing from them I would always keep it in repair, as it is now. God bless her, and rest her soul ! She was as good and as beautiful a woman as ever trod this earth.'

'Who was she?'

'The wife of an officer in my old regiment, sir. I was in her husband's troop. He's been out twice since the regiment went home, only to visit this grave; for he has long since sold out of the service, and is a rich gentleman. The last time he came was about five years ago. He comes what you call incog.; nobody knows who he is, and he never calls on anybody. All that he now does in this country is to come here—stop for three days and nights—putting up at the dak bungalow, and spending his time here, crying. It is there that he stands—where you stand now—fixing his eyes on the tablet, and sometimes laying his head down on the stone, and calling out her name: "Ellen ! Ellen ! My own dear Ellen!" He did love her surely, sir.'

'Judging from the age of the lady—twenty-three, and the date of her death—he must be rather an old man now.'

'Yes, sir. He must be more than sixty; but his love for her memory is just as strong as ever. She died of a fever, poor thing. And for that business,' he again pointed with his stick to a tomb admirably preserved, 'I used to get two pounds ten shillings a year. That is the tomb of a little girl of five years old, the daughter of a civilian. The parents are now dead. They must be, for I have not heard of 'em or received anything from 'em for more than six years past.'

'Then, who keeps the tomb in repair?'

'I do, sir. When I am here with my trowel and mortar, and whitewash, why shouldn't I make the outside of the little lady's last home on earth, as bright and as fair as those of her friends and neighbours? I have a nursery of 'em, as I call it, over in yonder corner—the children's corner. Some of 'em are paid for—others not; but when I'm there, doing what's needful, I touch 'em up all alike—bless their dear little souls. And somehow or other every good action meets its own reward, and often when we least expect it. Now, for instance, sir, about three years and a half ago, I was over there putting the nursery in good order, when up comes a grey-headed gentleman, and looks about the graves. Suddenly he stopped opposite to one and began to read, and presently he took out his pocket-handkerchief and put it to his eyes.

"Did you know that little child, sir?" said I, when it was not improper to speak. "Know it?" said he, "Yes. It was my own little boy." "Dear me, sir!" I answered him. "And you are, then, Lieutenant Statterleigh?" "I was," said he, "but I am now the colonel of a regiment that has just come to India, and is now stationed at Dinapore. But tell me, who keeps this grave in order?" "I do, sir," says I. "At whose expense?" says he. "At nobody's, sir," says I. "It is kept in order by the dictates of my own conscience. Your little boy is in good company here; and while I am whitening the tombs of the other little dears, I have it not in my heart to pass by his, without giving it a touch also."

'Blest, if he didn't take me to the house where he was staying, and give me five hundred rupees! That sort of thing has happened to me more than five or six times in my life—not that I ever hope or think of being paid for such work and labour when I am about it.'

'That must have been a magnificent affair,' said I, pointing to a heap of red stone and marble. 'But how comes it in ruins?'

'It is just as it was left, sir. The lady died. Her husband, a judge here, took on terribly; and ordered that tomb for her. Some of the stone was brought from Agra, some from Delhi; but before it was put together and properly erected he married again, and the work was stopped. I was present at the funeral. There was no getting him away after the service was over, and at last they had to resort to force and violence, in fact, to carry him out of the yard. But the shallowest waters, as the proverb says, sir, always make the most noise, while those are the deepest that flow on silently. Yonder is a funny tomb, sir,' continued the old man, again pointing with his stick. 'There!–close to the tomb of the lady which I first showed you.'

'How do you mean, funny?' I asked, observing nothing particular in the structure.

'Well, sir, it is funny only on account of the history of the two gentlemen whose remains it covers,' replied the old man, leading me to the tomb. 'One of these young gentlemen, sir, was an officer—a lieutenant—in the Bengal Horse Artillery; the other was an ensign in a Royal Regiment of the Line. There was a ball; and by some accident that beautiful lady of our regiment had engaged herself to both of them for the same dance. When the time came, both went up and claimed her hand. Neither of them would give way; and the lady not wishing to offend either by showing a preference, and finding herself in a dilemma, declined to dance with either. Not satisfied with this, they retired to the veranda, where they had some high words, and the next morning they met—behind the church there—and fought a duel, in which both of them fell, mortally wounded. They had scarcely time to shake hands with one another, when they died. In those days matters of the kind were very easily hushed up; and it was given out—though everybody knew to the contrary—that one had died of fever, and the other of cholera; and they were both buried side by side in one grave; and this tomb was erected over them at the joint expense of the two regiments to which they belonged. I get ten rupees a year for keeping this grave in order.'

'Who pays you?'

'A gentleman in Calcutta, a relation of one of them. I'll tell you what it is, sir. This foolish affair, which ended so fatally, sowed the seeds of the fever that carried off that beautiful and good woman, yonder. She was maddened by the thought of being the cause of the quarrel in which they lost their lives. I knew them both, sir, from seeing them so often on the parade-ground, and at the band-stand; very fine young men they were, sir. Yes; here they sleep in peace.'

'Whose tombs are those?' I asked, pointing to some two or three hundred, which were all exactly alike, and in three straight lines: in other words, three deep.

'Those are the tombs of the men of the Cameronians, sir. These graves are all uniform, as you observe. Fever made sad havoc with that regiment. They lost some three companies in all. Behind them are the tombs of the men of the Buffs, and behind them the tombs of the men of other Royal Regiments of Infantry—all uniform, you see, sir; but those of each regiment, rather differently shaped. To the right, flanking the infantry tombs, are the tombs of the men of the Cavalry, Eighth and Eleventh Dragoons, and Sixteenth Lancers. In the rear of the Cavalry are the tombs of the Horse and Foot Artillery men—all uniform, you see, sir. Egad! If they could rise just now, what a pretty little army they would form—of all ranks—some thousands of 'em, and well officered, too, they would be; and here a man to lead them. This is the tomb of Major General Considine, one of the most distinguished men in the British army. He was the officer that the Duke of Wellington fixed upon to bring the Fifty-third Foot into good order, when they ran riot in Gibraltar, some years ago. This is the tomb of General Considine, rotting and going rapidly to decay, though it was only built in the year eighteen hundred and forty-five.

'A great deal of money is squandered in the churchyards in India. Tombs are erected, and at a great expense frequently. After they are once put up it is very seldom that they are visited or heeded. Tens of thousands of pounds have been thrown away on the vast pile of bricks and mortar and stone that you now see within this enclosure; and, with the exception of a few, all are crumbling away. A Hindoo said to me the other day, in this graveyard, "Why don't you English burn your dead, as we do, instead of leaving their graves here, to tell us how much you can neglect them, and how little you care for them? What is the use of whitening a few sepulchres amidst this mass of black ruin?" I had no answer to give the fellow, sir. Indeed, the same thought had often occurred to me, while at work in this wilderness.

'Do you not think, sir, that the government, through its own executive officers, ought to expend a few hundred pounds every year on these yards, in order to avert such a scandal and disgrace? I do not speak interestedly. I have as much already on my hands as I can perform, if not more; but I do often think that there is really some reason in the Hindoo's remarks. All these graves that you see here so blackened and left to go to ruin, are the graves of men who have served their country and died in its service. Very little money would keep the yard free from this grass and these rank weeds, and very little more would make all these tombs fit to be seen; for neither labour nor whitewash is expensive in this part of the world. One would hardly suppose, on looking about him just now, that the sons and daughters of some of the best families in England are buried here, and that in a very short time no one will be able to distinguish the spot where each is lying: so defaced and so much alike will all the ruins become. What, sir, I repeat, is the use of throwing away money in building tombs, if they are not kept in repair? Instead of laying out fifty or a hundred pounds on a thing like this, why not lay out only five pounds on a single head-stone, and put the rest out at interest to keep it up?'

'Or a small slab with an iron railing round it?'

'Ah, sir; but then you would require an European to remain here, and a couple of native watchmen to see that the railings were not carried off by the villagers. As it is, they never allow an iron railing to remain longer than a week, or so long as that. They watch for an opportunity, jump over this low wall, and tear them down, or wrench them off and away with them.'

'But surely there is someone to watch the yard?'

'Yes, two sweepers. And when it is found out that a grave has been plundered of its railings, or that the little marble tablet which some have, has been taken away, they deny all knowledge of the matter, and are simply discharged, and two others are put into their places. It would not be much to build a comfortable little bungalow for an European—a man like myself, for instance—and give the yard into his charge, holding him responsible for any damage done, and requiring him to see that the grave of every Christian—man, woman, and child—is kept in good order. But horrible as is the condition of this churchyard—looking as it does, for the most part, more like a receptacle for the bodies of felons than those of good and brave soldiers and civilians, and their wives and children—it is really nothing when compared with the graveyard at Kernaul.

'Kernaul you know, sir, was our great frontier station some twenty years ago. It was, in fact, as large a station as Umballah now is. It had its church, its playhouse, its barracks for cavalry, infantry, and artillery, its mess-houses, magnificent bungalows, and all the rest of it. For some reason or other—but what that reason was I could never discover, nor anybody else to my knowledge—the station was abandoned with all its buildings, which cost the government and private individuals lakhs and lakhs of rupees. You may be pretty sure that the villagers were not long in plundering every house that was unprotected. Away went the doors and windows, the venetians, and every bar, bolt, nail, or bit of iron upon which they could lay their fingers; not content with this, the brutes set fire to many or nearly all of the thatched bungalows, in the hope of picking up something amongst the ruins. The church—the largest and best in the Upper Provinces, with no one to take care of it—was one of the first places that suffered. Like the other buildings, it was despoiled of its doors, windows, benches, bolts, nails, etc., and they carried away every marble tablet therein erected, and removeable without much difficulty. And the same kind of havoc was made in the burial-ground—the tombs were smashed, some of the graves, and especially the vaults, opened; and plainly enough was it to be seen that the low caste men had broken open the coffins and examined their contents, in the hope of finding a ring, or an earring, or some other ornament on the person of the dead.

'I went there a year ago on some business connected with the grave of a lady whose husband wished her remains to be removed to Meerut, and placed in the same vault with those of his sister, who died here about eighteen months since. I was not successful, however. There was no trace of her tomb. It was of stone, and had been taken away bodily, to pave the elephant shed or camel yard, perhaps, of some rich native in the neighbourhood. Looking around me, as I did, and remembering Kernaul when it was crowded with Europeans, it seemed to me as though the British had been turned out of the country by the natives, and that the most sacred spot in the cantonment had been desecrated out of spite or revenge. And it is just what they would do if ever they got the upper hand.'

(Whilst I write, it has just occurred to me that this old soldier and his family perished in the massacre at Meerut on the tenth of May. He was, in some way, related to, or connected by marriage with Mrs Courtenay, the keeper of the hotel, who, with her nieces was so barbarously murdered on that disastrous occasion.)

'Why, bless my soul!' exclaimed the old man, stooping down and picking up something, 'If the old gentleman hasn't shed his skin again! This is the skin of a very large snake, a cobra capella, that I have known for the last thirteen years. He must be precious old from his size, the slowness of his movements, and the bad cough he has had for the last four or five years. Last winter he was very bad indeed, and I thought he was going to die. He was then living in the ruins of old General Webster's vault, and coughing continually, just like a man with the asthma. However, I strewed a lot of fine ashes and some bits of wool in the ruin to keep him warm by night, and some fine white sand at the entrance, upon which he used to crawl out and bask, when the sun had made it hot enough; and when the warm weather set in he got all right again.'

'Rather a strange fancy of yours, to live upon such amicable terms with the great enemy of the human race?'

'Well, perhaps it is. But he once bit and killed a thief who came here to rob a child's grave of the iron railings, which its parents, contrary to my advice, had placed round it, and ever since then I have liked the snake, and have never thought of molesting him. I have had many an opportunity of killing him (if I had wished to do it) when I have caught him asleep on the tombstones, in the winter's sun. I could kill him this very day—this very hour—if I liked, for I know where he is at this very moment. He is in a hole, close to the Ochterlony monument there, in that corner of the yard. But why should I hurt him? He has never offered to do me any harm, and when I sing, as I sometimes do when I am alone here at work on some tomb or other, he will crawl up, and listen for two or three hours together. One morning, while he was listening, he came in for a good meal which lasted him some days.'

'How was that?'

'I will tell you, sir. A minar was chased by a small hawk, and in despair came and perched itself on the top of a most lofty tomb at which I was at work. The hawk, with his eyes fixed intently on his prey, did not, I fancy, see the snake lying motionless in the grass; or if he did see him he did not think he was a snake, but something else—my crowbar, perhaps. After a little while the hawk pounced down, and was just about to give the minar a blow and a grip, when the snake suddenly lifted his head, raised his hood, and hissed. The hawk gave a shriek, fluttered, flapped his wings with all his might, and tried very hard to fly away. But it would not do. Strong as the eye of the hawk was, the eye of the snake was stronger. The hawk for a time seemed suspended in the air; but at last he was obliged to come down, and sit opposite to the old gentleman (the snake) who commenced, with his forked tongue, and keeping his eyes upon him all the while, to slime his victim all over. This occupied him for at least forty minutes, and by the time the process was over the hawk was perfectly motionless. I don't think he was dead. But he was very soon, however, for the old gentleman put him into a coil or two, and crackled up every bone in the hawk's body. He then gave him another sliming, made a big mouth, distended his neck till it was as big a round as the thickest part of my arm, and down went the hawk like a shin of beef into a beggarman's bag.'

'And what became of the minar?'

'He was off like a shot, sir, the moment his enemy was in trouble, and no blame to him. What a funny thing nature is altogether, sir! I very often think of that scene when I am at work here.'

'But this place must be infested with snakes?'

'I have never seen but that one, sir, and I have been here for a long time. Would you like to see the old gentleman, sir? As the sun is up, and the morning rather warm, perhaps he will come out, if I pretend to be at work and give him a ditty. If he does not, we will look in upon him.'

'Come along,' said I.

I accompanied the old man to a tomb, close to the monument beneath which the snake was said to have taken up his abode. I did not go very near to the spot, but stood upon a tomb with a thick stick in my hand, quite prepared to slay the monster if he approached me; for from childhood I have always had an instinctive horror of reptiles of every species, caste and character.

The old man began to hammer away with his mallet and chisel, and to sing a very quaint old song which I had never heard before, and have never heard since. It was a dialogue or duet between the little finger and the thumb, and began thus. The thumb said:

'Dear Rose Mary Green!
When I am king, little finger, you shall be queen.'

The little finger replied:

'Who told you so, Thummy, Thummy?
Who told you so?'

The thumb responded:

'It was my own heart, little finger, who told me so!

The thumb then drew a very flattering picture of the life they would lead when united in wedlock, and concluded, as nearly as I can remember, thus:

Thumb:
'And when you are dead, little finger, as it may hap,
You shall be buried, little finger, under the tap.'

Little Finger:
'Why, Thummy, Thummy? Why, Thummy, Thummy? Why, Thummy, Thummy—Why?'

Thumb:
'That you may drink, little finger, when you are dry.'

But this ditty did not bring out the snake. I remarked this to the old man, who replied: 'He hasn't made his toilet yet—hasn't rubbed his scales up, sir; but he'll be here presently. You will see. Keep your eye on that hole, sir. I am now going to give him a livelier tune, which is a great favourite of his,' and forthwith he struck up an old song, beginning:

'Twas in the merry month of May,
When bees from flower to flower did hum.'

Out came the snake before the song was half over! Before it was concluded he had crawled slowly and (if I dare use such a word) rather majestically, to within a few paces of the spot where the old man was standing.

'Good morning to you, sir,' said the old man to the snake. 'I am happy to see you in your new suit of clothes. I have picked up your old suit, and I have got it in my pocket, and a very nice pair of slippers my old wife will make out of it. The last pair that she made out of your rejected apparel were given as a present to Colonel Cureton, who, like myself, very much resembled the great General Blücher in personal appearance. Who will get the pair of which I have now the makings, Heaven only knows. Perhaps old Brigadier White, who has also a Blücher cut about him. What song would you like next? Kathleen Mavourneen? Yes, I know that is a pet song of yours; and you shall have it.'

The old man sung the melody with a tenderness and feeling which quite charmed me as well as the snake, who coiled himself up and remained perfectly still. Little reason as I had to doubt the truth of any of the old man's statements, I certainly should have been sceptical as to the story of the snake if I had not witnessed the scene I have attempted to describe.

'Well, sir,' said the old man, coming up to me, after he had made a salaam to the snake and left him, 'it is almost breakfast-time, and I will, with your permission, bid you good morning.'

A Ghost

Lafcadio Hearn

Perhaps the man who never wanders away from the place of his birth may pass all his life without knowing ghosts; but the nomad is more than likely to make their acquaintance. I refer to the civilized nomad, whose wanderings are not prompted by hope of gain, nor determined by pleasure, but simply compelled by certain necessities of his being—the man whose inner secret nature is totally at variance with the stable conditions of a society to which he belongs only by accident. However intellectually trained, he must always remain the slave of singular impulses which have no rational source, and which will often amaze him no less by their mastering power than by their continuous savage opposition to his every material interest . . . . These may, perhaps, be traced back to some ancestral habit—be explained by self-evident hereditary tendencies. Or perhaps they may not. In which event, the victim can only surmise himself the *Imago* of some pre-existent larval aspiration—the full development of desires long dormant in a chain of more limited lives . . . .

Assuredly the nomadic impulses differ in every member of the class—take infinite variety from individual sensitiveness to environment: the line of least resistance for one being that of greatest resistance for another; no two courses of true nomadism can ever be wholly the same. Diversified of necessity both impulse and direction, even as human nature is diversified. Never since consciousness of time began were two beings born who possessed exactly the same quality of voice, the same precise degree of nervous impressibility, or, in brief, the same combination of those viewless force-storing molecules which shape and poise themselves in sentient substance. Vain, therefore, all striving to particularize the curious psychology of such existences: at the very utmost it is possible only to describe such impulses and perceptions of nomadism as lie within the very small range of one's own observation. And whatever in these be strictly personal can have little interest or value except in so far as it holds something in common with the great general experience of restless lives. To such experience may belong, I think, one ultimate result of all those irrational partings, self-wreckings, sudden isolations, abrupt severances from all attachment, which form the history of the nomad . . . the knowledge that a strange silence is ever deepening and expanding about one's life, and that in that silence there are ghosts.

II

. . . Oh! the first vague charm, the first sunny illusion of some fair city—when vistas of unknown streets all seem leading to the realization of a hope you dare not even whisper; when even the shadows look beautiful, and strange facades appear to smile good omen through lights of gold! And those first winning relations with men, while you are still a stranger, and only the better and the brighter side of their nature is turned to you! . . . All is yet a delightful, luminous indefiniteness—sensation of streets and of men—like some beautifully tinted photograph slightly out of focus . . . .

Then the slow solid sharpening of details all about you, thrusting through illusion and dispelling it, growing keener and harder day by day, through long dull seasons, while your feet learn to remember all asperities of pavements, and your eyes all physiognomy of buildings and of persons, failures of masonry, furrowed lines of pain. Thereafter only the aching of monotony intolerable, and the hatred of sameness grown dismal, and dread of the merciless, inevitable, daily and hourly repetition of things; while those impulses of unrest, which are Nature's urgings through that ancestral experience which lives in each one of us—outcries of sea and peak and sky to man—ever make wider appeal . . . . Strong friendships may have been formed but there finally comes a day when even these can give no consolation for the pain of monotony, and you feel that in order to live you must decide, regardless of result, to shake for ever from your feet the familiar dust of that place . . . .

And, nevertheless, in the hour of departure you feel a pang. As train or steamer bears you away from the city and its myriad associations, the old illusive impression will quiver back about you for a moment—not as if to mock the expectation of the past, but softly, touchingly, as if pleading to you to stay; and such a sadness, such a tenderness may come to you, as one knows after reconciliation with a friend misapprehended and unjustly judged . . . . But you will never more see those streets—except in dreams.

Through sleep only they will open again before you; steeped in the illusive vagueness of the first long-past day; peopled only by friends outreaching to you. Soundlessly you will tread those shadowy pavements many times, to knock in thought, perhaps, at doors which the dead will open to you . . . . But with the passing of years all becomes dim—so dim that even asleep you know 'tis only a ghost-city, with streets going to nowhere. And finally whatever is left of it becomes confused and blended with cloudy memories of other cities—one endless bewilderment of filmy architecture in which nothing is distinctly recognizable, though the whole gives the sensation of having been seen before . . . ever so long ago.

Meantime, in the course of wanderings more or less aimless, there has slowly grown upon you a suspicion of being haunted—so frequently does a certain hazy presence intrude itself upon the visual memory. This, however, appears to gain rather than to lose in definiteness: with each return its visibility seems to increase . . . . And the suspicion that you may be haunted gradually develops into a certainty.

III

You are haunted whether your way lie through the brown gloom of London winter or the azure splendour of an equatorial day; whether your steps be tracked in snows, or in the burning black sand of a tropic beach, whether you rest beneath the swart shade of Northern pines, or under spidery umbrages of palm: you are haunted ever and everywhere by a certain gentle presence. There is nothing fearsome in this haunting . . . the gentlest face . . . the kindliest voice—oddly familiar and distinct, though feeble as the hum of a bee . . . .

But it tantalizes—this haunting—like those sudden surprises of sensation *within* us, though seemingly not *of* us, which some dreamers have sought to interpret as inherited remembrances, recollections of pre-existence . . . . Vainly you ask yourself: 'Whose voice?—whose face?' It is neither young nor old, the Face: it has a vapoury indefinableness that leaves it a riddle; its diaphaneity reveals no particular tint; perhaps you may not even be quite sure whether it has a beard. But its expression is always gracious, passionless, smiling—like the smiling of unknown friends in dreams, with infinite indulgence for any folly, even a dream-folly . . . . Except in that you cannot permanently banish it, the presence offers no positive resistance to your will: it accepts each caprice with obedience; it meets your every whim with angelic patience. It is never critical, never makes plaint even by a look, never proves irksome: yet you cannot ignore it, because of a certain queer power it possesses to make something stir and quiver in your heart—like an old vague sweet regret—something buried alive which will not die . . . . And so often does this happen that desire to solve the riddle becomes a pain, that you finally find yourself making supplication to the Presence, addressing to it questions which it will never answer directly, but only by a smile or by words having no relation to the asking—words enigmatic, which make mysterious agitation in old forsaken fields of memory . . . even as a wind betimes, over wide wastes of marsh, sets all the grasses whispering about nothing. But you will question on, untiringly, through the nights and days of years:

'Who are you?—what are you?—what is this weird relation that you bear to me? All you say to me I feel that I have heard before—but where?—but when? By what name am I to call you, since you will answer to none that I remember? Surely you do not live: yet I know the sleeping places of all my dead—and yours I do not know! Neither are you any dream—for dreams distort and change; and you, you are ever the same. Nor are you any hallucination; for all my senses are still vivid and strong . . . . This only I know beyond doubt—that you are of the Past: you belong to memory—but to the memory of what dead suns? . . .'

Then, some day or night, unexpectedly, there comes to you at last, with a soft swift tingling shock as of fingers invisible, the knowledge that the Face is not the memory of any one face, but a multiple image formed of the traits of many dear faces—superimposed by remembrance, and interblended by affection into one ghostly personality—infinitely sympathetic, phantasmally beautiful: a Composite of recollections! And the Voice is the echo of no one voice, but the echoing of many voices, molten into a single utterance—a single impossible tone—thin through remoteness of time, but inexpressibly caressing.

IV

Thou most gentle Composite! Thou nameless and exquisite Unreality, thrilled into semblance of being from out the sum of all lost sympathies! Thou Ghost of all dear vanished things . . . with thy vain appeal of eyes that looked for my coming, and vague faint pleading of voices against oblivion, and thin electric touch of buried hands, . . . must thou pass away for ever with my passing, even as the Shadow that I cast, O thou Shadowing of Souls? . . .

I am not sure . . . . For there comes to me this dream, that if aught in human life hold power to pass—like a swerved sunray through interstellar spaces—into the infinite mystery . . . to send one sweet strong vibration through immemorial Time . . . might not some luminous future be people with such as thou? . . . And in so far as that which makes for us the subtlest charm of being can lend one choral note to the Symphony of the Unknowable Purpose—in so much might there not endure also to greet thee, another Composite One—embodying, indeed, the comeliness of many lives, yet keeping likewise some visible memory of all that may have been gracious in this thy friend . . . ?

The Brown Hand

Arthur Conan Doyle

Everyone knows that Sir Dominick Holden, the famous Indian surgeon, made me his heir, and that his death changed me in an hour from a hard-working and impecunious medical man to a well-to-do landed proprietor. Many know also that there were at least five people between the inheritance and me, and that Sir Dominick's selection appeared to be altogether arbitrary and whimsical. I can assure them, however, that they are quite mistaken, and that, although I only knew Sir Dominick in the closing years of his life, there were, none the less, very real reasons why he should show his goodwill towards me. As a matter of fact, though I say it myself, no man ever did more for another than I did for my Indian uncle. I cannot expect the story to be believed, but it is so singular that I should feel that it was a breach of duty if I did not put it upon record—so here it is, and your belief or incredulity is your own affair.

Sir Dominick Holden, C.B., K.C.S.I., and I don't know what besides, was the most distinguished Indian surgeon of his day. In the Army originally, he afterwards settled down into civil practice in Bombay, and visited, as a consultant, every part of India. His name is best remembered in connection with the Oriental Hospital which he founded and supported. The time came, however, when his iron constitution began to show signs of the long strain to which he had subjected it, and his brother practitioners (who were not, perhaps, entirely disinterested upon the point) were unanimous in recommending him to return to England. He held on so long as he could, but at last he developed nervous symptoms of a very pronounced character, and so came back, a broken man, to his native county of Wiltshire. He bought a considerable estate with an ancient manor-house upon the edge of Salisbury Plain, and devoted his old age to the study of Comparative Pathology, which had been his learned hobby all his life, and in which he was a foremost authority.

We of the family were, as may be imagined, much excited by the news of the return of this rich and childless uncle to England. On his part, although by no means exuberant in his hospitality, he showed some sense of his duty to his relations, and each of us in turn had an invitation to visit him. From the accounts of my cousins it appeared to be a melancholy business, and it was with mixed feelings that I at last received my own summons to appear at Rodenhurst. My wife was so carefully excluded in the invitation that my first impulse was to refuse it, but the interests of the children had to be considered, and so, with her consent, I set out one October afternoon upon my visit to Wiltshire, with little thought of what that visit was to entail.

My uncle's estate was situated where the arable land of the plains begins to swell upwards into the rounded chalk hills which are characteristic of the county. As I drove from Dinton Station in the waning light of that autumn day, I was impressed by the weird nature of the scenery. The few scattered cottages of the peasants were so dwarfed by the huge evidences of prehistoric life, that the present appeared to be a dream and the past to be the obtrusive and masterful reality. The road wound through the valleys, formed by a succession of grassy hills, and the summit of each was cut and carved into the most elaborate fortifications, some circular, and some square, but all on a scale which has defied the winds and the rains of many centuries. Some call them Roman and some British, but their true origin and the reasons for this particular tract of country being so interlaced with entrenchments have never been finally made clear. Here and there on the long, smooth, olive-coloured slopes there rose small, rounded barrows or tumuli. Beneath them lie the cremated ashes of the race which cut so deeply into the hills, but their graves tell us nothing save that a jar full of dust represents the man who once laboured under the sun.

It was through this weird country that I approached my uncle's residence of Rodenhurst, and the house was, as I found, in due keeping with its surroundings. Two broken and weather-stained pillars, each surmounted by a mutilated heraldic emblem, flanked the entrance to a neglected drive. A cold wind whistled through the elms which lined it, and the air was full of drifting leaves. At the far end, under the gloomy arch of trees, a single yellow lamp burned steadily. In the dim half-light of the coming night I saw a long, low building stretching out two irregular wings, with deep eaves, a sloping gambrel roof, and walls which were criss-crossed with timber balks in the fashion of the Tudors. The cheery light of a fire flickered in the broad, latticed window to the left of the low-porched door, and this, as it proved, marked the study of my uncle, for it was thither that I was led by his butler in order to make my host's acquaintance.

He was cowering over his fire, for the moist chill of an English autumn had set him shivering. His lamp was unlit, and I only saw the red glow of the embers beating upon a huge, craggy face, with a Red Indian nose and cheek, and deep furrows and seams from eye to chin, the sinister marks of hidden volcanic fires. He sprang up at my entrance with something of an old-world courtesy and welcomed me warmly to Rodenhurst. At the same time I was conscious, as the lamp was carried in, that it was a very critical pair of light-blue eyes which looked out at me from under shaggy eyebrows, like scouts beneath a bush, and that this outlandish uncle of mine was carefully reading off my character with all the ease of a practised observer and an experienced man of the world.

For my part I looked at him, and looked again, for I had never seen a man whose appearance was more fitted to hold one's attention. His figure was the framework of a giant, but he had fallen away until his coat dangled straight down in a shocking fashion from a pair of broad and bony shoulders. All his limbs were huge and yet emaciated, and I could not take my gaze from his knobby wrists, and long, gnarled hands. But his eyes—those peering, light-blue eyes—they were the most arrestive of any of his peculiarities. It was not their colour alone, nor was it the ambush of hair in which they lurked; but it was the expression which I read in them. For the appearance and bearing of the man were masterful, and one expected a certain corresponding arrogance in his eyes, but instead of that I read the look which tells of a spirit cowed and crushed, the furtive, expectant look of the dog whose master has taken the whip from the rack. I formed my own medical diagnosis upon one glance at those critical and yet appealing eyes. I believed that he was stricken with some mortal ailment, that he knew himself to be exposed to sudden death, and that he lived in terror of it. Such was my judgement—a false one, as the event showed; but I mention it that it may help you to realize the look which I read in his eyes.

My uncle's welcome was, as I have said, a courteous one, and in an hour or so I found myself seated between him and his wife at a comfortable dinner, with curious, pungent delicacies upon the table, and a stealthy, quick-eyed Oriental waiter behind his chair. The old couple had come round to that tragic imitation of the dawn of life when husband and wife, having lost or scattered all those who were their intimates, find themselves face to face and alone once more, their work done, and the end nearing fast. Those who have reached that stage in sweetness and love, who can change their winter into a gentle, Indian summer, have come as victors through the ordeal of life. Lady Holden was a small, alert woman with a kindly eye, and her expression as she glanced at him was a certificate of character to her husband. And yet, though I read a mutual love in their glances, I read also mutual horror, and recognized in her face some reflection of that stealthy fear which I had detected in his. Their talk was sometimes merry and sometimes sad, but there was a forced note in their merriment and a naturalness in their sadness which told me that a heavy heart beat upon either side of me.

We were sitting over our first glass of wine, and the servants had left the room, when the conversation took a turn which produced a remarkable effect upon my host and hostess. I cannot recall what it was which started the topic of the supernatural, but it ended in my showing them that the abnormal in psychical experiences was a subject to which I had, like many neurologists, devoted a great deal of attention. I concluded by narrating my experiences when, as a member of the Psychical Research Society, I had formed one of a committee of three who spent the night in a haunted house. Our adventures were neither exciting nor convincing, but, such as it was, the story appeared to interest my auditors in a remarkable degree. They listened with an eager silence, and I caught a look of intelligence between them which I could not understand. Lady Holden immediately afterwards rose and left the room.

Sir Dominick pushed the cigar-box over to me, and we smoked for some little time in silence. That huge, bony hand of his was twitching as he raised it with his cheroot to his lips, and I felt that the man's nerves were vibrating like fiddle-strings. My instincts told me that he was on the verge of some intimate confidence, and I feared to speak lest I should interrupt it. At last he turned towards me with a spasmodic gesture like a man who throws his last scruple to the winds.

'From the little that I have seen of you it appears to me, Dr Hardacre,' said he, 'that you are the very man I have wanted to meet.'

'I am delighted to hear it, sir.'

'Your head seems to be cool and steady. You will acquit me of any desire to flatter you, for the circumstances are too serious to permit of insincerities. You have some special knowledge upon these subjects, and you evidently view them from that philosophical standpoint which robs them of all vulgar terror. I presume that the sight of an apparition would not seriously discompose you?'

'I think not, sir.'

'Would even interest you, perhaps?'

'Most intensely.'

'As a psychical observer, you would probably investigate it in as impersonal a fashion as an astronomer investigates a wandering comet?'

'Precisely.'

He gave a heavy sigh.

'Believe me, Dr Hardacre, there was time when I could have spoken as you do now. My nerve was a byword in India. Even the Mutiny never shook it for an instant. And yet you see what I am reduced to—the most timorous man, perhaps, in all this county of Wiltshire. Do not speak too bravely upon this subject, or you may, find yourself subjected to as long-drawn a test as I am—a test which can only end in the madhouse or the grave.'

I waited patiently until he should see fit to go farther in his confidence. His preamble had, I need not say, filled me with interest and expectation.

'For some years, Dr Hardacre,' he continued, 'my life and that of my wife have been made miserable by a cause which is so grotesque that it borders upon the ludicrous. And yet familiarity has never made it more easy to bear—on the contrary, as time passes my nerves become more worn and shattered by the constant attrition.

'If you have no physical fears, Dr Hardacre, I should very much value your opinion upon this phenomenon which troubles us so.'

'For what it is worth my opinion is entirely at your service. May I ask the nature of the phenomenon?'

'I think that your experiences will have a higher evidential value if you are not told in advance what you may expect to encounter. You are yourself aware of the quibbles of unconscious cerebration and subjective impressions with which a scientific sceptic may throw a doubt upon your statement. It would be as well to guard against them in advance.'

'What shall I do, then?'

'I will tell you. Would you mind following me this way?' He led me out of the dining-room and down a long passage until we came to a terminal door. Inside there was a large, bare room fitted as a laboratory, with numerous scientific instruments and bottles. A shelf ran along one side, upon which there stood a long line of glass jars containing pathological and anatomical specimens.

'You see that I still dabble in some of my old studies,' said Sir Dominick. 'These jars are the remains of what was once a most excellent collection, but unfortunately I lost the greater part of them when my house was burned down in Bombay in '92. It was a most unfortunate affair for me—in more ways than one. I had examples of many rare conditions, and my splenic collection was probably unique. These are the survivors.'

I glanced over them, and saw that they really were of a very great value and rarity from a pathological point of view: bloated organs, gaping cysts, distorted bones, odious parasites—a singular exhibition of the products of India.

'There is, as you see, a small settee here,' said my host. 'It was far from our intention to offer a guest so meagre an accommodation, but since affairs have taken this turn, it would be a great kindness upon your part if you would consent to spend the night in this apartment. I beg that you will not hesitate to let me know if the idea should be at all repugnant to you.'

'On the contrary,' I said, 'it is most acceptable.'

'My own room is the second on the left, so that if you should feel that you are in need of company a call would always bring me to your side.'

'I trust that I shall not be compelled to disturb you.'

'It is unlikely that I shall be asleep. I do not sleep much. Do not hesitate to summon me.'

And so with this agreement we joined Lady Holden in the drawing-room and talked of lighter things.

It was no affectation upon my part to say that the prospect of my night's adventure was an agreeable one. I have no pretence to greater physical courage than my neighbours, but familiarity with a subject robs it of those vague and undefined terrors which are the most appalling to the imaginative mind. The human brain is capable of only one strong emotion at a time, and if it be filled with curiosity or scientific enthusiasm, there is no room for fear. It is true that I had my uncle's assurance that he had himself originally taken this point of view, but I reflected that the breakdown of his nervous system might be due to his forty years in India as much as to any psychical experiences which had befallen him. I, at least, was sound in nerve and brain, and it was with something of the pleasurable thrill of anticipation with which the sportsman takes his position beside the haunt of his game that I shut the laboratory door behind me, and partially undressing, lay down upon the rug-covered settee.

It was not an ideal atmosphere for a bedroom. The air was heavy with many chemical odours, that of methylated spirit predominating. Nor were the decorations of my chamber very sedative. The odious line of glass jars with their relics of disease and suffering stretched in front of my very eyes. There was no blind to the window, and a three-quarter moon streamed its white light into the room, tracing a silver square with filigree lattices upon the opposite wall. When I had extinguished my candle this one bright patch in the midst of the general gloom had certainly an eerie and discomposing aspect. A rigid and absolute silence reigned throughout the old house, so that the low swish of the branches in the garden came softly and smoothly to my ears. It may have been the hypnotic lullaby of this gentle susurrus, or it may have been the result of my tiring day, but after many dozings and many efforts to regain my clearness of perception, I fell at last into a deep and dreamless sleep.

I was awakened by some sound in the room, and I instantly raised myself upon my elbow on the couch. Some hours had passed, for the square patch upon the wall had slid downwards and sideways until it lay obliquely at the end of my bed. The rest of the room was in deep shadow. At first I could see nothing, presently, as my eyes became accustomed to the faint light, I was aware, with a thrill which all my scientific absorption could not entirely prevent, that something was moving slowly along the line of the wall. A gentle, shuffling sound, as of soft slippers, came to my ears, and I dimly discerned a human figure walking stealthily from the direction of the door. As it emerged into the patch of moonlight I saw very clearly what it was and how it was employed. It was a man, short and squat, dressed in some sort of dark-grey gown, which hung straight from his shoulders to his feet. The moon shone upon the side of his face, and I saw that it was chocolate-brown in colour, with a ball of black hair like a woman's at the back of his head. He walked slowly, and his eyes were cast upwards towards the line of bottles which contained those gruesome remnants of humanity. He seemed to examine each jar with attention, and then to pass on to the next. When he had come to the end of the line, immediately opposite my bed, he stopped, faced me, threw up his hands with a gesture of despair, and vanished from my sight.

I have said that he threw up his hands, but I should have said his arms, for as he assumed that attitude of despair I observed a singular peculiarity about his appearance. He had only one hand! As the sleeves drooped down from the upflung arms I saw the left plainly, but the right ended in a knobby and unsightly stump. In every other way his appearance was so natural, and I had both seen and heard him so clearly, that I could easily have believed that he was an Indian servant of Sir Dominick's who had come into my room in search of something. It was only his sudden disappearance which suggested anything more sinister to me. As it was I sprang from my couch, lit a candle, and examined the whole room carefully. There were no signs of my visitor, and I was forced to conclude that there had really been something outside the normal laws of nature in his appearance. I lay awake for the remainder of the night, but nothing else occurred to disturb me.

I am an early riser, but my uncle was an even earlier one, for I found him pacing up and down the lawn at the side of the house. He ran towards me in his eagerness when he saw me come out from the door.

'Well, well!' he cried. 'Did you see him?'

'An Indian with one hand?'

'Precisely.'

'Yes, I saw him'—and I told him all that occurred. When I had finished, he led the way into his study.

'We have a little time before breakfast,' said he. 'It will suffice to give you an explanation of this extraordinary affair—so far as I can explain that which is essentially inexplicable. In the first place, when I tell you that for four years I have never passed one single night, either in Bombay, aboard ship, or here in England without my sleep being broken by this fellow, you will understand why it is that I am a wreck of my former self. His programme is always the same. He appears by my bedside, shakes me roughly by the shoulder, passes from my room into the laboratory, walks slowly along the line of my bottles, and then vanishes. For more than a thousand times he has gone through the same routine.'

'What does he want?'

'He wants his hand.'

'His hand?'

'Yes, it came about in this way. I was summoned to Peshawur for a consultation some ten years ago, and while there I was asked to look at the hand of a native who was passing through with an Afghan caravan. The fellow came from some mountain tribe living away at the back of beyond somewhere on the other side of Kaffiristan. He talked a bastard Pushtoo, and it was all I could do to understand him. He was suffering from a soft sarcomatous swelling of one of the metacarpal joints, and I made him realize that it was only by losing his hand that he could hope to save his life. After much persuasion he consented to the operation, and he asked me, when it was over, what fee I demanded. The poor fellow was almost a beggar, so that the idea of a fee was absurd, but I answered in jest that my fee should be his hand, and that I proposed to add it to my pathological collection.

'To my surprise he demurred very much to the suggestion, and he explained that according to his religion it was an all-important matter that the body should be reunited after death, and so make a perfect dwelling for the spirit. The belief is, of course, an old one, and the mummies of the Egyptians arose from an analogous superstition. I answered him that his hand was already off, and asked him how he intended to preserve it. He replied that he would pickle it in salt and carry it about with him. I suggested that it might be safer in my keeping than his, and that I had better means than salt for preserving it. On realizing that I really intended to carefully keep it, his opposition vanished instantly. 'But remember, sahib,' said he, 'I shall want it back when I am dead.' I laughed at the remark, and so the matter ended. I returned to my practice, and he no doubt in the course of time was able to continue his journey to Afghanistan.

'Well, as I told you last night, I had a bad fire in my house at Bombay. Half of it was burned down, and, among other things, my pathological collection was largely destroyed. What you see are the poor remains of it. The hand of the hillman went with the rest, but I gave the matter no particular thought at the time. That was six years ago.

'Four years ago—two years after the fire—I was awakened one

night by a furious tugging at my sleeve. I sat up under the impression that my favourite mastiff was trying to arouse me. Instead of this, I saw my Indian patient of long ago, dressed in the long, grey gown which was the badge of his people. He was holding up his stump and looking reproachfully at me. He then went over to my bottles, which at that time I kept in my room, and he examined them carefully, after which he gave a gesture of anger and vanished. I realized that he had just died, and that he had come to claim my promise that I should keep his limb in safety for him.

'Well, there you have it all, Dr Hardacre. Every night at the same hour for four years this performance has been repeated. It is a simple thing in itself, but it has worn me out like water dropping on a stone. It has brought a vile insomnia with it, for I cannot sleep now for the expectation of his coming. It has poisoned my old age and that of my wife, who has been the sharer in this great trouble. But there is the breakfast gong, and she will be waiting impatiently to know how it fared with you last night. We are both much indebted to you for your gallantry, for it takes something from the weight of our misfortune when we share it, even for a single night, with a friend, and it reassures us to our sanity, which we are sometimes driven to question.'

This was the curious narrative which Sir Dominick confided to me—a story which to many would have appeared to be a grotesque impossibility, but which, after my experience of the night before, and my previous knowledge of such things, I was prepared to accept as an absolute fact. I thought deeply over the matter, and brought the whole range of my reading and experience to bear upon it. After breakfast, I surprised my host and hostess by announcing that I was returning to London by the next train.

'My dear doctor,' cried Sir Dominick in great distress, 'you make me feel that I have been guilty of a gross breach of hospitality in intruding this unfortunate matter upon you. I should have borne my own burden.'

'It is, indeed, that matter which is taking me to London,' I answered; 'but you are mistaken, I assure you, if you think that my experience of last night was an unpleasant one to me. On the contrary, I am about to ask your permission to return in the evening and spend one more night in your laboratory. I am very eager to see this visitor once again.'

My uncle was exceedingly anxious to know what I was about to do, but my fears of raising false hopes prevented me from telling him. I was back in my own consulting-room a little after luncheon, and was confirming my memory of a passage in a recent book upon occultism which had arrested my attention when I read it.

> In the case of earth-bound spirits, [said my authority], some one dominant idea obsessing them at the hour of death is sufficient to hold them in this material world. They are the amphibia of this life and of the next, capable of passing from one to the other as the turtle passes from land to water. The causes which may bind a soul so strongly to a life which its body has abandoned are any violent emotion. Avarice, revenge, anxiety, love and pity have all been known to have this effect. As a rule it springs from some unfulfilled wish, and when the wish has been fulfilled the material bond relaxes. There are many cases upon record which show the singular persistence of these visitors, and also their disappearance when their wishes have been fulfilled, or in some cases when a reasonable compromise has been effected.

'*A reasonable compromise effected*'—those were the words which I had brooded over all the morning, and which I now verified in the original. No actual atonement could be made here—but a reasonable compromise! I made my way as fast as a train could take me to the Shadwell Seamen's Hospital, where my old friend Jack Hewett was house-surgeon. Without explaining the situation I made him understand what it was that I wanted.

'A brown man's hand!' said he, in amazement. 'What in the world do you want that for?'

'Never mind. I'll tell you some day. I know that your wards are full of Indians.'

'I should think so. But a hand—'He thought a little and then struck a bell.

'Travers,' said he to a student-dresser, 'what became of the hands of the Lascar which we took off yesterday? I mean the fellow from the East India Dock who got caught in the steam winch.'

'They are in the *post-mortem* room, sir.'

'Just pack one of them in antiseptics and give it to Dr Hardacre.'

And so I found myself at Rodenhurst before dinner with this curious outcome of my day in town. I still said nothing to Sir Dominick, but I slept that night in the laboratory, and I placed the Lascar's hand in one of the glass jars at the end of my couch.

So interested was I in the result of my experiment that sleep was out of the question. I sat with a shaded lamp beside me and waited patiently for my visitor. This time I saw him clearly from the first. He appeared beside the door, nebulous for an instant, and then hardening into as distinct an outline as any living man. The slippers beneath his grey gown were red and heelless, which accounted for the low, shuffling sound which he made as he walked. As on the previous night he passed slowly along the line of bottles until he paused before that which contained the hand. He reached up to it, his whole figure quivering with expectation, took it down, examined it eagerly, and then, with a face which was convulsed with fury and disappointment, he hurled it down on the floor. There was a crash which resounded through the house, and when I looked up the mutilated Indian had disappeared. A moment later my door flew open and Sir Dominick rushed in.

'You are not hurt?' he cried.

'No—but deeply disappointed.'

He looked in astonishment at the splinters of glass, and the brown hand lying upon the floor.

'Good God!' he cried. 'What is this?'

I told him my idea and its wretched sequel. He listened intently, but shook his head.

'It was well thought of,' said he, 'but I fear that there is no such easy end to my sufferings. But one thing I now insist upon. It is that you shall never again upon any pretext occupy this room. My fears that something might have happened to you—when I heard that crash—have been the most acute of all the agonies which I have undergone. I will not expose myself to a repetition of it.'

He allowed me, however, to spend the remainder of that night where I was, and I lay there worrying over the problem and lamenting my own failure. With the first light of morning there was the Lascar's hand still lying upon the floor to remind me of my fiasco. I lay looking at it—as I lay suddenly an idea flew like a bullet through my head and brought me quivering with excitement out of my couch. I raised the grim relic from where it had fallen. Yes, it was indeed so. The hand was the *left* hand of the Lascar.

By the first train I was on my way to town, and hurried at once to the Seamen's Hospital. I remembered that both hands of the Lascar had been amputated, but I was terrified lest the precious organ which I was in search of might have been already consumed in the crematory. My suspense was soon ended. It had still been preserved in the *post-mortem* room. And so I returned to Rodenhurst in the evening with my mission accomplished and the material for a fresh experiment.

But Sir Dominick Holden would not hear of my occupying the laboratory again. To all my entreaties he turned a deaf ear. It offended his sense of hospitality and he could no longer permit it. I left the hand therefore, as I had done its fellow the night before, and I occupied a comfortable bedroom in another portion of the house, some distance away from the scene of my adventures.

But in spite of that my sleep was not destined to be uninterrupted. In the dead of night my host burst into my room, a lamp in his hand. His huge, gaunt figure was enveloped in a loose dressing-grown, and his whole appearance might certainly have seemed more formidable to a weak-nerved man than that of the Indian of the night before. But it was not his entrance so much as his expression which amazed me. He had turned suddenly younger by twenty years at the least. His eyes were shining, his features radiant, and he waved one hand in triumph over his head. I sat up astounded, staring sleepily at this extraordinary visitor. But his words soon drove the sleep from my eyes.

'We have done it! We have succeeded!' he shouted. 'My dear Hardacre, how can I ever in this world repay you?'

'You don't mean to say that it is all right?'

'Indeed I do. I was sure that you would not mind being awakened to hear such blessed news.'

'Mind! I should think not indeed. But is it really certain?'

'I have no doubt whatever upon the point. I owe you such a debt, my dear nephew, as I have never owed a man before, and never expected to. What can I possibly do for you that is commensurate? Providence must have sent you to my rescue. You have saved both my reason and my life, for another six months of this must have seen me either in a cell or a coffin. And my wife—it was wearing her out before my eyes. Never could I have believed that any human being could have lifted this burden off me.' He seized my hand and wrung it in his bony grip.

'It was only an experiment—a forlorn hope—but I am delighted from my heart that it has succeeded. But how do you know that it is all right? Have you seen something?'

He seated himself at the foot of my bed.

'I have seen enough,' said he. 'It satisfies me that I shall be troubled no more. What has passed is easily told. You know that at a certain hour this creature always comes to me. Tonight he arrived at the usual time, and aroused me with even more violence than is his custom. I can only surmise that his disappointment of last night increased the bitterness of his anger against me. He looked angrily at me, and then went on his usual round. But in a few minutes, I saw him, for the first time since this persecution began, return to my chamber. He was smiling. I saw the gleam of his white teeth through the dim light. He stood facing me at the end of my bed, and three times he made the low, Eastern salaam which is their solemn leave-taking. And the third time that he bowed he raised his arms over his head, and I saw his *two* hands outstretched in the air. So he vanished, and, as I believe, for ever.'

So that is the curious experience which won me the affection and the gratitude of my celebrated uncle, the famous Indian surgeon. His anticipations were realized, and never again was he disturbed by the visits of the restless hillman in search of his lost member. Sir Dominick and Lady Holden spent a very happy old age, unclouded, so far as I know, by any trouble, and they finally died during the great influenza epidemic within a few weeks of each other. In his lifetime he always turned to me for advice in everything which concerned that English life of which he knew so little; and I aided him also in the purchase and development of his estates. It was no great surprise to me, therefore, that I found myself eventually promoted over the heads of five exasperated cousins, and changed in a single day from a hard-working country doctor into the head of an important Wiltshire family. I, at least, have reason to bless the memory of the man with the brown hand, and the day when I was fortunate enough to relieve Rodenhurst of his unwelcome presence.

The Strange Ride of Morrowbie Jukes

Rudyard Kipling

Alive or dead—there is no other way.–*Native Proverb*

There is, as the conjurers say, no deception about this tale. Jukes by accident stumbled upon a village that is well-known to exist, though he is the only Englishman who has been there. A somewhat similar institution used to flourish on the outskirts of Calcutta, and there is a story that if you go into the heart of Bikanir, which is in the heart of the Great Indian Desert, you shall come across not a village but a town where the Dead who did not die but may not live have established their headquarters. And, since it is perfectly true that in the same Desert is a wonderful city where all the rich moneylenders retreat after they have made their fortunes (fortunes so vast that the owners cannot trust even the strong arm of the Government to protect them, but take refuge in the waterless sands), and drive sumptuous C-spring barouches, and buy beautiful girls and decorate their palaces with gold and ivory and Minton tiles and mother-o'-pearl, I do not see why Jukes' tale should not be true. He is a civil engineer, with a head for plans and distances and things of that kind, and he certainly would not take the trouble to invent imaginary traps. He could earn more by doing his legitimate work. He never varies the tale in the telling, and grows very hot and indignant when he thinks of the disrespectful treatment he received. He wrote this quite straightforwardly at first, but he has since touched it up in places and introduced Moral Reflections, thus:

In the beginning it all arose from a slight attack of fever. My work necessitated my being in camp for some months between Pakpattan and Mubarakpur—a desolate sandy stretch of country as every one who has had the misfortune to go there may know. My coolies were neither more nor less exasperating than other gangs, and my work demanded sufficient attention to keep me from moping, had I been inclined to so unmanly a weakness.

On the 23rd December, 1884, I felt a little feverish. There was a full moon at the time, and, in consequence, every dog near my tent was baying at it. The brutes assembled in twos and threes and drove me frantic. A few days previously I had shot one loud-mouthed singer and suspended his carcass *in terrorem* about fifty yards from my tent-door. But his friends fell upon, fought for, and ultimately devoured the body; and, as it seemed to me, sang their hymns of thanksgiving afterward with renewed energy.

The light-heartedness which accompanies fever acts differently on different men. My irritation gave way, after a short time, to a fixed determination to slaughter one huge black and white beast who had been foremost in song and first in flight throughout the evening. Thanks to a shaking hand and a giddy head I had already missed him twice with both barrels of my shot-gun, when it struck me that my best plan would be to ride him down in the open and finish him off with a hog-spear. This, of course, was merely the semi-delirious notion of a fever patient; but I remember that it struck me at the time as being eminently practical and feasible.

I therefore ordered my groom to saddle Pornic and bring him round quietly to the rear of my tent. When the pony was ready, I stood at his head prepared to mount and dash out as soon as the dog should again lift up his voice. Pornic, by the way, had not been out of his pickets for a couple of days; the night air was crisp and chilly; and I was armed with a specially long and sharp pair of persuaders with which I had been rousing a sluggish cob that afternoon. You will easily believe, then, that when he was let go he went quickly. In one moment, for the brute bolted as straight as a die, the tent was left far behind, and we were flying over the smooth sandy soil at racing speed.

In another we had passed the wretched dog, and I had almost forgotten why it was that I had taken horse and hog-spear.

The delirium of fever and the excitement of rapid motion through the air must have taken away the remnant of my senses. I have a faint recollection of standing upright in my stirrups, and of brandishing my hog-spear at the great white Moon that looked down so calmly on my mad gallop; and of shouting challenges to the camel-thorn bushes as they whizzed past. Once or twice, I believe, I swayed forward on Pornic's neck, and literally hung on by spurs—as the marks next morning showed.

The wretched beast went forward like a thing possessed, over what seemed to be a limitless expanse of moonlit sand. Next, I remember, the ground rose suddenly in front of us, and as we topped the ascent I saw the waters of the Sutlej shining like a silver bar below. Then Pornic blundered heavily on his nose, and we rolled together down some unseen slope.

I must have lost consciousness, for when I recovered I was lying on my stomach in a heap of soft white sand, and the dawn was beginning to break dimly over the edge of the slope down which I had fallen. As the light grew stronger I saw that I was at the bottom of a horseshoe-shaped crater of sand, opening on one side directly on to the shoals of the Sutlej. My fever had altogether left me, and, with the exception of a slight dizziness in the head. I felt no bad effects from the fall over night.

Pornic, who was standing a few yards away, was naturally a good deal exhausted, but had not hurt himself in the least. His saddle, a favourite polo one, was much knocked about, and had been twisted under his belly. It took me some time to put him to rights, and in the meantime I had ample opportunities of observing the spot into which I had so foolishly dropped.

At the risk of being considered tedious, I must describe it at length; inasmuch as an accurate mental picture of its peculiarities will be of material assistance in enabling the reader to understand what follows.

Imagine then, as I have said before, a horseshoe-shaped crater of sand with steeply graded sand walls about thirty-five feet high. (The slope, I fancy, must have been about sixty-five degrees.) This crater enclosed a level piece of ground about fifty yards long by thirty at its broadest part, with a rude well in the centre. Round the bottom of the crater, about three feet from the level of the ground proper, ran a series of eighty-three semi-circular, ovoid, square, and multilateral holes, all about three feet at the mouth. Each hole on inspection showed that it was carefully shored internally with drift-wood and bamboos, and over the mouth a wooden drip-board projected, like the peak of a jockey's cap, for two feet. No sign of life was visible in these tunnels, but a most sickening stench pervaded the entire amphitheatre—a stench fouler than any which my wanderings in Indian villages have introduced me to.

Having remounted Pornic, who was as anxious as I to get back to camp, I rode the base of the horseshoe to find some place whence an exit would be practicable. The inhabitants, whoever they might be, had not thought to put in an appearance, so I was left to my own devices. My first attempt to 'rush' Pornic up the steep sandbanks showed me that I had fallen into a trap exactly on the same model as that which the ant-lion sets for its prey. At each step the shifting sand poured down from above in tons, and rattled on the drip-boards of the holes like small shot. A couple of ineffectual charges sent us both rolling down to the bottom, half choked with the torrents of sand; and I was constrained to turn my attention to the river-bank.

Here everything seemed easy enough. The sand hills ran down to the river edge, it is true, but there were plenty of shoals and shallows across which I could gallop Pornic, and find my way back to *terra firma* by turning sharply to the right or the left. As I led Pornic over the sands I was startled by the faint pop of a rifle across the river; and at the same moment a bullet dropped with a sharp *'whit'* close to Pornic's head.

There was no mistaking the nature of the missile—a regulation Martini-Henry 'picket'. About five hundred yards away a country-boat was anchored in midstream; and a jet of smoke drifting away from its bows in the still morning air showed me whence the delicate attention had come. Was ever a respectable gentleman in such an impasse? The treacherous sand slope allowed no escape from a spot which I had visited most involuntarily, and a promenade on the river frontage was the signal for bombardment from some insane native in a boat. I'm afraid that I lost my temper very much indeed.

Another bullet reminded me that I had better save my breath to cool my porridge; and I retreated hastily up the sands and back to the horseshoe, where I saw that the noise of the rifle had drawn sixty-five human beings from the badger-holes which I had up till that point supposed to be untenanted. I found myself in the midst of a crowd of spectators—about forty men, twenty women, and one child who could not have been more than five years old. They were all scantily clothed in that salmon-coloured cloth which one associates with Hindu mendicants, and, at first sight, gave me the impression of a band of loathsome fakirs. The filth and repulsiveness of the assembly were beyond all description, and I shuddered to think what their life in the badger-holes must be.

Even in these days, when local self-government has destroyed the greater part of a native's respect for a Sahib, I have been accustomed to a certain amount of civility from my inferiors, and on approaching the crowd naturally expected that there would be some recognition of my presence. As a matter of fact there was; but it was by no means what I had looked for.

The ragged crew actually laughed at me—such laughter I hope I may never hear again. They cackled, yelled, whistled, and howled as I walked into their midst; some of them literally throwing themselves down on the ground in convulsions of unholy mirth. In a moment I had let go Pornic's head, and irritated beyond expression at the morning's adventure, commenced cuffing those nearest to me with all the force I could. The wretches dropped under my blows like nine-pins, and the laughter gave place to wails for mercy; while those yet untouched clasped me round the knees, imploring me in all sorts of uncouth tongues to spare them.

In the tumult, and just when I was feeling very much ashamed of myself for having thus easily given way to my temper, a thin, high voice murmured in English from behind my shoulder: 'Sahib! Sahib! Do you not know me? Sahib, it is Gunga Dass, the telegraph-master.'

I spun round quickly and faced the speaker.

Gunga Dass (I have, of course, no hesitation in mentioning the man's real name) I had known four years before as a Deccanee Brahmin loaned by the Punjab Government to one of the Khalsia States. He was in charge of a branch telegraph-office there, and when I had last met him was a jovial, full-stomached, portly government servant with a marvellous capacity for making bad puns in English—a peculiarity which made me remember him long after I had forgotten his services to me in his official capacity. It is seldom that a Hindu makes English puns.

Now, however, the man was changed beyond all recognition. Caste-mark, stomach, slate-coloured continuations, and unctuous speech were all gone. I looked at a withered skeleton, turbanless and almost naked, with long matted hair and deep-set codfish-eyes. But for a crescent-shaped scar on the left cheek—the result of an accident for which I was responsible—I should never have known him. But it was indubitably Gunga Dass, and—for this I was thankful—an English-speaking native who might at least tell me the meaning of all that I had gone through that day.

The crowd retreated to some distance as I turned toward the miserable figure, and ordered him to show me some method of escaping from the crater. He held a freshly plucked crow in his hand, and in reply to my question climbed slowly on a platform of sand which ran in front of the holes, and commenced lighting a fire there in silence. Dried bents, sand-poppies, and driftwood burn quickly; and I derived much consolation from the fact that he lit them with an ordinary sulphur-match. When they were a bright glow, and the crow was neatly spitted in front thereof, Gunga Dass began without a word of preamble:

'There are only two kinds of men, Sar. The alive and the dead. When you are dead you are dead, but when you are alive you live.' (Here the crow demanded his attention for an instant as it twirled before the fire in danger of being burned to cinder.)

'If you die at home and do not die when you come to the ghât to be burned you come here.'

The nature of the reeking village was made plain now, and all that I had known or read of the grotesque and the horrible paled before the fact just communicated by the ex-Brahmin. Sixteen years ago, when I first landed in Bombay, I had been told by a wandering Armenian of the existence, somewhere in India, of a place to which such Hindus as had the misfortune to recover from trance or catalepsy were conveyed and kept, and I recollect laughing heartily at what I was then pleased to consider a traveller's tale. Sitting at the bottom of the sand-trap, the memory of Watson's Hotel, with its swinging punkahs, white-robed attendants, and the sallow-faced Armenian, rose up in my mind as vividly as a photograph, and I burst into a loud fit of laughter. The contrast was too absurd!

Gunga Dass, as he bent over the unclean bird, watched me curiously. Hindus seldom laugh, and his surroundings were not such as to move Gunga Dass to any undue excess of hilarity. He removed the crow solemnly from the wooden spit and as solemnly devoured it. Then he continued his story, which I give in his own words:

'In epidemics of the cholera you are carried to be burned almost before you are dead. When you come to the riverside the cold air, perhaps, makes you alive, and then, if you are only little alive, mud is put on your nose and mouth and you die conclusively. If you are rather more alive, more mud is put; but if you are too lively they let you go and take you away. I was too lively, and made protestation with anger against the indignities that they endeavoured to press upon me. In those days I was Brahmin and proud man. Now I am dead man and eat'—here he eyed the well-gnawed breast bone with the first sign of emotion that I had seen in him since we met—'crows, and other things. They took me from my sheets when they saw that I was too lively and gave me medicines for one week, and I survived successfully. Then they sent me by rail from my place to Okara Station, with a man to take care of me; and at Okara Station we met two other men, and they conducted we three on camels, in the night, from Okara Station to this place, and they propelled me from the top to the bottom, and the other two succeeded, and I have been here ever since two and a half years. Once I was Brahmin and proud man, and now I eat crows.'

'There is no way of getting out?'

'None of any kind at all. When I first came I made experiments frequently and all the others also, but we have always succumbed to the sand which is precipitated upon our heads.'

'But surely,' I broke in at this point, 'the river-front is open, and it is worthwhile dodging the bullets; while at night'—

I had already matured a rough plan of escape which a natural instinct of selfishness forbade me from sharing with Gunga Dass. He, however, divined my unspoken thought almost as soon as it was formed; and, to my intense astonishment, gave vent to a long low chuckle of derision—the laughter, be it understood, of a superior or at least of an equal.

'You will not'—he had dropped the Sir completely after his opening sentence—'make any escape that way. But you can try. I have tried. Once only.'

The sensation of nameless terror and abject fear which I had in vain attempted to strive against overmastered me completely. My long fast—it was now close upon ten o'clock, and I had eaten nothing since tiffin on the previous day—combined with the violent and unnatural agitation of the ride had exhausted me, and I verily believe that, for a few minutes, I acted as one mad. I hurled myself against the pitiless sand-slope. I ran round the base of the crater, blaspheming and praying by turns. I crawled out among the sedges of the river-front, only to be driven back each time in an agony of nervous dread by the rifle-bullets which cut up the sand round me—for I dared not face the death of a mad dog among that hideous crowd—and finally fell, spent and raving, at the curb of the well. No one had taken the slightest notice of an exhibition which makes me blush hotly even when I think of it now.

Two or three men trod on my panting body as they drew water, but they were evidently used to this sort of thing, and had no time to waste upon me. The situation was humiliating. Gunga Dass, indeed, when he had banked the embers of his fire with sand, was at some pains to throw half a cupful of fetid water over my head, an attention for which I could have fallen on my knees and thanked him, but he was laughing all the while in the same mirthless, wheezy key that greeted me on my first attempt to force the shoals. And so, in a semi-comatose condition, I lay till noon. Then, being only a man after all, I felt hungry, and intimated as much to Gunga Dass, whom I had begun to regard as my natural protector. Following the impulse of the outer world when dealing with natives, I put my hand into my pocket and drew out four annas. The absurdity of the gift struck me at once, and I was about to replace the money.

Gunga Dass, however, was of a different opinion, 'Give me

the money,' said he; 'all you have, or I will get help, and we will kill you!' All this as if it were the most natural thing in the world!

A Briton's first impulse, I believe is to guard the contents of his pockets; but a moment's reflection convinced me of the futility of differing with the one man who had it in his power to make me comfortable; and with whose help it was possible that I might eventually escape from the crater. I gave him all the money in my possession, Rs. 9-8-5—nine rupees eight annas and five pie—for I always keep small change as bakshish when I am in camp. Gunga Dass clutched the coins, and hid them at once in his ragged loin-cloth, his expression changing to something diabolical as he looked round to assure himself that no one had observed us.

'*Now* I will give you something to eat,' said he.

What pleasure the possession of my money could have afforded him I am unable to say; but inasmuch as it did give him evident delight I was not sorry that I had parted with it so readily, for I had no doubt that he would have had me killed if I had refused. One does not protest against the vagaries of a den of wild beasts; and my companions were lower than any beasts. While I devoured what Gunga Dass had provided, a coarse chapatti and a cupful of the foul well-water, the people showed not the faintest sign of curiosity—that curiosity which is so rampant, as a rule, in an Indian village.

I could even fancy that they despised me. At all events they treated me with the most chilling indifference, and Gunga Dass was nearly as bad. I plied him with questions about the terrible village, and received extremely unsatisfactory answers. So far as I could gather, it had been in existence from time immemorial—whence I concluded that it was at least a century old—and during that time no one had ever been known to escape from it. (I had to control myself here with both hands, lest the blind terror should lay hold of me a second time and drive me raving round the crater.) Gunga Dass took a malicious pleasure in emphasizing this point and in watching me wince. Nothing that I could do would induce him to tell me who the mysterious 'They' were.

'It is so ordered,' he would reply, 'and I do not yet know any one who has disobeyed the orders.'

'Only wait till my servants find that I am missing,' I retorted, 'and I promise you that this place shall be cleared off the face of the earth, and I'll give you a lesson in civility, too, my friend.'

'Your servants would be torn in pieces before they came near this place; and, besides, you are dead, my dear friend. It is not your fault, of course, but none the less you are dead *and* buried.'

At irregular intervals supplies of food, I was told, were dropped down from the land side into the amphitheatre, and the inhabitants fought for them like wild beasts. When a man felt his death coming on he retreated to his lair and died there. The body was sometimes dragged out of the hole and thrown on to the sand, or allowed to rot where it lay.

The phrase 'thrown on to the sand' caught my attention, and I asked Gunga Dass whether this sort of thing was not likely to breed a pestilence.

'That,' said he, with another of his wheezy chuckles, 'you may see for yourself subsequently. You will have much time to make observations.'

Whereat, to his great delight, I winced once more and hastily continued the conversation:—'And how do you live here from day to day? What do you do?' The question elicited exactly the same answer as before—coupled with the information that 'this place is like your European heaven; there is neither marrying nor giving in marriage.'

Gunga Dass had been educated at a Mission School, and, as he himself admitted, had he only changed his religion 'like a wise man', might have avoided the living grave which was now his portion. But as long as I was with him I fancy he was happy.

Here was a Sahib, a representative of the dominant race, helpless as a child and completely at the mercy of his native neighbours. In a deliberate lazy way he set himself to torture me as a schoolboy would devote a rapturous half-hour to watching the agonies of an impaled beetle, or as a ferret in a blind burrow might glue himself comfortably to the neck of a rabbit. The burden of his conversation was that there was no escape 'of no kind whatever,' and that I should stay here till I died and was 'thrown on to the sand.' If it were possible to forejudge the conversation of the Damned on the advent of a new soul in their abode, I should say that they would speak as Gunga Dass did to me throughout that long afternoon. I was powerless to protest or answer; all my energies being devoted to a struggle against the inexplicable terror that threatened to overwhelm me again and again. I can compare the feeling to nothing except the struggles of a man against the overpowering nausea of the Channel passage—only my agony was of the spirit and infinitely more terrible.

As the day wore on, the inhabitants began to appear in full strength to catch the rays of the afternoon sun, which were now sloping in at the mouth of the crater. They assembled in little knots, and talked among themselves without even throwing a glance in my direction. About four o'clock, as far as I could judge, Gunga Dass rose and dived into his lair for a moment, emerging with a live crow in his hands. The wretched bird was in a most draggled and deplorable condition, but seemed to be in no way afraid of its master. Advancing cautiously to the river front, Gunga Dass stepped from tussock to tussock until he had reached a smooth patch of sand directly in the line of the boat's fire. The occupants of the boat took no notice. Here he stopped, and with a couple of dexterous turns of the wrist, pegged the bird on its back with outstretched wings. As was only natural, the crow began to shriek at once and beat the air with its claws. In a few seconds the clamour had attracted the attention of a bevy of wild crows on a shoal a few hundred yards away, where they were discussing something that looked like a corpse. Half a dozen crows flew over at once to see what was going on, and also, as it proved, to attack the pinioned bird. Gunga Dass, who had lain down on a tussock, motioned to me to be quiet, though I fancy this was a needless precaution. In a moment, and before I could see how it happened, a wild crow, who had grappled with the shrieking and helpless bird, was entangled in the latter's claws, swiftly disengaged by Gunga Dass, and pegged down beside its companion in adversity. Curiosity, it seemed, overpowered the rest of the flock, and almost before Gunga Dass and I had time to withdraw to the tussock, two more captives were struggling in the upturned claws of the decoys. So the chase—if I can give it so dignified a name—continued until Gunga Dass had captured seven crows. Five of them he throttled at once, reserving two for further operations another day. I was a good deal impressed by this, to me, novel method of securing food, and complimented Gunga Dass on his skill.

'It is nothing to do,' said he. 'Tomorrow you must do it for me. You are stronger than I am.'

This calm assumption of superiority upset me not a little, and I answered peremptorily—'Indeed, you old ruffian! What do you think I have given you money for?'

'Very well,' was the unmoved reply. 'Perhaps not tomorrow, nor the day after, nor subsequently; but in the end, and for many years, you will catch crows and eat crows, and you will thank your European God that you have crows to catch and eat.'

I could have cheerfully strangled him for this; but judged it best under the circumstances to smother my resentment. An hour later I was eating one of the crows; and, as Gunga Dass had said, thanking my God that I had a crow to eat. Never as long as I live shall I forget that evening meal. The whole population were squatting on the hard sand platform opposite their dens, huddled over tiny fires of refuse and dried rushes. Death, having once laid his hand upon these men and forborne to strike, seemed to stand aloof from them now; for most of our company were old men, bent and worn and twisted with years, and women aged to all appearance as the Fates themselves. They sat together in knots and talked—god only knows what they found to discuss—in low equable tones, curiously in contrast to the strident babble with which natives are accustomed to make day hideous. Now and then an access of that sudden fury which had possessed me in the morning would lay hold on a man or woman; and with yells and imprecations the sufferer would attack the steep slope until, baffled and bleeding, he fell back on the platform incapable of moving a limb. The others would never even raise their eyes when this happened, as men too well aware of the futility of their fellows' attempts and wearied with their useless repetition. I saw four such outbursts in the course of that evening.

Gunga Dass took an eminently business-like view of my situation, and while we were dining—I can afford to laugh at the recollection now, but it was painful enough at the time—propounded the terms on which he would consent to 'do' for me.

My nine rupees eight annas, he argued, at the rate of three annas a day, would provide me with food for fifty-one days, or about seven weeks; that is to say, he would be willing to cater for me for that length of time. At the end of it I was to look after myself. For a further consideration—*videlicet* my boots—he would be willing to allow me to occupy the den next to his own, and would supply me with as much dried grass for bedding as he could spare.

'Very well, Gunga Dass,' I replied; 'to the first terms I cheerfully agree but, as there is nothing on earth to prevent my killing you as you sit here and taking everything that you have,' (I thought of the two invaluable crows at the time), 'I flatly refuse to give you my boots and shall take whichever den I please.'

The stroke was a bold one, and I was glad when I saw that it had succeeded. Gunga Dass changed his tone immediately, and disavowed all intention of asking for my boots. At the time it did not strike me as at all strange that I, a civil engineer, a man of thirteen years' standing in the Service, and I trust, an average Englishman, should thus calmly threaten murder and violence against the man who had, for a consideration it is true, taken me under his wing. I had left the world, it seemed, for centuries. I was as certain then as I am now of my own existence, that the living dead men had thrown behind them every canon of the world which had cast them out; and that I had to depend for my own life on my strength and vigilance alone. The crew of the ill-fated Mignonette are the only men who would understand my frame of mind. 'At present,' I argued to myself, 'I am strong and a match for six of these wretches. It is imperatively necessary that I should, for my own sake, keep both health and strength until the hour of my release comes—if it ever does.'

Fortified with these resolutions, I ate and drank as much as I could, and made Gunga Dass understand that I intended to be his master, and that the least sign of insubordination on his part would be visited with the only punishment I had it in my power to inflict—sudden and violent death. Shortly after this I went to bed. That is to say, Gunga Dass gave me a double armful of dried bents which I thrust down the mouth of the lair to the right of his, and followed myself, feet foremost; the hole running about nine feet into the sand with a slight downward inclination, and being neatly shored with timbers. From my den, which faced the river-front, I was able to watch the waters of the Sutlej flowing past under the light of a young moon and compose myself to sleep as best I might.

The horrors of that night I shall never forget. My den was nearly as narrow as a coffin and the sides had been worn smooth and greasy by the contact of innumerable naked bodies, added to which it smelled abominably. Sleep was altogether out of question to one in my excited frame of mind. As the night wore on, it seemed that the entire amphitheatre was filled with legions of unclean devils that, trooping up from the shoals below, mucked the unfortunates in their lairs.

Personally I am not of an imaginative temperament—very few engineers are—but on that occasion I was as completely prostrated with nervous terror as any woman. After half an hour or so, however, I was able more to calmly review my chances of escape. Any exit by the steep sand walls, was, of course, impracticable. I had been thoroughly convinced of this some time before. It was possible, just possible, that I might, in the uncertain moonlight, safely run the gauntlet of the rifle shots. The place was so full of terror for me that I was prepared to undergo any risk in leaving it. Imagine my delight, then, when after creeping stealthily to the river-front I found that the infernal boat was not there. My freedom lay before me in the next few steps!

By walking out to the first shallow pool that lay at the foot of the projecting left horn of the horseshoe, I could wade across, turn the flank of the crater, and make my way inland. Without a moment's hesitation I marched briskly past the tussocks where Gunga Dass had snared the crows, and out in the direction of the smooth white sand beyond. My first step from the tufts of dried grass showed me how utterly futile was any hope of escape; for, as I put my foot down, I felt an indescribable drawing, sucking motion of the sand below. Another moment and my leg was swallowed up nearly to the knee. In the moonlight the whole surface of the sand seemed to be shaken with devilish delight at my disappointment. I struggled clear, sweating with terror and exertion, back to the tussocks behind me and fell on my face.

My only means of escape from the semicircle was protected with quick sand!

How long I lay I have not the faintest idea; but I was roused at last by the malevolent chuckle of Gunga Dass at my ear. 'I would advise you, Protector of the Poor,' (the ruffian was speaking English) 'to return to your house. It is unhealthy to lie down here. Moreover, when the boat returns, you will most certainly be rifled at.' He stood over me in the dim light of the dawn, chuckling and laughing to himself. Suppressing my first impulse to catch the man by the neck and throw him on to the quicksand, I rose sullenly and followed him to the platform below the burrows.

Suddenly, and futilely as I thought while I spoke, I asked: 'Gunga Dass, what is the good of the boat if I can't get out *anyhow*?' I recollect that even in my deepest trouble I had been speculating vaguely on the waste of ammunition in guarding an already well protected foreshore.

Gunga Dass laughed again and made answer: 'They have the boat only in daytime. It is for the reason that *there is a way*. I hope we shall have the pleasure of your company for much longer time. It is a pleasant spot when you have been here some years and eaten roast crow long enough.'

I staggered, numbed and helpless, toward the fetid burrow allotted to me, and fell asleep. An hour or so later I was awakened by a piercing scream—the shrill, high-pitched scream of a horse in pain. Those who have once heard that will never forget the sound. I found some little difficulty in scrambling out of the burrow. When I was in the open, I saw Pornic, my poor old Pornic, lying dead on the sandy soil. How they had killed him I cannot guess. Gunga Dass explained that horse was better than crow, and 'greatest good of greatest number is political maxim. We are now Republic, Mister Jukes, and you are entitled to a fair share of the beast. If you like, we will pass a vote of thanks. Shall I propose?'

Yes, we were a Republic indeed! A Republic of wild beasts penned at the bottom of a pit, to eat and fight and sleep till we died. I attempted no protest of any kind, but sat down and stared at the hideous sight in front of me. In less time almost than it takes me to write this, Pornic's body was divided, in some unclean way or other; the men and women had dragged the fragments on to the platform and were preparing their morning meal. Gunga Dass cooked mine. The almost irresistible impulse to fly at the sand walls until I was wearied laid hold of me afresh, and I had to struggle against it with all my might. Gunga Dass was offensively jocular till I told him that if he addressed another remark of any kind whatever to me I should strangle him where he sat. This silenced him till silence became insupportable, and I bade him say something.

'You will live here till you die like the other Feringhi,' he said, coolly, watching me over the fragment of gristle that he was gnawing.

'What other Sahib, you swine? Speak at once, and don't stop to tell me a lie.'

'He is over there,' answered Gunga Dass, pointing to a burrow-mouth about four doors to the left of my own. 'You can see for yourself. He died in the burrow as you will die, and I will die and as all these men and woman and the one child will also die.'

'For pity's sake tell me all you know about him. Who was he? When did he come, and when did he die?'

This appeal was a weak step on my part. Gunga Dass only leered and replied: 'I will not—unless you give me something first.'

Then I recollected where I was, and struck the man between the eyes, partially stunning him. He stepped down from the platform at once, and, cringing and fawning and weeping and attempting to embrace my feet, led me round to the burrow which he had indicated.

'I know nothing whatever about the gentleman. Your God be my witness that I do not. He was as anxious to escape as you were, and he was shot from the boat, though we all did all things to prevent him from attempting. He was shot here.' Gunga Dass laid his hand on his lean stomach and bowed to the earth.

'Well, and what then? Go on!'

'And then—and then, Your Honour, we carried him into his house and gave him water, and put wet cloths on the wound, and he laid down in his house and gave up the ghost.'

'In how long? In how long?'

'About half an hour, after he received his wound. I call Vishnu to witness,' yelled the wretched man, 'that I did everything for him. Everything which was possible, that I did!'

He threw himself down on the ground and clasped my ankles. But I had my doubts about Gunga Dass' benevolence, and kicked him off as he lay protesting.

'I believe you robbed him of everything he had. But I can find out in a minute or two. How long was the Sahib here?'

'Nearly a year and a half. I think he must have gone mad. But hear me swear, Protector of the Poor! Won't Your Honour hear me swear that I never touched an article that belonged to him? What is Your Worship going to do?'

I had taken Gunga Dass by the waist and had hauled him on to the platform opposite the deserted burrow. As I did so I thought of my wretched fellow-prisoner's unspeakable misery among all these horrors for eighteen months, and the final agony of dying like a rat in a hole, with a bullet-wound in the stomach. Gunga Dass fancied I was going to kill him and howled pitifully. The rest of the population, in the plethora that follows a full flesh meal, watched us without stirring.

'Go inside, Gunga Dass,' said I, 'and fetch it out.'

I was feeling sick and faint with horror now. Gunga Dass nearly rolled off the platform and howled aloud.

'But I am Brahmin, Sahib—a high-caste Brahmin. By your soul, by your father's soul, do not make me do this thing!'

'Brahmin or no Brahmin, by my soul and my father's soul, in you go!' I said, and, seizing him by the shoulders, I crammed his head into the mouth of the burrow, kicked the rest of him in, and, sitting down, covered my face with my hands.

At the end of a few minutes I heard a rustle and a creak; then Gunga Dass in a sobbing, choking whisper speaking to himself; then a soft thud—and I uncovered my eyes.

The dry sand had turned the corpse entrusted to its keeping into a yellow-brown mummy. I told Gunga Dass to stand off while I examined it. The body—clad in an olive-green bunting-suit much stained and worn, with leather pads on the shoulders—was that of a man between thirty and forty, above middle height, with light, sandy hair, long mustache, and a rough unkempt beard. The left canine of the upper jaw was missing, and a portion of the lobe of the right ear was gone. On the second finger of the left hand was a ring—a shield-shaped bloodstone set in gold, with a monogram that might have been either 'B.K.' or 'B.L.'. On the third finger of the right hand was a silver ring in the shape of a coiled cobra, much worn and tarnished. Gunga Dass deposited a handful of trifles he had picked out of the burrow at my feet, and, covering the face of the body with my handkerchief, I turned to examine these. I give the full list in the hope that it may lead to the identification of the unfortunate man:

1. Bowl of a briarwood pipe, serrated at the edge; much worn and blackened; bound with string at the screw.
2. Two patent-lever keys; wards of both broken.
3. Tortoise-shell-handled penknife, silver or nickel, name-plate, marked with monogram 'B.K.'.
4. Envelope, postmark undecipherable, bearing a Victorian stamp, addressed to 'Miss Mon-' (rest illegible)-'ham'-'nt.'
5. Imitation crocodile-skin notebook with pencil. First forty-five pages blank; four and a-half illegible; fifteen others filled with private memoranda relating chiefly to three persons—a Mrs L. Singleton, abbreviated several times to 'Lot Single,' 'Mrs S. May,' and 'Garmison,' referred to in places as 'Jerry' or 'Jack'.
6. Handle of small-sized hunting-knife. Blade snapped short. Buck's horn, diamond cut, with swivel and ring on the butt; fragment of cotton cord attached.

It must not be supposed that I inventoried all these things on the spot as fully as I have here written them down. The notebook first attracted my attention, and I put it in my pocket with a view to studying it later on. The rest of the articles I conveyed to my burrow for safety's sake, and there, being a methodical man, I inventoried them. I then returned to the corpse and ordered Gunga Dass to help me to carry it out to the river-front. While we were engaged in this, the exploded shell of an old brown cartridge dropped out of one of the pockets and rolled at my feet. Gunga

Dass had not seen it; and I fell to thinking that a man does not carry exploded cartridge-cases, especially 'browns', which will not bear loading twice, about with him when shooting. In other words, that cartridge-case has been fired inside the crater. Consequently there must be a gun somewhere. I was on the verge of asking Gunga Dass, but checked myself, knowing that he would lie. We laid the body down on the edge of the quicksand by the tussocks. It was my intention to push it out and let it be swallowed up—the only possible mode of burial that I could think of. I ordered Gunga Dass to go away.

Then I gingerly put the corpse out on the quicksand. In doing so, it was lying face downward, I tore the frail and rotten khaki shooting-coat open, disclosing a hideous cavity in the back. I have already told you that the dry sand had, as it were, mummified the body. A moment's glance showed that the gaping hole had been caused by a gun-shot wound; the gun must have been fired with the muzzle almost touching the back. The shooting-coat, being intact, had been drawn over the body after death, which must have been instantaneous. The secret of the poor wretch's death was plain to me in a flash. Someone of the crater, presumably Gunga Dass, must have shot him with his own gun—the gun that fitted the brown cartridges. He had never attempted to escape in the face of the rifle-fire from the boat.

I pushed the corpse out hastily, and saw it sink from sight literally in a few seconds. I shuddered as I watched. In a dazed, half-conscious way I turned to peruse the notebook. A stained and discoloured slip of paper had been inserted between the binding and the back, and dropped out as I opened the pages. This is what it contained: '*Four out from crow-clump: three left; nine out; two right; three back; two left; fourteen out; two left; seven out; one left; nine back; two right; six back; four right; seven back.*' The paper had been burned and charred at the edges. What it meant I could not understand. I sat down on the dried bents turning it over and over between my fingers until I was aware of Gunga Dass standing immediately behind me with glowing eyes and outstretched hands.

'Have you got it?' he panted. 'Will you not let me look at it also? I swear that I will return it.'

'Got what? Return what?' I asked.

'That which you have in your hands. It will help us both.' He stretched out his long, bird-like talons, trembling with eagerness.

'I could never find it,' he continued. 'He had secreted it about his person. Therefore I shot him, but nevertheless I was unable to obtain it.'

Gunga Dass had quite forgotten his little fiction about the rifle-bullet. I received the information perfectly calmly. Morality is blunted by consorting with the Dead who are alive.

'What on earth are you raving about? What is it you want me to give you?'

'The piece of paper in the notebook. It will help us both. Oh, you fool! You fool! Can you not see what it will do for us? We shall escape!'

His voice rose almost to a scream and he danced with excitement before me. I own I was moved at the chance of getting away.

'Don't skip! Explain yourself. Do you mean to say that this slip of paper will help us? What does it mean?'

'Read it aloud! Read it aloud! I beg and I pray you to read it aloud.'

I did so. Gunga Dass listened delightedly, and drew an irregular line in the sand with his fingers.

'See now! It was the length of his gun-barrels without the stock. I have those barrels. Four gun-barrels out from the place where I caught crows. Straight out; do you follow me? Then three left—Ah! how well I remember when that man worked it out night after night. Then nine out, and so on. Out is always straight before you across the quicksand. He told me so before I killed him.'

'But if you knew all this why didn't you get out before?'

'I did *not* know it. He told me that he was working it out a year and a half ago, and how he was working it out night after night when the boat had gone away, and he could get out near the quicksand safely. Then he said that we would get away together. But I was afraid that he would leave me behind one night when he had worked it all out, and so I shot him. Besides, it is not advisable that the men who once get in here should escape. Only I, and *I* am a Brahmin.'

The prospect of escape had brought Gunga Dass' caste back

to him. He stood up, walked about and gesticulated violently. Eventually I managed to make him talk soberly, and he told me how this Englishman had spent six months night after night in exploring, inch by inch, the passage across the quicksand; how he had declared it to be simplicity itself up to within about twenty yards of the river bank after turning the flank of the left horn of the horseshoe. This much he had evidently not completed when Gunga Dass shot him with his own gun.

In my frenzy of delight at the possibilities of escape I recollect shaking hands effusively with Gunga Dass, after we had decided that we were to make an attempt to get away that very night. It was weary work waiting throughout the afternoon.

About ten o'clock, as far as I could judge, when the Moon had just risen above the lip of the crater, Gunga Dass made a move for his burrow to bring out the gun-barrels whereby to measure our path. All the other wretched inhabitants had retired to their lairs long ago. The guardian boat drifted down-stream some hours before, and we were utterly alone by the crow-clump. Gunga Dass, while carrying the gun-barrels, let slip the piece of paper which was to be our guide. I stooped down hastily to recover it, and, as I did so, I was aware that the diabolical Brahmin was aiming a violent blow at the back of my head with the gun-barrels. It was too late to turn round. I must have received the blow somewhere on the nape of my neck. A hundred thousand fiery stars danced before my eyes, and I fell forwards senseless at the edge of the quicksand.

When I recovered consciousness, the Moon was going down, and I was sensible of intolerable pain in the back of my head. Gunga Dass had disappeared and my mouth was full of blood. I lay down again and prayed that I might die without more ado. Then the unreasoning fury which I have before mentioned laid hold upon me, and I staggered inland toward the walls of the crater. It seemed that some one was calling to me in a whisper—'Sahib! Sahib! Sahib!' exactly as my bearer used to call me in the morning. I fancied that I was delirious until a handful of sand fell at my feet. Then I looked up and saw a head peering down into the amphitheatre—the head of Dunnoo, my dog-boy, who attended to my collies. As soon as he had attracted my attention, he held up his hand and showed a rope. I motioned, staggering to and fro the while, that he should throw it down. It was a couple of leather punkah-ropes knotted together, with a loop at one end. I slipped the loop over my head and under my arms; heard Dunnoo urge something forward; was conscious that I was being dragged, face downward, up the steep sand slope, and the next instant found myself choked and half fainting on the sand hills overlooking the crater. Dunnoo, with his face ashy grey in the moonlight, implored me not to stay but to get back to my tent at once.

It seems that he had tracked Pornic's footprints fourteen miles across the sands to the crater; had returned and told my servants, who flatly refused to meddle with any one, white or black once fallen into the hideous Village of the Dead; whereupon Dunnoo had taken one of my ponies and a couple of punkah-ropes, returned to the crater, and hauled me out as I have described.

To cut a long story short, Dunnoo is now my personal servant on a gold mohur a month—a sum which I still think far too little for the services he has rendered. Nothing on earth will induce me to go near that devilish spot again, or to reveal its whereabouts more clearly than I have done. Of Gunga Dass I have never found a trace, nor do I wish to do. My sole motive in giving this to be published is the hope that someone may possibly identify, from the details and the inventory which I have given above, the corpse of the man in the olive-green hunting-suit.

The Mark of the Beast

Rudyard Kipling

East of Suez, some hold, the direct control of Providence ceases; Man being there handed over to the power of the Gods and Devil of Asia, and the Church of England Providence only exercising an occasional and modified supervision in the case of Englishmen.

This theory accounts for some of the more unnecessary horrors of life in India: it may be stretched to explain my story.

My friend Strickland of the Police, who knows as much of natives of India as is good for any man, can bear witness to the facts of the case. Dumoise, our doctor, also saw what Strickland and I saw. The inference which he drew from the evidence was entirely incorrect. He is dead now; he died in a rather curious manner, which has been elsewhere described.

When Fleete came to India, he owned a little money and some land in the Himalayas, near a place called Dharmsala. Both properties had been left him by an uncle, and he came out to finance them. He was a big, heavy, genial, and inoffensive man. His knowledge of natives was, of course, limited, and he complained of the difficulties of the language.

He rode in from his place in the hills to spend New Year in the station, and he stayed with Strickland. On New Year's Eve there was a big dinner at the club, and the night was excusably wet. When men foregather from the uttermost ends of the Empire, they have a right to be riotous. The Frontier had sent down a contingent o' Catch-'em-Alive-O's who had not seen twenty white faces for a year, and were used to ride fifteen miles to dinner at the next Fort at the risk of a Khyberee bullet where their drinks should lie. They profited by their new security, for they tried to play pool with a curled-up hedgehog found in the garden, and one of them carried the marker round the room in his teeth. Half a dozen planters had come in from the south and were talking 'horse' to the Biggest Liar in Asia, who was trying to cap all their stories at once. Everybody was there, and there was a general closing up of ranks and taking stock of our losses in dead or disabled that had fallen during the past year.

It was a very wet night, and I remember that we sang 'Auld Lang Syne' with our feet in the Polo Championship Cup, and our heads among the stars, and swore that we were all dear friends. Then some of us went away and annexed Burma, and some tried to open up the Soudan and were opened up by Fuzzies in that cruel scrub outside Suakim, and some found stars and medals, and some were married, which was bad, and some did other things which were worse, and the others of us stayed in our chains and strove to make money on insufficient experiences.

Fleete began the night with sherry and bitters, drank champagne steadily up to dessert, then raw, rasping Capri with all the strength of whisky, took Benedictine with his coffee, four or five whiskies and sodas to improve his pool strokes, beer and bones at half-past two, winding up with old brandy. Consequently, when he came out, at half-past three in the morning, into fourteen degrees of frost, he was very angry with his horse for coughing, and tried to leapfrog into the saddle. The horse broke away and went to his stables; so Strickland and I formed a Guard of Dishonour to take Fleete home.

Our road lay through the bazaar, close to a little temple of Hanuman, the Monkey-god, who is a leading divinity worthy of respect. All gods have good points, just as have all priests. Personally, I attach much importance to Hanuman, and am kind to his people—the great grey apes of the hills. One never knows when one may want a friend.

There was a light in the temple, and as we passed, we could hear voices of men chanting hymns. In a native temple, the priests rise at all hours of the night to do honour to their god. Before we could stop him, Fleete dashed up the steps, patted two priests on the back, and was gravely grinding the ashes of his cigar butt into the forehead of the red stone image of Hanuman. Strickland tried to drag him out, but he sat down and said solemnly:

'Shee that? Mark of the B—beasht! *I* made it. Ishn't it fine?'

In half a minute the temple was alive and noisy, and Strickland, who knew what came of polluting gods, said that things might occur. He, by virtue of his official position, long residence in the country, and weakness for going among the natives, was known to the priests and he felt unhappy. Fleete sat on the ground and refused to move. He said that 'good old Hanuman' made a very soft pillow.

Then, without any warning, a Silver Man came out of a recess behind the image of the god. He was perfectly naked in that bitter, bitter cold, and his body shone like frosted silver, for he was what the Bible calls 'a leper as white as snow'. Also he had no face, because he was a leper of some years standing and his disease was heavy upon him. We two stooped to haul Fleete up, and the temple was filling and filling with folk who seemed to spring from the earth, when the Silver Man ran in under our arms, making a noise exactly like the mewing of an otter, caught Fleete round the body and dropped his head on Fleete's breast before we could wrench him away. Then he retired to a corner and sat mewing while the crowd blocked all the doors.

The priests were very angry until the Silver Man touched Fleete. That nuzzling seemed to sober them.

At the end of a few minutes' silence one of the priests came to Strickland and said, in perfect English, 'Take your friend away. He has done with Hanuman, but Hanuman has not done with him.' The crowd gave room and we carried Fleete into the road.

Strickland was very angry. He said that we might all three have been knifed, and that Fleete should thank his stars that he had escaped without injury.

Fleete thanked no one. He said that he wanted to go to bed. He was gorgeously drunk.

We moved on, Strickland silent and wrathful, until Fleete was taken with violent shivering fits and sweating. He said that the smells of the bazaar were overpowering, and he wondered why slaughter-houses were permitted so near English residences. 'Can't you smell the blood?' said Fleete.

We put him to bed at last, just as the dawn was breaking, and Strickland invited me to have another whisky and soda. While we were drinking he talked of the trouble in the temple, and admitted that it baffled him completely. Strickland hates being mystified by natives, because his business in life is to overmatch them with their own weapons. He has not yet succeeded in doing this, but in fifteen or twenty years he will have made some progress.

'They should have mauled us,' he said, 'instead of mewing at us. I wonder what they meant. I don't like it one little bit.'

I said that the Managing Committee of the temple would in all probability bring a criminal action against us for insulting their religion. There was a section of the Indian Penal Code which exactly met Fleete's offence. Strickland said he only hoped and prayed that they would do this. Before I left I looked into Fleete's room and saw him lying on his right side, scratching his left breast. Then I went to bed cold, depressed, and unhappy, at seven o'clock in the morning.

At one o'clock I rode over to Strickland's house to inquire after Fleete's head. I imagined that it would be a sore one. Fleete was breakfasting and seemed unwell. His temper was gone, for he was abusing the cook for not supplying him with an underdone chop. A man who can eat raw meat after a wet night is a curiosity. I told Fleete this and he laughed.

'You breed queer mosquitoes in these parts,' he said, 'I've been bitten to pieces, but only in one place.'

'Let's have a look at the bite,' said Strickland. 'It may have gone down since this morning.'

While the chops were being cooked, Fleete opened his shirt and showed us, just over his left breast, a mark, the perfect double of the black rosettes—the five or six irregular blotches arranged in a circle—on a leopard's hide. Strickland looked and said. 'It was only pink this morning. It's grown black now.'

Fleete ran to a glass.

'By Jove!' he said, 'this is nasty. What is it?'

We could not answer. Here the chops came in, all red and juicy, and Fleete bolted three in a most offensive manner. He ate on his right grinders only, and threw his head over his right shoulder as he snapped the meat. When he had finished, it struck him that he had been behaving strangely, for he said apologetically, 'I don't think I ever felt so hungry in my life. I've bolted like an ostrich.'

After breakfast Strickland said to me, 'Don't go. Stay here, and stay for the night.'

Seeing that my house was not three miles from Strickland's this request was absurd. But Strickland insisted, and was going to say something when Fleete interrupted by declaring in a shamefaced way that he felt hungry again. Strickland sent a man to my house to fetch over my bedding and a horse, and we three went down to Strickland's stables to pass the hours until it was time to go out for a ride. The man who has a weakness for horses never wearies of inspecting them; and when two men are killing time in this way they gather knowledge and lies the one from the other.

There were five horses in the stables, and I shall never forget the scene as we tried to look them over. They seemed to have gone mad. They reared and screamed and nearly tore up their pickets; they sweated and shivered and lathered and were distraught with fear. Strickland's horses used to know him as well as his dogs; which made the matter more curious. We left the stable for fear of the brutes throwing themselves in their panic. Then Strickland turned back and called me. The horses were still frightened, but they let us 'gentle' and make much of them, and put their heads in our bosoms.

'They aren't afraid of *us*,' said Strickland. 'D'you know, I'd give three months' pay if *Outrage* here could talk.'

But *Outrage* was dumb, and could only cuddle up to his master and blow his nostrils, as is the custom of horses when they wish to explain things but can't. Fleete came up when we were in the stalls, and as soon as the horses saw him, their fright broke out afresh. It was all that we could do to escape from the place unkicked. Strickland said, 'They don't seem to love you, Fleete.'

'Nonsense,' said Fleete,'my mare will follow me like a dog.' He went to her; she was in a loose-box; but as he slipped the bars she plunged, knocked him down, and broke away into the garden. I laughed, but Strickland was not amused. He took his moustache in both fists and pulled at it till it nearly came out. Fleete, instead of going off to chase his property, yawned, saying that he felt sleepy. He went to the house to lie down, which was a foolish way of spending New Year's Day.

Strickland sat with me in the stables, and asked if I had noticed anything peculiar in Fleete's manner. I said that he ate his food like a beast; but that this might have been the result of living alone in the hills out of the reach of society as refined and elevating as ours for instance. Strickland was not amused. I do not think that he listened to me, for his next sentence referred to the mark on Fleete's breast and I said that it might have been caused by blister-flies, or that it was possibly a birthmark newly born and now visible for the first time. We both agreed that it was unpleasant to look at, and Strickland found occasion to say that I was a fool.

'I can't tell you what I think now,' said he, 'because you would call me a madman: but you must stay with me for the next few days, if you can. I want you to watch Fleete, but don't tell me what you think till I have made up my mind.'

'But I am dining out tonight,' I said.

'So am I,' said Strickland, 'and so is Fleete. At least if he doesn't change his mind.'

We walked about the garden smoking, but saying nothing—because we were friends, and talking spoils good tobacco—till our pipes were out. Then we went to wake up Fleete. He was wide awake and fidgeting about his room.

'I say, I want some more chops,' he said. 'Can I get them?' We laughed and said, 'Go and change. The ponies will be round in a minute.'

'All right,' said Fleete. 'I'll go when I get the chops—underdone ones, mind.'

He seemed to be quite in earnest. It was four o'clock, and we had had breakfast at one; still, for a long time, he demanded those underdone chops. Then he changed into riding clothes and went out into the veranda. His pony—the mare had not been caught—would not let him come near. All three horses were unmanageable—mad with fear—and finally Fleete said that he could stay at home and get something to eat. Strickland and I rode out wondering. As we passed the temple of Hanuman, the Silver Man came out and mewed at us.

'He is not one of the regular priests of the temple,' said Strickland. 'I think I should peculiarly like to lay my hands on him.'

There was no spring in our gallop on the racecourse that evening. The horses were stale, and moved as though they had been ridden out.

'The fright after breakfast has been too much for them,' said Strickland.

That was the only remark he made through the remainder of the ride. Once or twice I think he swore to himself; but that did not count.

We came back in the dark at seven o'clock, and saw that there were no lights in the bungalow. 'Careless ruffians my servants are!' said Strickland.

My horse reared at something on the carriage drive, and Fleete stood up under its nose.

'What are you doing, grovelling about the garden?' said Strickland.

But both horses bolted and nearly threw us. We dismounted by the stables and returned to Fleete, who was on his hands and knees under the orange bushes.

'What the devil's wrong with you?' said Strickland.

'Nothing, nothing in the world,' said Fleete, speaking very quickly and thickly. 'I've been gardening—botanizing you know. The smell of the earth is delightful. I think I am going for a walk—a long walk—all night.'

Then I saw that there was something excessively out of order somewhere, and I said to Strickland, 'I am not dining out.'

'Bless you!' said Strickland. 'Here, Fleete, get up. You'll catch fever there. Come in to dinner and let's have the lamps lit. We'll all dine at home.'

Fleete stood up unwillingly, and said, 'No lamps—no lamps. It's much nicer here. Let's dine outside and have some more chops—lots of 'em and underdone—bloody ones with gristle.'

'Come in,' said Strickland sternly. 'Come in at once.'

Fleete came, and when the lamps were brought, we saw that

he was literally plastered with dirt from head to foot. He must have been rolling in the garden. He shrank from the light and went to his room. His eyes were horrible to look at. There was a green light behind them, not in them, if you understand, and the man's lower lip hung down.

Strickland said, 'There is going to be trouble—big trouble—tonight. Don't change your riding things.'

We waited and waited for Fleete's reappearance, and ordered dinner in the meantime. We could hear him moving about his own room, but there was no light there. Presently from the room came the long-drawn howl of a wolf.

People write and talk lightly of blood running cold and hair standing up and things of that kind. Both sensations are too horrible to be trifled with. My heart stopped as though a knife had been driven through it, and Strickland turned white as the tablecloth.

The howl was repeated, and was answered by another howl far across the fields.

That set the gilded roof on the horror. Strickland dashed into Fleete's room. I followed, and we saw Fleete getting out of the window. He made beast-noises in the back of his throat. He could not answer us when we shouted at him. He spat.

I don't quite remember what followed, but I think that Strickland must have stunned him with the long boot-jack or else I should never have been able to sit on his chest. Fleete could not speak, he could only snarl, and his snarls were those of a wolf, not of a man. The human spirit must have been giving way all day and have died out with the twilight. We were dealing with a beast that had once been Fleete.

The affair was beyond any human and rational experience. I tried to say 'hydrophobia', but the word wouldn't come, because I knew that I was lying.

We bound this beast with leather thongs of the punkah-rope, and tied its thumbs and big toes together, and gagged it with a shoehorn, which makes a very efficient gag if you know how to arrange it. Then we carried it into the dining-room, and sent a man to Dumoise, the doctor, telling him to come over at once. After we had despatched the messenger and were drawing breath, Strickland said, 'It's no good. This isn't any doctor's work.' I, also, knew that he spoke the truth.

The beast's head was free, and it threw it about from side to side. Any one entering the room would have believed that we were curing a wolf's pelt. That was the most loathsome accessory of all.

Strickland sat with his chin in the heel of his fist, watching the beast as it wriggled on the ground, but saying nothing. The shirt had been torn open in the scuffle and showed the black rosette mark on the left breast. It stood out like a blister.

In the silence of the watching we heard something without mewing like a she-otter. We both rose to our feet, and, I answer for myself, not Strickland, felt sick—actually and physically sick. We told each other, as did the men in *Pinafore*, that it was the cat.

Dumoise arrived, and I never saw a little man so unprofessionally shocked. He said that it was a heartrending case of hydrophobia, and that nothing could be done. At least any palliative measures would only prolong the agony. The beast was foaming at the mouth. Fleete, as we told Dumoise, had been bitten by dogs once or twice. Any man who keeps half a dozen terriers must expect a nip now and again. Dumoise could offer no help. He could only certify that Fleete was dying of hydrophobia. The beast was then howling, for it had managed to spit out the shoe-horn. Dumoise said that he would be ready to certify to the cause of death, and that the end was certain. He was a good little man, and he offered to remain with us; but Strickland refused the kindness. He did not wish to poison Dumoise's New Year. He could only ask him not to give the real cause of Fleete's death to the public.

So Dumoise left, deeply agitated; and as soon as the noise of the cartwheels had died away, Strickland told me, in a whisper, his suspicions. They were so wildly improbable that he dared not say them out aloud; and I, who entertained all Strickland's beliefs, was so ashamed of owning to them that I pretended to disbelieve.

'Even if the Silver Man had bewitched Fleete for polluting the image of Hanuman, the punishment could not have fallen so quickly.'

As I was whispering this the cry outside the house rose again, and the beast fell into a fresh paroxysm of struggling till we were afraid that the thongs that held it would give way.

'Watch!' said Strickland. 'If this happens six times I shall take the law into my own hands. I order you to help me.'

He went into his room and came out in a few minutes with the barrels of an old shotgun, a piece of fishing-line, some thick cord, and his heavy wooden bedstead. I reported that the convulsions had followed the cry by two seconds in each case, and the beast seemed perceptibly weaker.

Strickland muttered. 'But he can't take away the life! He can't take away the life!'

I said, though I knew that I was arguing against myself. 'It may be a cat. It must be a cat. If the Silver Man is responsible, why does he dare to come here?'

Strickland arranged the wood on the hearth, put the gun barrels into the glow of the fire, spread the twine on the table and broke a walking stick in two. There was one yard of fishing-line, gut, lapped with wire, such as is used for *mahseer*-fishing, and he tied the two ends together in a loop.

Then he said, 'How can we catch him? He must be taken alive and unhurt.'

I said that we must trust in Providence, and go out softly with polo sticks into the shrubbery at the front of the house. The man or animal that made the cry was evidently moving round the house as regularly as a night watchman. We could wait in the bushes till he came by and knock him over.

Strickland accepted this suggestion, and we slipped out from a bathroom window into the front veranda and then across the carriage drive into the bushes.

In the moonlight we could see the leper coming round the corner of the house. He was perfectly naked, and from time to time he mewed and stopped to dance with his shadow. It was an unattractive sight, and thinking of poor Fleete, brought to such degradation by so foul a creature, I put away all my doubts and resolved to help Strickland from the heated gun barrels to the loop of twine—from the loins to the head and back again—with all tortures that might be needful.

The leper halted in the front porch for a moment and we

jumped out on him with the sticks. He was wonderfully strong, and we were afraid that he might escape or be fatally injured before we caught him. We had an idea that lepers were frail creatures, but this proved to be incorrect. Strickland knocked his legs from under him and I put my foot on his neck. He mewed hideously, and even through my riding boots I could feel that his flesh was not the flesh of a clean man.

He struck at us with his feet-stumps. We looped the lash of a dog whip round him, under the armpits and dragged him backwards into the hall and so into the dining-room where the beast lay. There we tied him with trunk straps. He made no attempt to escape, but mewed.

When we confronted him with the beast the scene was beyond description. The beast doubled backwards into a bow as though he had been poisoned with strychnine, and moaned in the most pitiable fashion. Several other things happened also, but they cannot be put down here.

'I think I was right,' said Strickland. 'Now we will ask him to cure this case.'

But the leper only mewed. Strickland wrapped a towel round his hand and took the gun barrels out of the fire. I put the half of the broken walking stick through the loop of fishing-line and buckled the leper comfortably to Strickland's bedstead. I understood then how men and women and little children can endure to see a witch burnt alive; for the beast was moaning on the floor, and though the Silver Man had no face, you could see horrible feelings passing through the slab that took its place, exactly as waves of heat play across red-hot iron-gun barrels for instance.

Strickland shaded his eyes with his hands for a moment and we got to work. This part is not to be printed.

The dawn was beginning to break when the leper spoke. His mewings had not been satisfactory up to that point. The beast had fainted from exhaustion and the house was very still. We unstrapped the leper and told him to take away the evil spirit. He crawled to the beast and laid his hand upon the left breast. That was all. Then he fell face down and whined, drawing in his breath as he did so.

We watched the face of the beast, and saw the soul of Fleete coming back into the eyes. Then a sweat broke out on the forehead and the eyes—they were human eyes—closed. We waited for an hour but Fleete still slept. We carried him to his room and bade the leper go, giving him the bedstead, and the sheet on the bedstead to cover his nakedness, the gloves and the towels with which we had touched him, and the whip that had been hooked round his body. He put the sheet about him and went out into the early morning without speaking or mewing.

Strickland wiped his face and sat down. A night-gong, far away in the city, made seven o'clock.

'Exactly four-and-twenty hours!' said Strickland. 'And I've done enough to ensure my dismissal from the service, besides permanent quarters in a lunatic asylum. Do you believe that we are awake?'

The red-hot gun barrel had fallen on the floor and was singeing the carpet. The smell was entirely real.

That morning at eleven we two together went to wake up Fleete. We looked and saw that the black leopard-rosette on his chest had disappeared. He was very drowsy and tired, but as soon as he saw us, he said, 'Oh! Confound you fellows. Happy New Year to you. Never mix your liquors. I'm nearly dead.'

'Thanks for your kindness, but you're over time,' said Strickland. 'Today is the morning of the second. You've slept the clock round with a vengeance.'

The door opened, and little Dumoise put his head in. He had come on foot, and fancied that we were laying out Fleete.

'I've brought a nurse,' said Dumoise. 'I suppose that she can come in for . . . what is necessary.'

'By all means,' said Fleete cheerily, sitting up in bed. 'Bring on your nurses.'

Dumoise was dumb, Strickland led him out and explained that there must have been a mistake in the diagnosis. Dumoise remained dumb and left the house hastily. He considered that his professional reputation had been injured, and was inclined to make a personal matter of the recovery. Strickland went out too. When he came back, he said that he had been to call on the Temple of

Hanuman to offer redress for the pollution of the god, and had been solemnly assured that no white man had ever touched the idol and that he was an incarnation of all the virtues labouring under a delusion. 'What do you think?' said Strickland.

I said, 'There are more things. . . .'

But Strickland hates that quotation. He says that I have worn it threadbare.

One other curious thing happened which frightened me as much as anything in all the night's work. When Fleete was dressed he came into the dining-room and sniffled. He had a quaint trick of moving his nose when he sniffled. 'Horrid doggy smell, here,' said he. 'You should really keep those terriers of yours in better order. Try sulphur, Strick.'

But Strickland did not answer. He caught hold of the back of a chair, and, without warning, went into an amazing fit of hysterics. It is terrible to see a strong man overtaken with hysteria. Then it struck me that we had fought for Fleete's soul with the Silver Man in that room, and had disgraced ourselves as Englishmen forever, and I laughed and gasped and gurgled just as shamefully as Strickland, while Fleete thought that we had both gone mad. We never told him what we had done.

Some years later, when Strickland had married and was a churchgoing member of society for his wife's sake, we reviewed the incident dispassionately, and Strickland suggested that I should put it before the public.

I cannot myself see that this step is likely to clear up the mystery; because, in the first place, no one will believe a rather unpleasant story, and, in the second, it is well-known to every rightminded man that the gods of the heathen are stone and brass, and any attempt to deal with them otherwise is justly condemned.

The Fire-Jogi

A.C. Renny

Many miles to the west of the Mechi river, in the practically impenetrable primal forests of the Nepal Tarai which stretch for many miles north and west till brought to an abrupt termination by the Kosi river, are to be found large game in a far greater variety and abundance than can be met with in the forests of the Indian Government.

Benighted one evening, it was my misfortune to be compelled to spend the night in the fork of a tree; my only solace being an experienced, but garrulous shikari chowkidar and a plentiful supply of smokes. We were well out of the reach of carnivora, but fair game for the most voracious mosquitoes it has ever been my lot to meet. Smoking, slapping and swearing were useless deterrents, they had found good feeding grounds and were unsparing. Our faces and hands were tingling from their bites and the chowkidar, congratulating them on the sharpness of their needles, prognosticated a horrible death for us from a malignant fever, the germs of which had been injected into our blood.

What I looked like, I could not tell, but when the first streak of dawn lit up the Eastern sky and I could indistinctly make out the chowkidar's muffled face, it appeared to have swollen to twice the size. Consoling myself that I could not be as bad, I waited for the strengthening of the morning light—and when the light had gained in strength I was well repaid for all the inconvenience of having spent a dreadful night, for the animals that had crossed from the Nepal forests into the reserves of the Nirpania Government blocks, commenced to return again.

It is no exaggeration to say that every animal walking on four feet was represented. They came on singly, in pairs and in batches, the last lot being lesser game such as pigs, deer, hare and porcupine.

'This thing I have never seen before, huzoor,' remarked the chowkidar.

'And will never see again unless you come a second time to give the mosquitoes a feed,' I answered.

What that chowkidar said about the origin of mosquitoes and their subsequent relations will not bear repeating. It took a little over an hour for the animals to cross over, and as the last snuggled into the forest undergrowth, the mighty orb rose to light the world.

We got down in silence and wended our way home. I, to my bungalow, the chowkidar to his scolding wife whose wrath combined with the bites of the mosquitoes seem to be the two topics occupying his troubled mind. He began telling me of the wretched life he led and I could barely suppress a laugh at times.

Three days after, a planter friend arrived to spend a few days with me. When I related my story and came to the part where I had seen a veritable Noah's Ark emptying itself, his eyes glowed with excitement.

'If you can persuade the chowkidar to take you, for I refuse point blank to repeat the experience, and as you are only armed to shoot a *jungli murghi*, keep to it, for without a permit no shooting is allowed.'

'I'll get at the chowkidar this evening; bribe him if possible,' he returned.

'Wish you luck,' I answered, 'the money will probably do it.' But when the chowkidar arrived to report in the evening and was asked, then coaxed and threatened and finally offered a bribe, he was adamant. Turning to me he said, 'not because of the mosquitoes, huzoor, but because of the fire-jogi.'

'The fire-jogi, never heard of him.

'Neither had I, huzoor, but when I explained to my wife where and how we had spent the night, she said it was a pity I had not been consumed by the fire-jogi. I looked at her in surprise, but when I asked her to explain what she meant, she referred me to Dhanbir Sirdar.'

'Have you questioned Dhanbir?'

'I have, huzoor, for the woman's wild talk haunted me all day. It was last evening I met Dhanbir and taking him aside, questioned him.'

'What had he to say?'

'It is not good to talk of, huzoor, you and I have had a narrow escape from an enemy of mankind.'

'It may not be good to talk of, but we wish to hear what he had to say. If any misfortune follows, we are prepared to take the responsibility.'

'He says, huzoor, not a hundred yards from where we sat, a most mysterious occurrence takes place every night. We were too busy with the mosquitoes to take note of our surroundings. It is as well, huzoor, for very few have seen the fire-jogi and the few have met with misfortune shortly after. In the day he is a jogi at night a fire.'

'Tosh! twaddle,' exclaimed my friend. 'Look here, can you get us someone to show us this strange man. We only desire to see him, after that we will investigate on our own account. Five rupees I will gladly pay for this.'

A *tharoo* was brought to us the next day. A *tharoo* is an indigenous dweller of the Nepal Tarai, and because of his living in the Tarai, he is immune from the deadly Tarai fever. Take him away from his environments and curiously enough he immediately goes down, with the fever. Time alone cures them as it does most things and we find them employed all over India as elephant drivers. The chowkidar brought him up and introduced him to us. 'This man, for the consideration of the money offered, is prepared to show you the fire-jogi.'

My friend was impatient to be off. I restrained him, saying, 'look here, let me question this man and if his answers are satisfactory, we engage him. If not, the fire-jogi can wait a bit or go hang.'

Turning to the *tharoo* I asked him if he had ever seen the jogi. 'Often,' came his prompt reply. 'He has been in the same place for years and intends remaining until he can coax an elephant to be his friend and not continue as his enemy.'

'Quite satisfactory!' I exclaimed. 'We can start now if you wish it.'

Taking our revolvers unknown to anyone, we followed the *tharoo*. He led us to the same jungle in which the chowkidar and I had spent our wretched night and going two hundred yards inside, suddenly turned to the right and disappeared through an opening in the undergrowth. We did the same and coming to a clearing observed a jogi, ash-smeared and naked, with matted hair and emaciated features calmly sitting on a tiger skin in deep contemplation. In front of him, prostrated, we saw the *tharoo*.

As we approached, the venerable old priest raised his head and looked at us. 'Curiosity has made you brave all danger to see me.'

'True, sadhuji,' I answered, before my friend could bring out an irreverent reply. 'I have heard of you only today and have lost no time to pay my respects.'

'Lie not, O sahib, there is much to be gained in truthfulness. Who am I to you that you should trespass into my little domain to pay your respects? From me you can hide naught. Curiosity compelled you and curiosity will not be satisfied until I have explained why I am in this jungle by myself and why men call me the fire-jogi.'

My friend, who understood something of the conversation, was furious. The jogi, however, looking him calmly in the face, smilingly said, 'Young man, many summers are needed to gain some wisdom of the mysteries of this land, and not understanding much, you become wrathful. Your wrath is nothing to me. Be calm always and that which you do not understand, endeavour to learn, loss of temper repays not. This sahib, your friend, has been long in the land and understands somewhat of our ways but even to him much is hidden. He knows, if we admonish we mean no harm.'

'Jogiji,' I replied, 'my friend is young and inexperienced, all things seem known to you and your surmise is correct. We have come to see you and hear your story and if it please you we will keep it to ourselves.'

'It matters naught, sahib, if the whole world knows my story, but I must ask you, if you repeat it, that no mention be made of my domain, as my sole desire is peace. Later, I may leave this and go once more among men, but that cannot be till I have made friends with the only enemy I have in all the world. He is an ungrateful elephant, who even now is watching us from a distance.'

It was unpleasant news and we could not help looking around. The jogi laughed. 'There is nothing to fear, friends, his approach will be made known by those who watch over me.'

'Watch over you,' I repeated, 'we see nothing.'

'Nor will you till I intend,'and the old man whistled softly at first and then louder.

Immediately from each side of us an animal made an appearance, a fine tiger and a leopard. Snarling and growling at us they took up their stations on either side of the aged man. 'These be my watchmen, sahib. The leopard is old,' and placing his hand lovingly on the tiger's neck, he continued, 'and this one replaces his father as you will come to know. The elephant, my enemy, comes not when these two are on guard. Should both go away, he would kill us all.'

My friend looked at me and I at him. We found ourselves in a distinctly unpleasant place, simply to satisfy our curiosity and were far from comfortable.

'Years ago,' droned the voice of the jogi, 'many years ago, disappointed with living among men, I forsook the world and sought the security and silence of this jungle. Because of its nearness to human dwellings none suspect my dwelling place. I abode here at first with some trepidation, but for the last ten years I have dwelt in peace. My dwelling at first was up that tree, a fine and roomy one, and there through intercession and prayer, I acquired the influence over animals as you see; now the denizens of the jungle know me and are friendly, all but one, sahib. A call from me will bring many here, all except the elephant, who is filled with hatred for me, because in doing him a kind action he suffered some pain.

'One day he came to me limping badly. After examining his feet carefully, I found a large bamboo splinter had become embedded in the flesh between his toes. "*Hatiji*," I said "a cure can be effected, but not without pain."

"I will mind not the pain so long as you can guarantee to free me of it eventually."

'Sahib, I extracted the thorn and in doing so nearly met with my death, for the ungrateful creature, enraged at my methods, sought my life. The leopard you see and the father of this fine tiger sprang at him, enabling me to escape by climbing a tree. Since then of all the animals and creeping things in this jungle, he alone is my enemy. Creeping up silently another night he nearly did me to death. I have studied deeply and for protection I have acquired great powers and using one of them, I turn myself into a fire at night. It is the only protection, for elephants fear fire alone.

'Come some night and you will behold me a fire, from it I will speak with you, but remember, I leave the coming to you entirely, for great risk is attached to entering these jungles at night. On an elephant you have determined to come, let this *tharoo* drive the beast. Go now, friends, the hour grows late, I will send the tiger to protect you as far as the edge of the forest. Farewell.'

I thanked the aged jogi and with my friend took our departure in silence, the *tharoo* following. As we neared the forest edge, a streak of yellow shot past us, we knew it to be the tiger, who had obeyed his master's instructions and guarded us. Once out of the forest, Maclaude could restrain himself no longer. He swore badly to begin with and then came out with a long-drawn-out, 'I'll be hanged! If I was to tell anyone in the Duars what you and I had seen today, I would be put into the same category as Ananias and Baron Munchausen.'

'Mythical and mystical India,' I said, 'shall we ever know it. We see what we are allowed to see, things superficial, but always, the undercurrents remain hidden from us. When you hear a fire actually talking—well.'

'Fire talking, man alive, sure you do not for a moment believe that cock and bull story.'

'On the contrary every word of it. Two days hence, at sunset, we will start out, driven here by the *mahaut* to whom, I must remind you, you owe five rupees.'

'O come, I say, it's Rs. 2-8 each.'

'You bargained for five and I have paid him on my own account and you must abide by the conditions made before starting. Remember you named the price.'

I never saw a five rupee G.C. note parted with more reluctantly.

Two nights went by and during the morning of the day we were to set out at sunset, my friend was suffering from nerves.

'Chuck it,' I suggested.

'Not for anything on earth,' came the reply.

When the hour arrived to set out, and were glad after an hour's swaying from side to side to know we had arrived at the sadhu's abode. With the sinking of the sun all light had died out in the forest. Silently the *mahaut* moved the animal towards the sadhu's seat and halted ten yards from it. The tiger skin, the tongs and gourd bowl were in their place, but no signs could be seen of the sadhu. In front of the tiger skin a fire glowed brightly and as we watched it, it shot into a flame. 'So you have braved the dangers of the forest to satisfy your curiosity—Welcome.'

'Say nothing, huzoor,' warned the *tharoo* in a whisper. A minute went by and the same voice spoke: 'O, sons of white men, who show no fear yet feel it. I, the jogi, speak to you from out of the fire. I waited for you, until I could wait no longer, for at the setting of the sun came my enemy, an earlier visit than usual, and I was compelled to avoid him by the only means I have. He still hovers at a distance and watches us, but as long as I glow with a brightness, he will do no harm.

There was no other voice in the forest depth and from the fire alone the jogi's voice floated towards us.

'The young man desires to spend the night in the forest to see from where I appear at dawn. My fire-talk leaves him sceptical of any powers. The glow will die down when I call my guards.'

A loud whistle rang through the forest and was answered by the roar of the tiger. They came almost immediately, paying no heed to our presence and took up their stations on either side of the tiger skin. The glow of the fire now began perceptibly to lessen, we watched it fascinated. It had nearly gone out and it appeared as if the tiger had actually laughed. Looking round in the direction of the empty tiger skin, we were surprised to see the aged jogi calmly sitting on it, watching us.

'I am here, young man, from the fire have I come, believe me or not. I am here to bid you farewell for I will never see you two together again. I send an elephant to show your animal the way. My fire dies down, I must replenish it again with my body. Farewell.'

The fire immediately glowed brighter, the tiger skin was again empty and from the depths of the forest, the breaking of boughs and the trumpeting of an enraged elephant gave us an idea why the jogi had hurried us away.

The *tharoo* turned our elephant and hurried us out. As we neared the edge into lesser darkness, for the first time we perceived that the jogi had not failed us in providing a guide.

Two years after, when taking the short cut between Gyabari and Kurseong, I saw the sadhu sitting near the monolithic monuments of the *Lepchas*. I saluted him and was about to pass on when he stopped me.

'Your friend?' he simply asked.

'Dead,' I answered.

'It is as I foretold. I was not to see you two together again. Pass on for you will only be in time to catch your train and without a meal you must do until you reach your abode. We will meet again on Mahakhal's Hill.'

Truth to tell I was glad to get away, for since our experience in the Darjeeling Tarai, the very thought of the fire-jogi made my flesh creep. I had seen many extraordinary things in my life, but like the chowkidar, said to myself, 'This thing I have never seen.'

I hurried up the hill and was only in time to catch the train I had left at Gyabari.

The Fourth Man

Hilton Brown

Whatever may be obscure or questionable about this history, there is nothing either the one or the other in the record of the establishment known once as 'Sammy's Hotel' and thereafter as the 'Scandal Bay Mahal'. On no material point concerning it is there any divergence of opinion.

To those who travel between England and the Orient, whether on duty or on pleasure, Scandal Bay is a well-known milestone. It is one of those places, not infrequent in the Far East and the Far West, which after remaining unchanged for some two thousand years have changed out of all recognition in as many days. Thirty years ago—twenty years ago almost—Scandal Bay was a strip of delightful beach on the South-West coast of India, a fishing village and Sammy's Hotel. Today it is a strip of delightful beach, a fishing village and the stark remains of the Scandal Bay Mahal. In the interval the Mahal has come, prospered, perished.

Two questions arise. In the first place—why was it called Scandal Bay, which is not and never can have been a native name? That I can answer but I will not, because there are still in these parts many friends and even relatives of the principal lady involved in the transaction. It is, in any case, quite a separate story. The second question—what caused the change in its destinies?—I can answer readily and will. Eight miles south of Scandal Bay is Kalashi which was, until the beginning of this century a third-rate port visited only by coasting steamers which lay far out and negotiated with the shore through the medium of lighters. Then came Barrow—the great Sir Alexis Barrow—and discovered that there existed at Kalashi the material for a first-class harbour where all the big east-going liners could call. As happens when the dreamer is big enough and has big enough friends, his dream took shape. The oriental traveller put in at Kalashi after the wearisome landless trek across the Arabian Sea and found it a place of no amenities. As did the rare old-time resident of Kalashi, he chartered a vehicle and drove north to Scandal Bay where he found a divinely-appointed bathing beach and an infernally-appointed hotel masquerading in the mouldering remains of a forty-year-old bungalow. He clamoured for better things and a Bombay syndicate descended on the place, bought up the descendant of the original 'Sammy' and scrapped the bungalow. Hence rose the 'Mahal' which had a glorious dining-room open on three sides, European sanitation and I know not all what. For some years the oriental traveller swarmed to it.

Now for the proper understanding of this tale it is necessary to go back a little—back to the original Sammy. Sammy was the butler of one Maclagan who was collector of the district of Quilay for twelve years somewhere in the eighties and nineties. His name may have been Ramaswami or Muniswami or Thambuswami or any other Swami and when Maclagan, retiring in the fullness of the years, pensioned him off and set him up in the little bungalow at Scandal Bay which he, Maclagan, in those spacious days had built, the place may have been called Ramaswami's Hotel or Thambuswami's. In those days there was no such place as Scandal Bay, for the Scandal had not happened; it was called Kapil, as the fishing village is called still. In those days again Kalashi was a place of no importance and the few Europeans who inhabited it—there may have been a dozen and a half all told—were mainly agents of Madras firms and shipping companies. To such 'Ramaswami' and 'Thambuswami' were inconvenient mouthfuls; they shortened him presently and by accepted usage to Sammy. And in the nineties and in the early years of this century the thing to do at the weekend was to make up a select party—it had to be select because Sammy's accommodation was limited in the extreme—and drive down to Scandal Bay (which was then just earning its name) and bathe and play cards and drink such liquor as Sammy provided. Wild nights there have been on that gentle moonlit beach while the villagers of Kapil went about their peaceful ways.

At the dead-centre between century and century, Kalashi was at its very lowest ebb. Trade was bad; one or two agencies had closed down, one or two steamship lines had ceased to call. The Government had transferred the collector's headquarters from Kalashi to Amay, dealing thereby an almost fatal blow. Barrow still tarried in the womb of time and nobody had yet seen the enormous protective advantages of the great sheering headland the local Europeans called Noah's Ark. The place was dying—was almost already dead. At this time the European population—leaving out the Missionaries who do not come into this tale—was reduced to a bare half dozen of whom four were old and established friends. These were Brent, the Agent of the Asiatic Bank; Hartle and Macrae, merchants; and the strange man Ranken, whom they called The Doctor, was not an old man—not more than forty and I think he must have established himself rather by force of personality than by any real length of residence. He was an institution in the Kalashi Club when Macrae first saw it; and in these days he used sometimes to be called 'The Major', but he discouraged this and it dropped. Whether or not he was ever a major I cannot say; he was indeed a doctor, but if you ask me why a doctor of any qualifications at all should choose to settle in a place of the miserable prospects and pretensions then appertaining to Kalashi, again I cannot say. He had doubtless his own reasons. He was, as I have said, a man of about forty, very tall, in good hard condition in spite of what he drank and a fine horseman. He had unruly reddish hair and an unkempt moustache, a dissolute mouth and nostrils and a wild uncertain eye. There is an enlarged photograph of him, said to be a very good likeness, in the Kalashi Club; it used to be in the billiard room but men took to saying that the uneasy eyes of it spoiled their breaks and it hangs now in an obscure dark corner just outside the bar. If you take it into the light and look at it you will see a man hag-ridden and tormented from within who made things worse for himself by trying too hard to make them better.

Weekend after weekend, by unalterable routine, Brent, Hartle, Macrae and Ranken drove down to Scandal Bay and commandeered Sammy's till Monday. They left Kalashi after tiffin on

Saturdays and drove down in separate *jatkas*—a most uncomfortable method but part of the game. The *jatkas* raced and the last man in paid for the Saturday night's dinner. All Sunday they bathed in the sea and played whist, which passed with the later night into poker. They did not go to bed at all on Sunday night—this at least was the theory of the game—but played till dawn, bathed, breakfasted and went back to Kalashi and such work as awaited them. They drank, I imagine, colossally. This they did fifty-two weeks in the year; none of them ever went away even in the depth of the hot weather; none of them had any womenkind—at any rate of his own race; if strangers came to Kalashi they were not encouraged to join the Four. As a four they cornered Sammy's and—this is important indeed from the point of view of this story—but for them Sammy's must have closed and perished.

You may call them four very bad men or you may call them four extraordinary asses—it is according to your point of view. You might also call them, as I am inclined to call them, four tragic and pitiable figures. Brent, if left to himself, would have spent his Sundays as a naturalist; he was very interested in birds and wanted to take up Indian butterflies. Hartle, if he had had any money and if circumstances had been different, would have married a nice honest girl and spent his Sundays in a nursery. Neither of them really cared for the weekends at Sammy's in their hearts. Macrae had reached the appalling stage when a bottle of whisky represented all the remaining entertainment and all the possible adventure the world could still offer him; but even he would have drunk that bottle contentedly in the Kalashi Club and would not have driven out eight miles into a wild region of combing breakers and singing coco-palms to do it. It was Ranken, The Doctor, that wild uneasy spirit, that man without rest, who dominated the other three. It was Ranken who said that, come what might, they must spend their weekends at Sammy's; and sick or ill, hot weather or cold, monsoon rain or April sunshine, to Sammy's they went. It was Ranken really who kept Sammy's going.

To Sammy's these four went without break for perhaps two years; then, as so often happens in India, established custom disintegrated very suddenly. It began with a terrible Saturday afternoon, a nightmare of an afternoon. The *jatkas* were racing as usual and it was a very close thing—a neck and neck finish down the last slight gradient into Kapil. Half-way down it the left wheel of Macrae's *jatka* came off, and the resulting smash would have done credit to a Roman chariot race. The driver flew clear but Macrae and the *jatka* and the pony went over and over and over. The Doctor did what he could, but a fractured skull is a fractured skull and there ended Macrae.

It broke up Hartle, ever too soft of nature for these wild doings. Macrae's head and face had been unspeakably battered in the smash; and in the stark sunshine of a March afternoon, the blood and the dust and the sweat and the pony with a broken leg waving and kicking horribly must have been a dreadful sight enough. Hartle said he could not stop seeing it; he took to drinking—real drinking—for a couple of days at the end of which time he was picked out of a ditch by a missionary to whom thenceforward he transferred his allegiance. Whether or not Ranken, The Doctor, would have tried to find another two men in place of Hartle and Macrae I do not know: at all events things were settled by the sudden transfer of Brent to a distant agency. A man was sent in his place and a man was sent in Macrae's place but they were both youngsters and Ranken, for all his unease, for all his desperate need of comrades and subalterns, was no seducer of boys. Besides, the fourth man was still to seek.

'I like four,' said Ranken, as he had said it many a time. 'It's a good number. If you can't get a four, then keep to yourself.' This, in view of what I shall have to tell, seems important. At any rate Ranken put his preaching into practice, for he quitted Kalashi and lived, day in day out, alone by himself at Sammy's.

The Recording Angel, whose business it is to know all things, must know what sort of life Ranken lived during those weeks at Sammy's; but there are matters of which it is better for mortals to know little. Whatever he was or had been, he was a man of education and intelligence; how then did he get through these endless days from the hour when the chirupping squirrels—Sammy's was infested by squirrels—roused him at dawn till the more merciful hour when the unclouded crimson disc of the sun went down into the sea? He drank, no doubt; but he was a man on whom drink took little effect. His conversation could at times, they said, be brilliant; but he is indeed a brilliant talker who can converse for weeks with himself. The Recording Angel must know also what it was that tormented him; what past dreadfulness, what loss or folly, what commission or omission it was that left him fevered and in perpetual unease. That I do not myself know—nor did anybody—but I will wager that it had full play at him during these weeks. He had craved his company, his 'four' and he sat alone at Sammy's from morning till night—and very possibly from night till morning—looking out upon a most beautiful blue and most absolutely empty sea. What weeks these must have been!

I have said 'weeks' repeatedly, and of course it could hardly last for more. However it may be with the dead, the living at least are not called upon to endure hell. Ranken, The Doctor, who was at one time also called The Major, and of whose past no man knows more than that it horrified himself unbearably, took pistol and finished it on the top front veranda of Sammy's Hotel on the 17th of May, 1901. I don't know what else he could have done.

Sammy's—or rather Sammy's son, for the original Sammy was long since gathered to his fathers—wept bitterly and not altogether from motives of self-interest. Brent, Hartle and Macrae had loved Ranken after their fashion—Sammy too after his.

'Master always very kind to me,' wailed Sammy, 'And always he is coming to our hotel. Always he is bringing friends. Too many peoples coming. Aiyo! Who will come now? Aiyo! How I will live!'

Four months later came Barrow, the great Sir Alexis of harbour fame, and solved Sammy's problem among others more considerable.

II

Of the enormous, the incredible metamorphosis that befell Kalashi—the piers, groins, moles, jetties, cranes, railway-lines and swinging bridges that emerged out of nothing at the bidding of Sir Alexis—I have no call to write. I am concerned solely with the metamorphosis that befell Sammy's Hotel.

The original Sammy was a good, capable, efficient butler; at any rate Maclagan, who was no doubt a man of some discernment, appears to have thought so. His son, on whom the title of Sammy devolved, may even have risen to cook's matey; but easy days came upon him too young and with fatal results. There being no rent to pay and the staff being furnished almost entirely by the family, quite occasional visitors sufficed to run Sammy's at a profit; and a single weekend, as conceived by the Four and spent by them, kept all the Sammy's in comfort and plenty for some time. Those regular weekends, week after week for a couple of years, demoralized Sammy altogether. Moreover, the Four were that beau ideal and delight of the Indian servant—a master who is prepared to establish a procedure and stick to it without deviation for an indefinite period. I imagine the Four's dinner hardly altered: 'Clear Soup, Fry Fish, Chops, Malabar Pudding, Ramkin Toast,' probably served them time after time after time. To drink, whisky and 'bilewater'. As a result, Sammy had no occasion to learn and never did in fact learn the rudiments of running a hotel. When the Harbour opened and the boom came, he at first expected great things; then found it all rather a nuisance. Strange Europeans appeared, clad and speaking as he had never known; tendering English money; asking for the most impossible and incomprehensible things; grumbling over deficiencies nobody had ever noticed before. It was all work, work, work and never anybody satisfied; and if they paid blindly and one made big money—who wanted all that money? Sammy found himself sighing for the comfortable sufficiency of the old days and for the Four contented with their unvarying routine.

Then one day came a Parsee gentleman in black alpaca and a strangely-shaped hat; and presently the Bombay syndicate materialized and bought up the place with stock and goodwill. Sammy sold gladly and cheaply on condition that all the Sammy family, their heirs and assigns, were provided with employment in the new hotel for life. These were for the time being Sammy—that is, Sammy II, son of Sammy I—Sammy's mother, over seventy who had once been ayah to Maclagan's sister, Sammy's brother Thambi and his brother-in-law Muni, and Sammy's son, Sammy III, aged twenty. All these, except the last, had inhabited the 'Hotel' since Maclagan left it. The syndicate also took over an aged waiter called Kuppan and some odds-and-ends of syces, malis and the like.

Now began the great days of Kapil. Over the demolished ruins of Sammy's there rose the vast facade of the Scandal Bay Mahal. It was a wonder of a place containing English baths and what not; taxis lounged in its yard; its great dining-room, open on three sides, hummed with lunches, teas, dinners. Outside Colombo there was no place like it. Goanese cooks laboured in its kitchens, a 'European' manager (but he was Eurasian really) called Bowler strolled round in dignified supervision and Sammy II as head steward presided over its tables.

Now, if this story is true at all, it must be true throughout; therefore we must suppose that Odd Things went on in the Scandal Bay Mahal from the first. In India Odd Things often do go on for a long time, however, and nobody speaks of them. At all events the first time the Odd Things broke through the surface was one evening after the Mahal had been running for nearly three years; it was the evening when old Crinshaw the planter and his married daughter Mrs Reeve and his grand-nephew young Jack Willis came there to dine.

As Europeans go in the East, old Crinshaw was very old—quite seventy; and since his daughters married and his wife died he had lived a lost, hermitish life on a rather remote coffee plantation up in the Yevamalais. He was as odd and crotchety as any old man in these conditions has a right to be; but it was never said—at least it never had been said up to that particular night—that there was anything wrong with his head. Personally, I do not believe there was. On the other hand, he was on his way to England for the last time, Mrs Reeve and young Willis looking after him, and the Yevamalai planters had given him rather an expansive send-off and no doubt he was in an excited state. This condition dinner in the unaccustomed glare and glitter of the Scandal Bay Mahal would doubtless not ameliorate; but I doubt if it would account for his springing up suddenly at table, upsetting a good glass of Burgundy, and crying out—

'By God, there's Ranken! Just going out.'

Amiable young Willis sprang up too. 'Shall I try and catch him?' Then he saw Mrs Reeve's alarmed eyes and sat down again.

'If that isn't too provoking,' piped old Crinshaw, 'I'd ha' liked to ha' seen Ranken. One of the old lot here.'

Mrs Reeve laid a hand on his sleeve. 'You must be dreaming, father. Mr Ranken—'

'Dammit, I saw him!' the old man shrilled. 'He was sitting at that table with these three other fellows and they all got up and went out together. He'd his back to me or I'd have seen him sooner. I'd know that tousled hair anywhere.'

Jack Willis sat in silent bewilderment but Mrs Reeve could not keep the tactless anxiety out of her eyes. The old man saw it.

'You think I'm wrong, eh? You think I'm wandering? I'll show you. Here—you—steward!'

'Mr Ranken stayin' here now?'

Sammy never moved a muscle. 'No, master. No Mr Ranken staying here now.'

The old man glared at him. 'You're wrong. I saw him. You give him my salaams.'

'Very well, sir,' said Sammy, 'I giving master's message.'

A quarter of an hour later Mrs Reeve and Willis took old Crinshaw away; by that time he had forgotten about Ranken. (Apparently he forgot about him altogether; on the voyage, where Mrs Reeve watched him narrowly, he gave no further cause for anxiety. Nor, so far as I know, ever afterwards).

Sammy from a corner of the veranda watched the party go; with him stood his brother Thambi, long and long barman at Sammy's. They spoke together in rapid Malayalam.

Said Sammy, 'Old Mr Crinshaw saw our *dorai* tonight. It is very strange.'

'I saw him all the time,' said Thambi.

Sammy snorted. 'So did I. Of course. But others did not see him. The three with whom he sat down did not see him. Why should the old Crinshaw *dorai* see?'

Thambi shrugged, 'Who knows? He is an old man. He knew

our *dorai,* Ranken *dorai,* long ago. The old man goes away to England. Perhaps Ranken *dorai* showed himself.'

Sammy shook his head. 'I do not like. If other people see they will not like. Bad, bad.'

They parted, Thambi muttering, 'Bad, bad,' in dreary agreement.

Sammy said nothing. Thambi said nothing; so it must have been old Kuppan the waiter who chattered. For next morning Sammy was summoned to the presence of a very angry Bowler. Mr Bowler had served some time as a steward in Australia and spoke with a fine blend of chi-chi and Melbourne.

'What's all this,' said he, 'What's this you all been sayin'? Abaht seein' dead folks in the 'otel. Eh?'

'Not folks,' corrected Sammy slowly, 'Only our *dorai.* Only Ranken *dorai.* Oftentimes he coming.'

'Ye blinkin' idiot!' said Mr Bowler. 'How much arrack you taking drinking, eh?'

'I never drinking arrack,' said Sammy (which was true; for years he had drunk nothing but the best brandy). 'But that Ranken *dorai* sometimes coming.' He plucked up his courage. 'Old times, long times ago, that Ranken *dorai* and three other *dorais* coming every week. That Ranken *dorai* always liking to sit four at table. Now sometimes when three gentlemen sitting at a table, that Ranken *dorai* coming and sitting down beside them.'

Mr Bowler permitted himself a sneer. 'Makin' a fourth, like.'

'Ranken *dorai* always liking to have four *dorais* at table,' persisted Sammy. 'Now when he see three other *dorais,* sometimes he coming and sitting down there. I seeing, sometimes my brother seeing. Kuppan also seeing. But these three *dorais* not seeing. Nobody else seeing. So no troubles coming.'

'Fourth man, eh?' repeated Mr Bowler. 'Aw, go to 'ell. Cheese it, for the love o' Mike. You give me a pine.'

Sammy salaamed.

III

Those professing a knowledge of psychic affairs—which I do not—have told me that there is a theoretical explanation for the succeeding events at Scandal Bay. It has been put to me like this. Supposing there are a number of men playing billiards together and the balls are in a certain position; there will be a number of angles which everyone will see but there will be one angle which only one man present will see—persuming, that is, that the right man *is* present. That man could therefore play a shot which none of the others could attempt; but once the shot was played they would all see that the angle had existed, that the shot was 'on'. So with any given spiritualistic materialization; one single man who for no reason of association, foreknowledge or anything else is just naturally *en rapport* will be able to see that materialization whether he wishes it or not, whether *it* wishes it or not. And once he had seen it, others might see it too.

That is the theory and I daresay there may be something in it. I proceed to narrate events, however—the events that occurred on the night of young Raglan's dinner-party.

This was something over a year after old Crinshaw's disturbing appearance and the Mahal had done better and better in the interval. No guest had made any allusion to a Fourth Man; there *was* no Fourth Man, never could have been. In Mr Bowler's memory, however, he remained green and flourishing. Bowler was one of those fortunate individuals whose jokes never pall, whose good stories are always good. Every now and then he would meet Sammy and say—'Seen any spooks today, eh?'

Sammy was imperturbable. 'Sometimes I seeing. Only that *dorai*, that Ranken *dorai*.'

'An' your brother seeing an' all,' said Bowler. 'Cor! You mike me ike.'

Sammy strove mentally; what seemed so natural in Malayalam was so hard to express, sounded so silly in English. Sammy's English got worse with the years rather than better.

'I think a good thing that *dorai* coming. Always bringing luck that *dorai*. Long times ago, old times, that *dorai* doing me plenty good, always helping this place. I like that *dorai* to come. I think better he not go away.'

Mr Alastair Raglan was a young—a very young—man who was coming East to join a bank in Singapore. As a suffering community of fellow-passengers on the boat had realized, he fancied himself. He dressed immaculately and grumbled wearily at everything, giving the impression that in his previous experience perfection itself had been hardly good enough. To women over the few girls on the ship he was a pest. With him were associated throughout the voyage Messrs Palliser and Sweete, concerning whom the only thing important is that Master Palliser was leaving the ship at Kalashi to join a West Coast firm. It was on the strength of this that Master Raglan's fatigued brain conceived the idea of a dinner-party at Scandal Bay.

'It'll probably be a putrid dinner,' he said languidly, 'but anything's better than this ship's garbage.'

'Oh, rather,' said Master Palliser. Master Sweete yawned.

Messrs Raglan, Palliser and Sweete reached the Scandal Bay Mahal about eight of the evening and ordered cocktails; they ordered more cocktails. It was an occasion the momentousness of which seemed to increase as the minutes passed; the first of the trio was at grips with reality, was about to launch himself definitely into the East. The East, so far a mere abstraction, was now outside the door. All three young men were a little strung up, a little apprehensive, a little homesick; for which reason they were outwardly more assured, more noisy, more contemptuous than ever. But they had to have their cocktails, as children going into a tunnel must have sweets.

At last—it was nearly nine—Raglan, the host, stood up. 'What about a spot of food?'

He led the way from the veranda into the big open dining-room. Palliser and Sweete followed a little way behind. Sweete was making eyes at a girl in a blue dress and not watching Raglan at all. Palliser, the guest of the evening, had done himself rather well before leaving the ship; admittedly he observed the universe something indistinctly. At all events the three young men seemed to walk into a curious kind of mental fog; not one of them was clear as to whether the three sat down at the table and the fourth man joined them or whether he was already sitting at the table when they reached it. Palliser thought that they all three sat down and there was no fourth man and then suddenly there was; at the moment he put this down to the cocktails.

The first thing that emerged clearly out of the fog was Raglan calling angrily for the steward. Raglan, apparently, had seen the fourth man at once, all the time.

'Steward! Steward! I say, steward.' Sammy came hurriedly alongside.

'I reserved this table. Why haven't you kept it?' There was no doubt about the fourth man by this time; there he sat, opposite Palliser, eyeing them curiously. People were looking round at Raglan's outcry; they saw him too.

The second thing that emerged from the fog was Sammy's face; it was one mask of inarticulate terror.

'I—I keeping this table,' he stammered.

'Then why is this gentleman sitting here?' said Raglan.

The fourth man spoke. He was dressed in spotless but clearly darzi-made evening dress—the old all-white evening dress that passed out of usage in South India with the nineteenth century. He wore the old-fashioned long-ended white tie. He had a quantity of tousled ruddy hair and a moustache that drooped dissolutely over a slack mouth. He had extraordinary, disconcerting eyes—eyes that looked as if they would shed tears if all possible tears had not been shed long since. His voice was odd—bell-like, with an echo in it.

'I always sit here,' he said.

'Are you staying in this hotel?' said Raglan.

'I always stay in this hotel,' said the fourth man.

'Then I don't understand—.' Raglan turned on the shivering steward. 'If this gentleman—.'

The fourth man spoke again.

'I'll go if you like.' Without giving them time to answer he turned those tortured eyes on Sammy. 'Am I to go?' he asked.

Sammy's answer was to drop the salver he was carrying with a crash like a gong and to rush into the pantry with a kind of wail.

'Upon my soul—' began Raglan. He was standing up, very pale, his hands twitching. Everyone in the room was watching by now; people at distant tables were standing up to see what was happening. Far away down the aisle of tables appeared the hurrying figure of Bowler.

The fourth man fixed Raglan with those intolerable eyes. 'Shall I go?' he said.

Raglan's assurance had deserted him. He stammered like a schoolboy.

'Perhaps—. If you don't mind—.'

Bowler came hurrying up; the fourth man drew himself out of his chair—tall, gaunt, somehow terrible.

'It's all right,' he said, 'I'm going.'

In his white evening dress he walked the whole length of that long room and out through the pillared veranda in the direction of the sea. Everyone in the room saw and watched him go, striding out, his hands in his pockets his eyes looking straight ahead. . . . Raglan found himself sitting down in his chair.

'A little mistake, Sir,' Bowler was saying. 'Had a drop, Sir, perhaps. What will you drink, Sir?'

'I've ordered champagne,' gasped Raglan. 'Bring it. Quick.'

For the first time in their young lives those immaculate sticklers for procedure, Messrs Raglan, Palliser and Sweete, committed the unpardonable solecism of drinking champagne with their soup.

IV

The immediate result of Master Raglan's dinner-party was, of course, the departure of Sammy, his brother, his brother-in-law, Sammy III and the old mother. Kuppan would have joined them but he had died the year before; the surviving mali followed Sammy. Sammy's view of the case, once expressed, was repeated without variation.

'We sending Ranken *dorai* away. Now plenty trouble coming.'

'I'm glad to see yer backs, 'said Bowler, 'I'd ha' fired ye anyway. Seein' spooks an' makin' up fours. Enough to give the plice a bad nime.'

But the name was given already. Raglan and Sweete went on next day and never came back; but Palliser, as you will remember, stayed in Kalashi. He told the story often and dined out on it and became popular; so it was only a question of time till he told it one evening to a grey-eyed, grey-haired, grey-faced stranger in the Club who said—.

'My name's Hartle. If there's anything in anything, that man you saw was Ranken.'

And of course there were others—besides Hartle who had known The Doctor, many others who had heard of him. The old dreary story of Sammy's Hotel and the Four and their dreadful inhuman weekends went round and round. Neither those who had known Ranken nor those who had not, showed much desire to meet The Fourth Man. Hostesses said—'Scandal Bay? Ye-es, of course it's very nice and the food's quite good, but *I* wouldn't give a party there, my dear. *No!*'

'Curse them Sammy's,' said Bowler striving to account to his Parsee proprietors for enormously diminished returns, 'Givin' the plice a bad nime.' But one month later Bowler himself lay dead at Scandal Bay—of some obscure species of ptomaine poisoning; and four guests lay dead with him and nearly a score of others escaped but narrowly. So the bad name already given went worse. There was a fire, too, and a particularly distressing bathing tragedy. Someone coined the name Suicide Bay—and it stuck. Scandal Bay Mahal went into the market—and found buyers shy as snipe.

Today you may take a taxi from anywhere in Kalashi and drive northwards along the level road through the continuous chiaroscuro of coconut plantations. Presently you will cross a little ridge of laterite outcrop, and then you will run down that final easy gradient which was the last vista Macrae's eyes saw on earth. You will look out over the beautifully blue, appallingly empty sea that served the same purpose for Ranken's. You will find the divinely-appointed beach and the fishing-village of Kapil with its inhabitants going about their peaceful ways as they went about them all through this history. And dominating the foreshore and depressing it and shutting it off as with a barrier from all things human you will see the long, pretentious facade of the Mahal, sun-blistered, rain-begrimed, shuttered, blind, dead. There was no final catastrophe; it just decayed and perished and there it will stand till it falls down. It just decayed and began perishing from the night when Ranken, The Doctor, went out of it towards the sea and made Fourth Man to threes at its tables no more.

There is one more question which stands out and you will ask it. You will say—why Raglan? Why Raglan, who was barely born when The Doctor shot himself, who was Ranken's antithesis, hard where he was soft and soft where he was hard? Why (following our theory) should this callow creature be the one man of all men so closely *en rapport* that he could see the invisible and make it appear? And why in the course of his insignificant life should he come for one short hour to Scandal Bay and produce these vast and irrevocable effects?. . . .

Why Raglan?

There you have me.

The Werewolf

C.A. Kincaid

It was a terribly hot afternoon in July some fifty years ago in Upper Sind. In the Deccan cooling showers had turned the hard earth, baked by the summer winds, into a perfect paradise. The soil there was bright with long green grass. The hills rose emerald to the sky, although their summits were often veiled by the monsoon mists; and delightful breezes swept over the glad earth to the great joy of foreign sojourners in the Indian plateau. Even in the Punjab and the Gangetic valley heavy rain had fallen in if the air seemed stuffy to the traveller from southern India, his eyes rejoiced in the rich foliage and endless maize fields. While his ears listened joyfully to the murmuring sound of new-born streams, as they tinkled and splashed on their way to join the brimming rivers.

In Upper Sind the landscape was quite different. Rain hardly ever falls there except in the cold weather and while more favoured parts of India revel in the monsoon, none of it reaches that strange land. Irrigated by canals from the Indus, the fields are in winter gay with young wheat and he who visits Upper Sind in January may well think that he has reached some heavenly spot. But let him go there in July or August and he will soon change his opinion. All day long the hot wind roars driving the mercury up to 120 degrees in the shade; nor is there much relief at night. The hot wind drops, but the thermometer still marks over a hundred; the sandflies and mosquitoes buzz all night and moonbeams like the rays of a powerful electric headlight pour down on the would-be sleeper's face making slumbering exceedingly difficult.

In the middle of this sunsplashed region is Sehwan, formerly an important town, but now greatly sunk in importance. One thing it still claims with justice: that it is one of the hottest places on earth.

A Persian poet once in the bitterness of his heart asked the Almighty why, after making Sehwan and Sibi, he thought it worthwhile to make Hell. The afternoon on which this story opens was well worthy of Sehwan's ancient reputation. The train steamed slowly into Sehwan station from Sukkur. The railway on the left bank of the Indus had not then been built, so the railtrack passed through Sehwan on its way to Karachi and the seacoast. The last carriage on the train was the saloon of the traffic superintendent. It was far roomier than the ordinary first-class carriages, as befitted the quarters of senior railway official; but nothing could keep out the heat or make the interior cool. The shutters were closed. A railway coolie pulled a diminutive punka fixed in the roof, but he merely stirred into motion the heavy, hot air. There were two occupants of the saloon; one was the traffic superintendent, Frank Bollinger; the other was a Major Sinclair, whom he had known for some years. He had invited his friend to share the saloon instead of sweltering in the first-class compartment and sharing it with two missionaries, their wives and baby.

'I shall be devoutly thankful,' said Bollinger, 'when we get out of this Hell into the monsoon area.'

'When will that be?'

'Once we pass the Lakhi gorge it will be better. They say the monsoon dies there and so they call the gorge the gate of Hell. It is true that once past that frightful mass of heated limestone, one does begin to feel a breath of cooler air. It gradually grows in strength; so we ought to get a good night on our way to Karachi.'

'I am very glad to hear that. I could not sleep a wink in this part of the world, could you?'

'Oh! I have had such a long experience of hot nights that I might; but thank God! there will be no need to make the experiment.'

Just then the train drew up in Sehwan station. The stationmaster, Isarmal, who had known Bollinger in earlier days, came running up to pay his respects. His face beamed all over with the pleasure that an Indian almost always feels at meeting a former English friend. Bollinger remembered well the little stationmaster and was also very glad to see him and have a chat over old times.

To let the two old acquaintances have their talk out, Major Sinclair got out of the carriage and strolled about on the platform. After Bollinger and Isarmal had been gossiping together for about a quarter of an hour, the former said suddenly:

'I say, Mr Isarmal, why are we staying here so long? I never remember waiting more than five minutes at Sehwan before.'

'I am afraid, sir—I am very sorry, sir—the river has breached the line some four miles down and the train cannot go on until tomorrow morning.'

'Do you mean to say that we shall have to stay all night in this inferno? I am afraid the Major Sahib will not like that at all. He was grumbling at the heat when the train was moving; what he'll say when he hears that we will have to pass the night in a stationary train, I can't think. He will swear horribly.'

'Yes indeed, sir,' said Mr Isarmal, anxious to agree to everything his English friend said, 'the Major Sahib will swear horribly.'

Just then all doubts were settled by the arrival of Sinclair in a frightful temper. After so varied an outburst of blasphemy that it filled Bollinger with respectful awe, he shouted:

'Damn it all, Bollinger, have you heard that we have to spend the night in this hellhole?'

'Yes; I'm awfully sorry, old chap; but it cannot be helped. The Indus is in flood and it is just as capricious as a spoilt harlot. Still it will only be for one night and you'll be able to wipe out your arrears of sleep, when we near Karachi.'

'My dear chap, I'm not going to sleep in your saloon. I have just been talking to the khansama of the rest-house. He says it is up on the top of a hill and all night one gets a cool breeze from the river. He'll give us dinner and he'll call us at 6 a.m. so that we shan't miss the train. He'll put our beds out in the open and he swears that we'll be able to sleep like tops.'

Just then the khansama himself came up. He was a powerfully built Panjabi Musulman with a long black beard and very strange yellow eyes. His face in repose had a villainous expression. He had a smile that rarely came off, but it was a very unpleasant one; it was rather like the smile of a savage Alsatian fawning on its master. He could speak a little broken English, which in the case of poor linguists like Major Sinclair was a great attraction. On reaching the saloon he stood at the door and addressing Bollinger very deferentially, said:

'The Major Sahib, he coming to rest-house. Sahib, please come too, and have good night in cool breeze. I give good dinner and you get good sleep and I wake you 6 a.m. Madras time. Down here too dammed hot, you get no sleep at all, Sahib.'

Bollinger could not help thinking of the old nursery rhyme 'Won't you walk into my parlour said the spider to the fly' and anyway he had no wish to leave his comfortable saloon and a dinner served by his own servants for a hard bed and a doubtful meal at a rest-house half a mile away. He politely thanked the khansama.

'No, Khansama; I shall be quite all right here. It may be hot, but I doubt whether it will be any cooler on the top of your Himalayan peak. After all, I have been there and it is only about thirty feet high and my dinner will be better than any you can give me.'

The khansama's yellow eyes flashed disagreeably, but he continued as before to smile in his canine way and to repeat mechanically:

'Sahib, I give you very good dinner. A cool breeze will blow all night. You get good sleep and tomorrow I call you at 6 a.m. Madras time.'

At last Bollinger said impatiently: 'It's no use going on jabbering like that. I'm just not going to your rest-house. I'm going to stay here and there's an end of it.'

Suddenly Sinclair broke in: 'Well, I'm not. I'm damned if I'm going to spend the night in your sardine box.' Turning to his butler, he said: 'Here, boy, get my luggage out of the saloon and put it in a tonga and tell the man to drive to the rest-house. You can come with the khansama in another.'

Bollinger, taken aback, replied with stiff courtesy: 'My dear Sinclair, you must, of course, please yourself. I shall stay in the old sardine box and you'll have a good dinner and a capital night. Goodnight!'

The Major, without troubling to answer, walked off with the

khansama and Bollinger resumed his talk with Mr Isarmal the stationmaster.

When the khansama and Sinclair had passed out of sight Isarmal suddenly said in a low earnest voice: 'Thank God, you did not go, sahib, with that terrible man. If you had you would be as good as dead already. The Major Sahib will not be alive tomorrow.'

'What on earth are you talking about, Isarmal?'

'It is that khansama, sir. He is not really a man, but a—a—a—I have forgotten the English word; we call it in Sindi a *lakhibaghar*.'

'A hyena, you mean,' said Bollinger, who knew some Sindi.

'Yes, sahib, he turns himself every night into a hyena and eats anyone whom he finds sleeping alone on a cot in the open. We say that he is the reincarnation of a horrible man called Anu Kasai.'

'Oh, you mean that fellow who ate Bodlo Bahar?'

'Yes. I see the sahib knows the story. Bodlo Bahar was the disciple of our great Sehwan saint, Lal Shabaz. One day he disappeared. The following morning one of the saint's disciples saw that the bits of mutton that he was cooking for his dinner were jumping about strangely in his pot. Other disciples had the same tale to tell. So Lal Shabaz said: 'It must be our Bodlo Bahar,' and went to the Governor of Sehwan. He asked from whom they had bought the mutton. They all said, 'From the butcher Anu Kasai.' Now this wicked man had once been very prosperous, but he had fallen on evil days; and having no money to buy sheep he used to murder strangers and sell their flesh as mutton. The Governor arrested Anu Kasai and searched his shop and house. They were full of human bones. He had for months escaped punishment, but he was caught when he killed a saint like Bodlo Bahar.'

'How did the Governor punish him?'

'He walled him up in the battlements of Sehwan fort, that is the hill on which the rest-house now stands. As you pass it you can see a sort of hollow in the side of it. That is where they walled up Anu the butcher.'

'But what is this talk of the khansama being his reincarnation?'

'Well, sahib, he has only been here three or four months and yet several people in the town have disappeared. Whenever they have done so, a large hyena has been seen galloping through

Sehwan. Not only that, but two Chota Sahibs (subordinate Europeans) who went to the rest-house also have disappeared. The khansama said the same in both cases. They dined and slept outside the rest-house, but when he brought the tea next morning they had vanished. We say the khansama turns himself into a hyena and eats them during the night. You will never see the Major Sahib again, I am afraid; but thank God you are here! Still at night close the doors and windows of your saloon, otherwise that khansama may attack you even here. We always shut ourselves in at night, although it is so hot.'

Bollinger was far too wise to laugh at the stationmaster's story. He did not believe that the khansama and the hyena were the same: but remembering his villainous expression he did think it possible that he was a murderer; and after Isarmal had left he began to wonder what he should do.

At last he determined to go to the rest-house and share the danger, if any, with Sinclair. He had no gun, but he had a long heavy hunting knife that, had it been a bit sharper, would have been a very efficient weapon. He did not bother to take his servant as he did not wish to have him on his hands too. In the glare of the setting sun he walked along the dusty limestone road and then up the steep side of the old fort, now the rest-house. He noticed as he walked a depression in the fort wall and said to himself that that must be the place where they walled up Anu Kasai. At last he reached the top of the old fort. He arrived just as Sinclair was sitting down to dinner outside the building. It certainly was far cooler than in the station siding, for a cool breeze blew from the river.

'Come along, Bollinger, I am so glad you have come,' said Sinclair cordially. 'You must dine with me. We can get a good night here in the breeze. I say, I'm awfully sorry for having been so grumpy just now. I cannot make out what came over me.'

'Oh, that's all right!' said Bollinger cheerily, wondering secretly what Sinclair would think of Isarmal's tale. The khansama also welcomed Bollinger and made ready a place for him. He then served an excellent dinner and after dinner began to put the two officers' cots outside.

'Oh, don't do that, we shall sleep inside.'

'It will be damned hot, almost as hot as in your saloon below.'

'Oh no, we shall leave the windows open and so get a through draught. The stationmaster tells me that the place is alive with scorpions and one may well get stung if one sleeps outside.'

Sinclair looked towards the khansama, but he made no objection, so Sinclair said 'Very well; but it will be so hot that we shall not get a wink of sleep.'

'Oh well, no matter, we'll play piquet until midnight. After that it will cool down sufficiently for us to sleep indoors.'

'Right-o!' said Sinclair gloomily, wishing Bollinger in the infernal regions.

From nine on the two men played cards and Bollinger deliberately played badly so that Sinclair might win and remain interested in the game. The simple device succeeded and Sinclair was so pleased that at 11 p.m. he was still absorbed in the piquet. Just then someone tried the door, but Bollinger had bolted it. A few seconds later the khansama appeared at the window in front of which had been fixed wire netting to keep the numerous pigeons from soiling the rooms.

'I have brought iced lemonade for the Sahib,' said the khansama with an obsequious grin. Bollinger thought that he had never seen any man with such an odious expression and his yellow eyes were twinkling as if with some horrible anticipation.

'All right,' said Sinclair. 'I'll open the door.' He rose, and before Bollinger could stop him he had drawn the bolt. Bollinger pushed him aside and flung his weight against the door. It was too late. A huge paw and the muzzle of a monstrous hyena forced their way through the opening. Bollinger brought his knife down with all his strength on the paw. It was too blunt to cut deeply through the hair, but the blow was a heavy one and numbed the brute's limb. A bloodcurdling growl followed and the paw and snout were withdrawn. Bollinger slammed the door and shot the bolt.

'Thank God we got the better of that brute. I fancy we're rid of it for the night!'

Hearing a noise he looked round and cried, 'By God! we're not!' Through a gap in the netting of one of the windows the hyena had forced its head and in a few seconds would have been in the room. This time Bollinger decided to use the point and not the edge of his knife. He made a thrust at the brute's throat. It swung its head aside in time to avoid a fatal stab; nevertheless the knife scored a deep cut in its neck. It gave another bloodcurdling growl, dragged out its head and, with blood streaming from its wound, it raced off laughing in the diabolical way that hyenas do when hurt.

'By Jove! what an escape!' said Sinclair thankfully; 'but I suppose you fight that sort of brute every day.'

'No, thank Heaven, I don't,' and then Bollinger told Sinclair the stationmaster's story and how, on hearing it, he had come to the rest-house to see if his help was needed.

Sinclair went up to Bollinger and shook him cordially by the hand: 'Then my dear chap I owe you my life. I cannot say how grateful I feel. I shall never forget your help.'

The other smiled and said: 'Oh, nonsense! you'd have done the same for me. But, I say, didn't you bring your boy with you?'

'Yes, I did. I wonder where he is. I hope to goodness the khansama has not killed him.'

'Well, we had better go and look but we must be very wary, for if the hyena killed your boy he'll come back.'

'All right, come along. You've got a knife, haven't you? I'm afraid I've got nothing.'

The two men went to the back of the rest-house and there they found below a slight slope the dead body of Sinclair's Goanese servant. His throat was completely torn open. The hyena must have crept up noiselessly to the servant's bed and torn out his throat, killing him instantly. Then it must have again become the khansama and tried to enter the rest-house with the iced lemonade.

Sinclair stood sorrowfully by the dead man, who had been many years in his service and to whom he was greatly attached.

'I say, we can't do anything for the poor chap,' said Bollinger, 'so we had better go straight back to the rest-house. I have a horrid feeling that the brute is somewhere near, coming back to its kill. By God! there it is!'

He pointed to where a huge striped form was galloping straight for them. The two men ran for the rest-house as fast as they could; they only reached it in time through Bollinger throwing his coat at the brute's head and thus gaining a moment's respite.

'I wonder what it will do now,' said Sinclair, but it did nothing. It went slowly back to the body of the Goanese and began to crunch it up, every now and then breaking into screams of diabolical laughter when its neck hurt it.

'I wish to God I had a gun,' said Bollinger, 'but as we haven't let's try to get some sleep. One will sit up and watch while the other lies down. I'll sit up first.'

'All right,' said Sinclair, and lying down on one of the cots fell dead asleep in spite of the heat and his servant's death.

Bollinger sat in a chair and tried as best he could to keep awake. Still he must have dropped off for minute or so, for waking up with a start he saw in the bright moonlight the baleful glare of the hyena's eyes as it stared at him through the wire netting. He drew his knife and ran with a shout towards the netting but the hyena with a growl of fury jumped back and galloped off.

Sinclair woke and hearing what had happened said; 'We must both sit up, otherwise the brute will return and get us.'

The two friends sat and smoked and talked through the weary hours until about 5.30 a.m. when their troubles came to an end. A crowd of Sindis, led by Isarmal, came to the rest-house to see what had happened to the two Englishmen.

'God be praised!' exclaimed Isarmal earnestly. 'Nothing has happened and you are both safe!'

'We are safe, but look at this,' and Bollinger led the crowd of Sindis to the half-eaten remains of the unfortunate Goanese: 'The khansama killed him!'

Isarmal's face grew grim and turning to the rest of the crowd he cried: 'Brothers, we are Sindis. The khansama is a Panjabi and therefore of a race that we hate. He is clearly the reincarnation of Anu Kasai. When the train has gone we must deal with him.'

The two Englishmen walked back with Isramal to the station, where the train was standing; as they walked, Bollinger related the events of the night. Afterwards Isarmal repeated the story in Sindi to the men following him. On reaching the saloon nothing more was said. The two weary travellers got in and Isarmal, as he waved on the train, turned to the Sindis, who were mostly Musulmans, and cried: 'The Sahibs are safe, *Alhamdelilla* (God be praised)!'

After a hot, slow journey the Englishmen reached Karachi. On the way Bollinger said: 'I fancy the khansama has had a bad quarter of an hour. He is Panjabi and as Isarmal said of a race hated by the Sindis.'

'But why do the Sindis hate the Panjabis? I like them.'

'I really do not quite know. Perhaps like French and Germans Sindis and Panjabis live too near together. The Panjabis, too, are bigger men as a rule than the Sindis and they throw their weight about. The Sindis seem very much afraid of them. Indeed I remember hearing a Sindi proverb that says: "If one Panjabi comes, sit still and say nothing. If two come, then pack up your kit at once, abandon your house and clear out." Anyway Panjabis are not liked in these parts.'

'They don't seem to be!'

Two mornings after their arrival, Davidson, the District Superintendent of Police, burst unceremoniously into Bollinger's bungalow and onto the veranda, where he was having his *chota hazri* or morning tea.

'I'm sorry, Bollinger, but I must see you. I have just received an official report from the chief constable of Sehwan to the effect that the villagers, led by the stationmaster, broke into the khansama's house, dragged him out although he was very ill and walled him into the battlements of the old fort. He hints that you know something about it. In the meantime he has arrested the stationmaster, Isarmal I think he calls him.'

'Half a mo', Davidson! I fancy I have a letter from the stationmaster in my morning post. I'll open it.' Tearing open the envelope, Bollinger read aloud the following note, very short and quaintly expressed:

Honoured Sir,

The Chief Constable of Sehwan*, who is a Panjabi, is

---

* Sehwan was at this time a part of Karachi district.

troubling us because of the death of that Anu Kasai, the khansama. After Your Honour's departure we went to his house and found him very ill from a severe wound in the throat. We found in his house the property of the two missing Chota Sahibs; seeing this he became very obstinate and refused to answer our questions. Very soon he died. When dead, we put him where Anu Kasai was walled up. The Sahib knows the facts and will do the needful.

'Well, Bollinger, he says you know the facts, for goodness sake let me have them.'

Bollinger told the full story of the adventure and Sinclair supported him in every detail. Still, as told in an Englishman's house in Karachi, it did not sound very convincing.

'Hang it all, Bollinger! You can't expect me to believe this tale of a werewolf.'

'Well, Isarmal says that they found in the khansama's house the property of those two missing subordinates. That raises a presumption that he is a murderer anyway.'

'The chief constable says nothing about that.'

'He is a brother Panjabi and can scarcely be expected to. Look here, instead of arguing, let's go off and call on the commissioner.* He is Inspector-General of Police, as well as of everything else and we'll abide by his orders.'

'Right-o!' said the district superintendent and at 11 a.m. all three men met to call on Government House.

The commissioner was a big genial man who combined with a very cordial manner a vast amount of commonsense. He greeted all three men pleasantly. Then he turned to the D.S.P. who was in uniform:

'Well, Davidson, what's the trouble?'

---

* The governor of Sind was then called the Commissioner in Sind.

'I think, Sir, Bollinger had better tell you his yarn first and then I'll supplement it with my information.'

'Capital! Go ahead, Bollinger.'

The railwayman repeated his story and Sinclair confirmed it. Then Davidson showed the commissioner his chief constable's report and Bollinger produced Isarmal's letter.

The Commissioner's keen intellect grasped immediately all the facts and came at once to a decision.

'Look here, Bollinger, you can't expect me to accept as gospel your story of the werewolf or werehyena; but the khansama seems to have been a murderer all right. The discovery in his house of the property of the two subordinates points to that. I have often been worried as to what became of them. Again I do not see why we should not believe Isarmal's statement that they did not wall in the khansama until he was dead. Anyway it will be impossible to disprove it; for all the eye-witnesses will support Isarmal. In any case, if you go into the witness box, Bollinger, and tell your adventure with the khansama-cum-hyena, my administration will be the laughing stock of all India. Think how the young lions of the *Pioneer* will sharpen their wit at our expense. No! No, we must stop the prosecution at all costs. Look here, Davidson, you wire to the chief constable to drop the case and release Isarmal and any others he may have arrested. I shall myself transfer to some other district the chief constable; for he seems to have been very slack over the disappearance of the subordinates. Well, good morning.'

Isarmal was duly released and resumed his duties as stationmaster. But Bollinger did not forget him. Using his influence with the railway chiefs, he got Isarmal first promoted to be stationmaster of Radhan and then of Sukkur, a very important post. This Isarmal retained until his retirement. He lived for many years on an ample pension and nothing gave him greater pleasure than to tell the story of the Panjabi who could turn himself into a hyena and how he nearly ate up the two Sahibs. He gave ample credit to Bollinger Sahib for his courage and resource; but the person for whom he reserved the fullest commendation was none other than Mr Isarmal, late stationmaster of Sukkur.

The Tail-Light

F. R. Corson

'Dead men sometimes do tell tales,' said the quiet man in the corner, looking up from his book at a pause in the smoke-room conversation.

Every night since the *Ranpura* had left Bombay he had sat silent in his corner, had smoked one cigar and drunk one peg, before retiring at 10.30 to his cabin. Tall, spare and white-bearded, he was a noticeable figure in an age of smooth chins, and though unknown to most of his fellow-passengers, his seat at the captain's table and the deference shown to him by that officer marked him out as a person of consequence.

'Sometimes,' he went on, while the smoke-room listened attentively, 'sometimes they are permitted to return and to communicate with us, as I have good reason to know.'

'Donald Mackenzie, burra sahib of Bryce and Mackenzie,' whispered a Calcutta merchant to his neighbour. 'He comes out for three months every cold weather.'

'Will you not let us hear the story, Mr Mackenzie?' asked the High Court judge, voicing the general desire. 'I am afraid that I, for my part, am not a believer in the supernatural, but I am open to conviction.'

Mackenzie put down his book, looked at his watch, and carefully lit a fresh cigar before replying.

'When I was a young man in Inverness,' he began, 'I was of your opinion, Sir George; I did not believe in the supernatural, and I laughed at the old men with their tales of wraiths and the second-sight. Well, I know better now; the old men were right.'

'It happened thirty years ago, when I was an engine-driver on the Bengal and Behar Railway, and had only been in the country a few years. I had recently been put on passenger work, and was driving the Benares mail between Howrah and Mogul Sarai, up one night and down the next. One stormy night in the rains I had left Howrah up to time, and was running through the rocky hills beyond Asansol. It was a wild, wet night of pouring rain; the monsoon roared across the open country, and drove in gusts against the windows of the cab, making it very difficult to see the signals. We had passed Madhupur, and were climbing the long gradient beyond, when I caught sight of a red light far ahead, where no light should have been. This section of the line had been the scene of several accidents—was said to have been badly built in the beginning—and we drivers were always on the alert until clear of it.

'Shutting off steam I ran slowly towards the light, which presently resolved itself into a red lamp, carried by a white-clad figure standing in the middle of the track. As the locomotive came to a stand, I leaned from the cab, and shouted to the stranger to tell me what the matter was. There was no reply; the man, a European in a soiled white uniform, gazed at me in silence. In the glare of the headlight his face looked white and drawn; the drill coat, sodden with rain, clung closely to his spare figure; and I saw, with somewhat of a shock, that his right arm was missing. He had set down the red lamp between the metals, but made no attempt to move, so I jumped down from the cab and went forward to meet him. But the sleepers were slippery with rain; I missed my footing and fell heavily. I was up in a moment, but in those few seconds the white figure had gone.

'The head light showed the shining metals, the streaming, rain-lashed ballast, and the red lamp burning quietly in the middle of the track; that was all.

'I was puzzled and angry, for I thought someone was fooling me, but I picked up the lamp and went back to the engine. My Indian fireman seemed very reluctant to take the lamp, which was an ordinary railway tail-light, and besought me to leave it behind.

"Sahib!" he said, trembling and looking fearfully into the

darkness, "that was a *bhut*[*] which we saw, and not a man! It bodes no good to us and I am afraid. Do not take a *bhut's* gift or we shall surely perish."

"Nonsense, Ramjahn," I said angrily, "the sahib came to warn us, and has now gone back along the line. We will go on slowly and keep a good look out. As for the lamp, it is only a tail-light. See! It has the company's mark on it," and I showed him the letters 'B.B.R.' and the number 76321 stamped in the metal.

'He was somewhat reassured, and we moved on slowly, but I was ill at ease. Something was wrong on the line ahead, and I had received a warning, but who was the messenger, and where had he gone? I was no believer in apparitions, and in broad daylight would have scoffed at any such solution; but now, in the windy darkness and the driving rain, I was less confident.

'The man had certainly looked ghastly as he stood on the track. Could there have been an accident? Suddenly came the thought of the bridge, the great, mile-long Sardhana bridge, which lay seven miles ahead. What if the Barsi river, swollen by weeks of rain, had once more proved too strong and had swept away the mighty steel lattice bridge of today as, many years ago, it had destroyed an earlier structure? There was, I knew, no other passenger train due to meet us, but several up-goods were due to cross the bridge that night, and if it were down . . .?

'Resolutely I put away the thought and concentrated on watching the line ahead. By this time we had passed the summit, and were running slowly down the northern side; presently the long embankment of the bridge approach stretched before us.

'There is a station and a signal-box at Sardhana, and as I pulled up beside the latter, the Bengali stationmaster, umbrella in hand, hurried out to speak to me.

"Please to use great caution, Sir," he babbled nervously, "there is unforseen interruption of communication with North Bank. I apprehend calamitous incursion of River Barsi."

---

* Malignant spirit.

"Have you sent a man along the line to investigate?" I asked sharply.

"No, Sir. All subordinates are fearful tonight, and will not go. Besides, No. 17 up-goods is now overdue."

'Apparently the goods train should have passed the signal-box at 1.19, and it was now 2.5.

'There was little to be got from the Babu in his nervous state, so Roberts, the guard, and I decided to see for ourselves, and leaving the fireman on the engine, we set out across the bridge.

'It was not a pleasant walk by any means, and I quite sympathized with the "fearful" Indians as we battled our way through the windy darkness. From time to time, as the screaming gusts roared across the river and threatened to tear us from our hold, we crouched, blinded and deafened, gripping the lattice-work like drowning men.

'Roberts' hand-lamp, and the tail-light which I had brought with me, were soon extinguished, and we had to feel our way through the night, guiding ourselves by the hand-rail along the foot way of the bridge. Below us the river roared hungrily, swirling in foam round the stone piers, and licking upwards to the floor of the bridge, which was vibrating like a tense bow string. It was a tremendous effort to keep moving; I felt dazed and deafened by the never-ceasing roar, and had almost ceased to realize why we were there, when, far ahead, a light came into view.

"Thank God," I whispered, hardly realizing what I was saying,"that must be the North Bank."

'In ten more minutes, more dead than alive, we stood on firm ground, the Sardhana bridge, whole and unharmed, safely behind us. The light I had seen came from a point beside the track, where, in the shelter of a great tree, a dark figure crouched beside a charcoal brazier. Apparently alarmed at our arrival out of the night, the man sprang to his feet, and bolted. Not, however, before I had noticed that he wore a railwayman's belt.

'We had just succeeded in relighting our lamps, and Roberts, who had stumbled over an old tomb half-hidden in the grass, was swearing softly, when we saw a red light moving along the track, and a loud voice hailed us in English out of the darkness.

"Thank God you were stopped, Mackenzie," said the newcomer, when we explained who we were. "I'm Andrews, guard of No. 17 up-goods, which is derailed half a mile up the line. I'm afraid poor Brown is dead; he was pinned under his engine when she turned over. Ahmed Ali, his fireman, jumped clear, and is unhurt, so I sent him off to stop you; he has just come back without his lamp and scared out of his wits, but he seems to have stopped you all right. Where have you left the mail train?"

"We were held up seven miles the other side of the bridge," said Roberts slowly. "We left the train at Sardhana station."

"Seven miles beyond Sardhana!" repeated Andrews unbelievingly. "Why the thing's impossible! The fireman couldn't possibly have got there in time." He turned to the man, who was standing behind him. "Tell me what you did when I sent you to warn the stationmaster at Sardhana, Ahmed."

'The poor wretch was obviously very scared; his teeth chattered and he kept looking over his shoulder into the darkness.

"I will tell the Sahib all I know," he said at last, "but I am in great fear. After the train fell off the line, and Brown sahib was killed, I took the red lamp from the brake van, even such a lamp as this sahib is carrying, and went to warn the stationmaster at Sardhana. But there was a great wind, and I could not cross the bridge, else had I been blown into the river. So I put the lamp in the middle of the track and took shelter under the banyan tree yonder. Thrice was the lamp overset by the wind, and twice did I go and set it up. But when I went the third time, the lamp had gone, and I was sore afraid. Without doubt it was a *bhut* that took it, and men do not fight with *bhuts*! Then, after a long time came these two sahibs out of the night, and I was afraid and ran away."

'While the man was telling his story, I had been thinking of Brown, lying dead under his engine, and suddenly I had an idea.

"Is this the missing lamp?" I asked handing the fireman the one I was carrying.

'The man examined it for a moment, and I saw his hands tremble. "Allah be praised," he exclaimed at last. "Without a doubt it is the very lamp; I remember this twisted wire. But where did the sahib find it?"

'Then I told Andrews how it had come to be in my possession and of my strange encounter with the silent figure in white. At first he was inclined to be sceptical, but after examining the lamp, his tone changed. "Ahmed is right," he said, "for I remember the number of my lamp, and it was 76321. There is no possible doubt that this is the tail-light of the wrecked train, but how it came to be where you found it is a mystery. What is your theory, Mackenzie?"

"My theory is that Brown was trying to save the mail train, and that it was his ghost I saw."

"But Brown is not a one-armed man," objected Andrews, rather taken aback at my suggestion.

"Is it not conceivable that he lost an arm in the wreck?" I rejoined.

"Maybe, but why should he go seven miles up the line to stop you? No, I can't accept your theory, Mackenzie; it is too far-fetched. But it is time we thought about getting word through for a breakdown train. Do you feel like crossing the bridge again tonight?"

"We'll wait till it is light before we cross," said I.

'By now the storm was over, the rain had ceased, and dawn was at hand. We could distinguish the outline of the bridge against the sky, and as soon as it was light enough to think of crossing, Roberts and I left Andrews to return to his train, and started out towards the bridge.

'The river was as high as ever; a turbid, muddy, mile-wide torrent, bearing on its surface trees, houses, animals and flotsam of all kinds.

'Stranded against the third pier of the bridge was a mass of wreckage, from which projected beams and girders; evidently the remains of a considerable structure which had been washed down the river. We were hazarding guesses as to its nature, when Roberts stopped suddenly. "Look at the top of that pier, Mackenzie," he said in a queer, tense voice, "Do you notice anything peculiar about it?"

'I could see nothing wrong and said so. "Come here, then," he said, leading me down the railway embankment till we had a clear view of the bridge. "Now do you see what I mean?"

'From where we stood the line of mighty stone piers stretched like level stepping-stones across the river, whose sliding surface foamed, almost level with their tops! But the third stepping-stone was not level! Its upstream edge was below the water!

"My God, Roberts," I exclaimed, "the pier is giving way, the river has undermined it!"

'It was never satisfactorily established at what hour the mischief started, but there is little doubt that the mail train would have crashed into the river if we had attempted to cross that night. Whoever he was, the one-armed man had saved many lives.

'There is little more to add: Roberts and I returned to Sardhana, and gave the alarm, the mail train was diverted over another route, and engineers came up from Calcutta to inspect the damaged bridge.

'There was an enquiry, of which few details were allowed to reach the public; Brown, the dead driver, was buried at Monghyr, and the incident was forgotten.'

There was silence for a while after Mackenzie finished: then several men spoke together.

'What about the one-armed man, Sir? Did you ever discover who he was? Was it really the driver's ghost?'

Mackenzie finished his peg before replying; then, with an inclination towards the judge, he went on with the story.

'It was never ascertained who the man was, for no one could be found who had seen him that night. The affair had given rise to all sorts of rumours, however, and shortly after the enquiry, I was sent for by the Company's Agent, Mr Rutherford.

"I want to hear your version of what happened on the night of the 23rd of August," he said, when I was shown into his office. "Please give me the whole story."

"Before I begin, Sir," said I, "I would like to know where I stand. Is this another official enquiry?"

'Rutherford was an Aberdonian, and had a fine sense of humour. He laughed, and told me to tell him the whole story, "ghost and all". "I have a good reason for asking," he added with a smile, "May be I ken mair than ye think."

'He listened without comment while I told him the story, then, going to a bookcase he took down a red covered volume, turned to a marked page, and began to read aloud. As nearly as I can recollect this is what he read: "The rainy season of 1875 was notable for a regrettable accident, attended with considerable loss of life, when a span of the newly-built Sardhana bridge was swept away by the flooded Barsi river. The engine and five coaches of a passenger train which was crossing at the time were precipitated into the gap, whereby seventy persons were drowned.

"Among those who lost their lives was Mr Aneurin Edwards, the distinguished engineer who built the bridge. Although the private coach in which he was travelling remained, with six other vehicles, upon the bridge, Mr Edwards went forward to attempt the rescue of those left alive in the forepart of the train. When last seen he was trying to reach some survivors by means of a rope.

"Handicapped by the loss of his right arm, which was mauled by a tiger some years before, he is thought to have fallen, and been trapped by submerged wreckage. The body was recovered seven days later, and buried under a banyan tree on the north bank of the river, where a marble tomb to his memory is being erected at the expense of the Board of Directors."

"That is an extract from the history of the Company," said Rutherford, returning the book to its place. "That Edwards seems to have been a real sportsman: I should like to have met him."

"I rather think I have done so," said I.'

Fritz

Satyajit Ray

After having stared at Jayant for about a whole minute, I could not help asking him, 'Are you well? You appear a little dispirited today.'

Jayant quickly lost his slightly preoccupied air, gave me a boyish smile and said, 'No. On the contrary, I am feeling a lot better. This place is truly wonderful.'

'You've been here before. Didn't you know how good it was?'

'I had nearly forgotten,' Jayant sighed. 'Now some of my memories are slowly coming back. The bungalow certainly appears unchanged. I can even recognize some of the old furniture, such as these cane tables and chairs.'

The bearer came in with tea and biscuits on a tray. I poured.

'When did you come here last?'

'Thirty-one years ago. I was six then.'

We were sitting in the garden of the circuit house of Bundi. We had arrived only that morning. Jayant and I were old friends. We went to the same school and college. He now worked in the editorial division of a newspaper and I taught in a school. Although we had different jobs, it had not made any difference to our friendship. We had been planning a visit to Rajasthan for a long time. The main difficulty lay in both of us being able to get away together. That had, at last been made possible.

Most people go to Jaipur, Udaipur, Chittor in Rajasthan; but Jayant kept talking about going to Bundi. I had no objection for, having read Tagore's poem 'The Fort of Bundi', I was certainly familiar with the name of the place and felt a pleasurable excitement at the prospect of actually seeing the fort. Not many people came to Bundi. But that did not mean that there was not much to see there. It could be that, from the point of view of a historian, Udaipur, Jodhpur and Chittor had a lot more to offer; but simply as a beautiful place, Bundi was perfect.

However, Jayant's insistence on Bundi did puzzle me somewhat. I learnt the reason on the train when we were coming down. Jayant had, apparently, visited Bundi as a child and had always wanted to return after growing up, just to see how far the modern Bundi matched his memories. Jayant's father, Animesh Das Gupta, had worked in the Archaeological Department. His work sometimes took him to historical places, which is how Jayant had had the chance to come to Bundi.

The circuit house was really rather splendid. Built during the time of the British, it must have been at least a hundred years old. It was a single-storeyed building with a sloping tiled roof. The rooms had high ceilings and the skylights had long, dangling ropes which could be pulled to open and shut them. The veranda faced the east. Right opposite it was a huge garden with a large number of roses in full bloom. Behind these were a lot of trees which obviously housed a vast section of local birds. Parrots could be seen everywhere; and peacocks could be heard, but only outside the compound.

We had already been on a sightseeing tour of the town. The famous fort of Bundi was placed amidst the hills. We saw it from a distance that day but decided to go back to take a closer look. The only things that were reminders of the modern times were the electric poles. Otherwise it seemed as though we were back in old Rajputana.

The streets were cobbled, the houses had balconies hanging from the first floor. The carvings done on these and the wooden doors bore evidence of the work of master craftsmen. It was difficult to believe we were living in the age of machines.

I noticed Jayant had turned rather quiet after arriving in Bundi. Perhaps some of his memories had returned. It is easy enough to feel a little depressed when visiting a place one may have seen as a child. Besides, Jayant was certainly more emotional than most people. Everyone knew that.

He put his cup down on the table and said, 'You know,

Shankar, it is really quite strange. The first time I came here I used to sit cross-legged on these chairs. It seemed as though I was sitting on a throne. Now the chairs seem both small in size and very ordinary. The drawing-room here used to seem absolutely enormous. If I hadn't returned, those memories would have remained stuck in my mind for ever.'

I said, 'Yes, that's perfectly natural. As a child, one is small in size, so everything else seems large. One grows bigger with age, but the size of all the other things remains the same, doesn't it?'

We went for a stroll in the garden after tea. Jayant suddenly stopped walking and said, 'Deodar.'

I stared at him.

'A deodar tree. It ought to be here somewhere,' he said and began striding towards the far end of the compound. Why did he suddenly think of a deodar tree?

A few seconds later I heard his voice exclaiming jubilantly, 'Yes, it's here! Exactly where it was before!'

'Of course it's where it was before,' I said. 'Would a tree go roaming about?'

Jayant shook his head impatiently. 'No, that is not what I meant. All I meant was that the tree is where I thought it might be.'

'But why did you suddenly think of a tree?'

Jayant stared at the trunk of the tree, frowning. Then he shook his head slowly and said, 'I can't remember that now. Something had brought me near the tree. I had done something here. A European. . . .'

'European?'

'No, I can't recall anything at all. Memory is a strange business. . . .'

*

They had a good cook in the circuit house. Later in the evening, while we sat having dinner at the oval dining table, Jayant said, 'The cook they had in those days was called Dilawar. He had a scar on his left cheek and his eyes were always red. But he was an excellent cook.'

Jayant's memories began returning one by one soon after dinner when we went back to the drawing-room. He could recall where his father used to sit and smoke a cheroot; where his mother used to knit, and what magazines lay on the table.

And, slowly, in bits and pieces, he recalled the whole business about his doll.

It was not the usual kind of doll little girls play with. One of Jayant's uncles had brought for him, from Switzerland, a twelve-inch long figure of an old man, dressed in the traditional Swiss style. Apparently, it was very life-like. Although it was not mechanized, it was possible to bend and twist its limbs. Its face had a smile on it and, on its head, it wore a Swiss cap with a little yellow feather sticking out from it. Its clothes, especially in their little details, were perfect—belt, buttons, pockets, collars, socks. There were even little buckles on the shoes.

His uncle had returned from Europe shortly before Jayant left for Bundi with his parents. The little old man had been bought in a village in Switzerland. The man who sold him had said to Jayant's uncle jokingly, 'He's called Fritz. You must call him by this name. He won't respond to any other.'

Jayant said, 'I had a lot of toys when I was small. My parents gave me practically everything I wanted, perhaps because I was their only child. But once I had Fritz, I forgot all my other toys. I played only with him. A time came when I began to spend hours just talking to him. Our conversation had to be one-sided, of course, but Fritz had such a funny smile on his lips and a look in his eyes, that it seemed to me as though he could understand every word. Sometimes, I wondered if he would actually converse with me if I could speak to him in German. Now it seems like a childish fantasy, but at that time the whole thing was very real to me. My parents did warn me not to overdo things, but I listened to no one. I had not yet been put in a school, so I had all the time in the world for Fritz.'

Jayant fell silent. I looked at my watch and realized it was 9.30 p.m. It was very quiet outside. We were sitting in the drawing-room of the circuit house. An oil lamp burnt in the room.

I asked, 'What happened to the doll?'

Jayant was still deep in thought. His answer to my question came so late that, by that time, I had started to think that he had not heard me at all.

'I had brought it to Bundi. It was destroyed here.'

'Destroyed? How?'

Jayant sighed.

'We were sitting out on the lawn having tea. I had kept the doll by my side on the grass. I was not really old enough to have tea, but I insisted and, in the process, the cup tilted and some of the hot tea fell on my trouser. I ran inside to change and came back to find that Fritz had disappeared. I looked around and found quite soon that a couple of stray dogs were having a nice tug-of-war with Fritz between them. Although he didn't actually come apart, his face was battered beyond recognition and his clothes were torn. In other words, Fritz did not exist for me any more. He was dead.'

'And then?' Jayant's story intrigued me.

'What could possibly happen after that? I arranged his funeral, that's all.'

'Meaning?'

'I buried him under that deodar tree. I had wanted to make a coffin. Fritz was, after all, a European. But I could find nothing, not even a little box. So, in the end, I buried him just like that.'

At last, the mystery of the deodar tree was solved.

*

We went to bed at around ten. Our room was a large one, and our beds had been neatly made. Not being used to doing a lot of walking, I was feeling rather tired after the day's activities. Besides, the bed was very comfortable. I fell asleep barely ten minutes after hitting the pillow.

A slight noise woke me a little later. I turned on my side and found Jayant sitting up on his bed. The table lamp by his bed was on and, in its light, it was easy to see the look of anxiety on his face.

I asked, 'What is it? Are you not feeling well?'

Instead of answering my question, Jayant asked me one himself.

'Do you think this circuit house has got small animals? I mean, things like cats or mice?'

'I shouldn't be surprised if it does. Why?'

'Something walked over my chest. That's what woke me.'

'Rats and mice usually come in through drains. But I've never known them to climb on the bed.'

'This is the second time I've woken up actually. The first time I heard a shuffling noise near the window.'

'Oh, if it was near the window, it is more likely to be a cat.'

'Yes, but . . . .'

Jayant still sounded doubtful. I said, 'Didn't you see anything after you switched the light on?

'Nothing. But then, I didn't switch it on immediately after opening my eyes. To tell you the truth, I felt rather scared at first. But when I did switch it on, there was nothing to be seen.'

'That means whatever came in is still in the room.'

'Well . . . since both the doors are bolted from inside . . . .'

I rose quickly and searched under the bed, behind our suitcases and everywhere else in the room. I could not find anything. The door to the bathroom was closed. I opened it and was about to start another search when Jayant called out to me softly, 'Shankar!'

I came back to the room. Jayant was staring hard at the cover of his quilt. Upon seeing me, he pulled a portion of it near the lamp and said, 'Look at this!'

I bent over the cloth and saw tiny, brown circular marks on it.

I said, 'Well, these *could* have been made by a cat.'

Jayant did not say anything. It was obvious that something had deeply disturbed him. But it was 2.30 in the morning. I simply had to get a little more sleep, or I knew I would not stop feeling tired. And we had plans of doing a lot of sightseeing the following day.

So, after murmuring a few soothing words—such as, don't worry, I am here with you and who knows, those marks may have been on your quilt already when you went to bed—I switched off the light once more and lay down. I had no doubt that Jayant had only had a bad dream. All those memories of his childhood had upset him, obviously, and that was what had led to his dreaming of a cat walking on his chest.

I slept soundly for the rest of the night. If there were further disturbances, Jayant did not tell me about them. But I could see in the morning that he had not slept well.

'Tonight I must give him one of the tranquillizers I brought with me,' I thought.

We finished our breakfast by nine, as we had planned, and left for the fort. A car had already been arranged. It was almost nine-thirty by the time we reached it.

Some of Jayant's old forgotten memories began coming back again, though—fortunately—they had nothing to do with his doll. In fact, his youthful exuberance made me think he had forgotten all about it.

'There—there's that elephant on top of the gate!' he exclaimed, 'and the turrets! And here is the bed made of silver and the throne. Look at that picture on the wall—I saw it the last time!'

But within an hour, his enthusiasm began to wane. I was so engrossed myself that I did not notice it at first. But, while walking through a hall and looking at the chandeliers hanging from the ceiling, I suddenly realized Jayant was no longer walking by my side. Where was he?

We had a guide with us. 'Babu has gone out on the terrace,' he told me.

I came out of the hall and found Jayant standing absent-mindedly near a wall on the other side of the terrace. He did not seem to notice my presence even when I went and stood beside him. He started when I called him by his name.

'What on earth is the matter with you?' I asked. 'Why are you standing here looking morose even in a beautiful place like this? I can't stand it.' Jayant simply said. 'Have you finished seeing everything? If so, let's. . . .'

Had I been alone, I would definitely have spent a little more time at the fort. But one look at Jayant made me decide in favour of returning to the circuit house.

A road through the hills took us back to town. Jayant and I

were both sitting in the back of the car. I offered him a cigarette, but he refused. I noticed a veiled excitement in the movement of his hands. One moment he placed them near the window, then on his lap and, immediately afterwards, began biting his nails. Jayant was generally quiet by nature. This odd restlessness in him worried me.

After about ten minutes, I could not take it any more.

'It might help if you told me about your problem,' I said. Jayant shook his head.

'It's no use telling you for you're not going to believe me.'

'OK, even if I don't believe you, I can at least discuss the matter with you, can't I?'

'Fritz came into our room last night. Those little marks on my quilt were his footprints.'

There was very little I could do at this except put my hands on his shoulders and shake him. How could I talk sensibly to someone whose mind was obsessed with such an absurd idea?

'You didn't see anything for yourself, did you?' I said finally.

'No. But I could feel distinctly that whatever was walking on my chest had two feet, not four.'

As we came out of the car at the circuit house, I decided Jayant must be given a nerve tonic or some such thing. A tranquillizer might not be good enough. I could not allow a thirty-seven-year-old man to be so upset by a simple memory from his childhood.

I said to Jayant upon reaching our room, 'It's nearly 12 o'clock. Should we not be thinking of having a bath?'

'You go first,' said Jayant and flung himself on the bed.

An idea came to my mind in the bath. Perhaps this was the only way to bring Jayant back to normalcy.

If a doll had been buried somewhere thirty years ago and if one knew the exact spot, it might be possible to dig the ground there. No doubt most of it would have been destroyed, but it was likely that we'd find just a few things, especially if they were made of metal, such as the buckle of a belt or brass buttons on a jacket. If Jayant could actually be shown that was all that was left of his precious doll, he might be able to rid himself of his weird notions; otherwise, he would have strange dreams every night and talk of

Fritz walking on his chest. If this kind of thing was allowed to continue, he might actually go totally mad.

Jayant seemed to like my idea at first. But, after a little while, he said, 'Who will do the digging? Where will you find a spade?'

I laughed, 'Since there is a garden, there is bound to be a gardener. And that would mean there's a spade. If we offered him a little tip, I have no doubt that he would have no objection to digging a bit of the ground near the trunk of a tree at the far end.'

Jayant did not accept the idea immediately; nor did I say anything further. He went and had his bath after a little bit of persuasion. At lunch, he ate nothing except a couple of chapatis with meat curry, although I knew he was quite fond of his food.

After lunch we went and sat in the cane chairs on the veranda that overlooked the garden. There appeared to be no one else in the circuit house. There was something eerie about the silence that afternoon. All we could hear was the noise made by a few monkeys that sat on the gulmohar tree across the cobbled path.

Around 3 p.m., we saw a man come into the garden, carrying a watering can. He was an old man. His hair, moustaches and side-burns had all turned white.

'Will you ask him or should I?'

At this question from Jayant, I raised a reassuring hand and went straight to the gardener. After I had spoken to him, he looked at me rather suspiciously. Clearly, no one had ever made such a request. 'Why, Babu?' he asked. I laid a friendly hand on his shoulder and said, 'Don't worry about the reason. I'll give you five rupees. Please do as you're told.'

He relented at this, going so far as to give me a salute accompanied by a broad grin.

I beckoned to Jayant, who was still sitting on the veranda. He rose and began walking towards me. As he came closer, I saw the pallor of his face.

I did hope we would find at least a certain portion of the doll.

The gardener, in the meantime, had fetched a spade. The three of us made our way to the deodar tree.

Jayant pointed at the ground about a yard from the trunk of the tree and said, 'Here.'

'Are you sure?' I asked him.

Jayant nodded silently.

'How much did you dig?'

'At least eight inches.'

The gardener started digging. The man had a sense of humour. As he lifted his spade, he asked if there was hidden treasure under the ground and, if so, whether we would be prepared to share it with him. I had to laugh at this, but Jayant's face did not register even the slightest trace of amusement. It was the month of October and not at all warm in Bundi. Yet, the collar of his shirt was soaked in sweat. He was staring at the ground unblinkingly. The gardener continued to dig. Why was there no sign of the doll?

The raucous cry of a peacock made me turn my head for a moment and, in that instant, Jayant made a strange sound. I quickly looked at him. His eyes were bulging. He raised his right hand and pointed at the hole in the ground with a finger that was trembling visibly.

Then he asked in a voice turned hoarse with fear, 'What . . . what is that?'

The spade slipped from the gardener's hand. I, too, gaped at the ground, open-mouthed in amazement and disbelief.

There lay at our feet, covered in dust, lying flat on its back, a twelve-inch-long, pure white, perfect little human skeleton.

Anath Babu's Terror

Satyajit Ray

I met Anath Babu on a train to Ragunathpur, where I was going on holiday. I worked for one of the dailies in Calcutta. The pressure of work over the last few months had nearly killed me. I definitely needed a break. Besides, writing being my hobby, I had ideas for a couple of short stories that needed further thought. And I needed peace and quiet to think. So I applied for ten days' leave and left with a packet of writing paper in my suitcase.

There was a reason for choosing Raghunathpur. An old college mate of mine, Biren Biswas, had his ancestral home there. We were chatting in the Coffee House one evening, talking of possible places where one might spend one's holiday. Upon being told that I had applied for leave, Biren promptly offered me free accommodation in Raghunathpur. 'I would have gone with you,' he said, 'but you know how tied up I am at the moment. You won't have any problem, though. Bharadwaj will look after you. He's worked for our family for fifty years.'

Our coach was packed. Anathbandhu Mitra happened to be sitting right next to me. About fifty years of age, not very tall, hair parted in the middle, a sharp look in his eyes and an amused smile playing on his lips. But his clothes! He appeared to have dressed for a part in a play set fifty years ago. Nobody these days wore a jacket like that, or such collars, or glasses, or boots.

We began to chat. It turned out that he, too, was going to Raghunathpur. 'Are you also going on holiday?' I asked him. But he did not answer and seemed to grow a little pensive. Or it may be that he had failed to hear my question in the racket the train was making.

The sight of Biren's house pleased me very much. It was a nice house, with a strip of land in front that had both vegetables and flowers growing in it. There were no other houses nearby, so the possibility of being disturbed by the neighbours was non-existent.

Despite protests from Bharadwaj, I chose the room in the attic for myself. It was an airy little room, very comfortable and totally private. I moved my things upstairs and began to unpack. It was then that I realized I had left my razor blades behind. 'Never mind,' said Bharadwaj, 'Kundu Babu's shop is only a five minute walk from here. You'll get your "bilades" there.'

I left for the shop soon after tea, at around 4 p.m. It appeared that the place was used more or less like a club. About seven middle-aged men were seated inside on wooden benches, chatting away merrily. One of them was saying rather agitatedly, 'Well, it's not something I have only heard about. I saw the whole thing with my own eyes. All right, so it happened thirty years ago. But that kind of thing cannot get wiped out from one's memory, can it? I shall never forget what happened, especially since Haladhar Datta was a close friend of mine. In fact, even now I can't help feeling partly responsible for his death.'

I bought a packet of 7 O'Clock blades. Then I began to loiter, looking at things I didn't really need. The gentleman continued, 'Just imagine, my own friend laid a bet with me for just ten rupees and went to spend a night in that west room. I waited for a long time the next morning for him to turn up; but when he didn't, I went with Jiten Bakshi, Haricharan Saha and a few others to look for him in the Haldar mansion. And we found him in the same room—lying dead on the floor, stone cold, eyes open and staring at the ceiling. The naked fear I saw in those eyes could only mean one thing, I tell you: ghosts. There was no injury on his person, no sign of snake-bite or anything like that. So what else could have killed him but a ghost? *You* tell me?'

Another five minutes in the shop gave me a rough idea of what they were talking about. There was, apparently, a two-hundred-year-old mansion in the southern corner of Raghunathpur, which had once been owned by the Haldars, the local *zamindars*. It had lain abandoned for years. A particular room in this mansion that faced the west was supposed to be haunted.

Although in the last thirty years no one had dared to spend a night in it after the death of Haladhar Datta, the residents of Raghunathpur still felt a certain thrill thinking of the unhappy spirit that haunted the room. The reason behind this belief was both the mysterious death of Haladhar Datta, and the many instances of murders and suicides in the history of the Haldar family.

Intrigued by this conversation, I came out of the shop to find Anathbandhu Mitra, the gentleman I had met on the train, standing outside, a smile on his lips.

'Did you hear what they were saying?' he asked.

'Yes, I couldn't help it.'

'Do you believe in it?'

'In what? Ghosts?'

'Yes.'

'Well, you see, I have heard of haunted houses often enough. But never have I met anyone who has actually stayed in one and seen anything. So I don't quite . . . .'

Anath Babu's smile deepened.

'Would you like to see it?' he said.

'What?'

'That house.'

'See? How do you mean?'

'Only from the outside. It's not very far from here. A mile, at the most. If you go straight down this road, past the twin temples and then turn right, it's only a quarter of a mile from there.'

The man seemed interesting. Besides, there was no need to get back home quite so soon. So I left with him.

*

The Haldar mansion was not easily visible. Most of it was covered by a thick growth of wild plants and creepers. It was only the top of the gate that towered above everything else and could be seen a good ten minutes before one reached the house. The gate was really huge. The *nahabatkhana* over it was in shambles. A long drive led to the front veranda. A couple of statues and the remains of a fountain told us that there used to be a garden in the space between the house and the gate. The house was strangely structured. There was absolutely nothing in it that could have met even the lowest of aesthetic standards. The whole thing seemed only a shapeless heap. The last rays of the setting sun fell on its mossy walls.

Anath Babu stared at it for a minute. Then he said, 'As far as I know, ghosts and spirits don't come out in daylight. Why don't we,' he added, winking, 'go and take a look at that room?'

'That west room? The one . . . ?'

'Yes. The one in which Haladhar Datta died.'

The man's interest in the matter seemed a bit exaggerated.

Anath Babu read my mind.

'I can see you're surprised. Well, I don't mind telling you the truth. The only reason behind my arrival in Raghunathpur is this house.'

'Really?'

'Yes. I had learnt in Calcutta that the house was haunted. I came all the way to see if I could catch a glimpse of the ghost. You asked me on the train why I was coming here. I didn't reply, which must have appeared rude. But I had decided to wait until I got to know you a little better before telling you.'

'But why did you have to come all the way from Calcutta to chase a ghost?'

'I'll explain that in a minute. I haven't yet told you about my profession, have I? The fact is that I am an authority on ghosts and all things supernatural. I have spent the last twenty-five years doing research in this area. I have read everything that's ever been published on life after death, spirits that haunt the earth, vampires, werewolves, black magic, voodoo—the lot. I had to learn seven different languages to do this. There is a Professor Norton in London who has a similar interest. I have been in correspondence with him over the last three years. My articles have been published in well-known magazines in Britain. I don't wish to sound boastful, but I think it would be fair to say that no one in this country has as much knowledge about these things as I do.'

He spoke very sincerely. The thought that he might be telling lies or exaggerating things did not cross my mind at all. On the contrary, I found it quite easy to believe what he told me and my respect for the man grew.

After a few moments of silence, he said, 'I have stayed in at least three hundred haunted houses all over the country.'

'Goodness!'

'Yes. In places like Jabalpur, Cherrapunji, Kanthi, Katoa, Jodhpur, Azimganj, Hazaribagh, Shiuri, Barasat . . . and so many others. I've stayed in fifty-six dak bungalows, and at least thirty *neel kuthis.* Besides these, there are about fifty haunted houses in Calcutta and its suburbs where I've spent my nights. But . . . .'

Anath Babu stopped. Then he shook his head and said, 'The ghosts have eluded me. Perhaps they like to visit only those who don't want to have anything to do with them. I have been disappointed time and again. Only once did I feel the presence of something strange in an old building in Tiruchirapalli near Madras. It used to be a club during British times. Do you know what happened? The room was dark and there was no breeze at all. Yet, each time I tried to light a candle, someone—or something—kept snuffing it out. I had to waste twelve matchsticks. However, with the thirteenth I did manage to light the candle; but, as soon as it was lit, the spirit vanished. Once, in a house in Calcutta, too, I had a rather interesting experience. I was sitting in a dark room as usual, waiting for something to happen, when I suddenly felt a mosquito bite my scalp! Quite taken aback, I felt my head and discovered that every single strand of my hair had disappeared. I was totally bald! Was it really my own head? Or had I felt someone else's? But no, the mosquito bite was real enough. I switched on my torch quickly and peered into the mirror. All my hair was intact. There was no sign of baldness.

'These were the only two slightly queer experiences I've had in all these years. I had given up all hope of finding anything anywhere. But, recently, I happened to read in an old magazine about this house in Raghunathpur. So I thought I'd come and try my luck for the last time.'

We had reached the front door. Anath Babu looked at his watch and said, 'The sun sets today at 5.31 p.m. It's now 5.15. Let's go and take a quick look before it gets dark.'

Perhaps his interest in the supernatural was infectious. I readily accepted his proposal. Like him, I felt eager to see the inside of the house and that room in particular.

We walked in through the front door. There was a huge courtyard and what looked like a stage. It must have been used for pujas and other festivals. There was no sign now of the joy and laughter it must once have witnessed.

There were verandas, around the courtyard. To our right, lay a broken palanquin, and beyond it was a staircase going up.

It was so dark on the staircase that Anath Babu had to take a torch out of his pocket and switch it on. We had to demolish an invisible wall of cobwebs to make our way. When we finally reached the first floor, I thought to myself, 'If wouldn't be surprising at all if this house did turn out to be haunted.'

We stood in the passage and made some rough calculations. The room on our left must be the famous west room, we decided. Anath Babu said, 'Let's not waste any time. Come with me.'

There was only one thing in the passage: a grandfather clock. Its glass was broken, one of its hands was missing and the pendulum lay to one side.

The door to the west room was closed. Anath Babu pushed it gently with his forefinger. A nameless fear gave me goose-pimples. The door swung open.

But the room revealed nothing unusual. It may have been a living-room once. There was a big table in the middle with a missing top. Only the four legs stood upright. An easy chair stood near the window, although sitting in it now would not be very easy as it had lost one of its arms and a portion of its seat.

I glanced up and saw that bits and pieces of an old-fashioned, hand-pulled fan still hung from the ceiling. It didn't have a rope, the wooden bar was broken and its main body torn.

Apart from these objects, the room had a shelf that must once have held rifles, a pipeless hookah, and two ordinary chairs, also with broken arms.

Anath Babu appeared to be deep in thought. After a while, he said, 'Can you smell something?'

'Smell what?'

'Incense, oil and burning flesh . . . all mixed together. . . . ' I inhaled deeply, but could smell nothing beyond the usual musty smell that comes from a room that has been kept shut for a long time.

So I said, 'Why, no, I don't think I can . . . .'

Anath Babu did not say anything. Then, suddenly, he struck his left hand with his right and exclaimed, 'God! I know this smell well! There is bound to be a spirit lurking about in this house, though whether or not he'll make an appearance remains to be seen. Let's go!'

Anath Babu decided to spend the following night in the Haldar mansion. On our way back, he said, 'I won't go tonight because tomorrow is a moonless night, the best possible time for ghosts and spirits to come out. Besides, I need a few things which I haven't got with me today. I'll bring those tomorrow. Today I came only to make a survey.'

Before we parted company near Biren's house, he lowered his voice and said, 'Please don't tell anyone else about my plan. From what I heard today, people here are so superstitious and easily frightened that they might actually try to stop me from going in if they came to know of my intention. And,' he added, 'please don't mind that I didn't ask you to join me. One has to be alone, you see, for something like this . . . .'

*

I sat down the next day to write, but could not concentrate. My mind kept going back to the west room in that mansion. God knows what kind of experience awaited Anath Babu. I could not help feeling a little restless and anxious.

I accompanied Anath Babu in the evening, right up to the gate of the Haldar mansion. He was wearing a black high-necked jacket today. From his shoulder hung a flask and, in his hand, he carried the same torch he had used the day before. He took out a couple of small bottles from his pocket before going into the house. 'Look,' he said, 'this one has a special oil, made with my own formula. It is an excellent mosquito repellent. And this one here has carbolic acid in it. If I spread it in and around the room, I'll be safe from snakes.'

He put the bottles back in his pocket, raised the torch and touched his head with it. Then he waved me a final salute and walked in, his heavy boots clicking on the gravel.

I could not sleep well that night.

*

As soon as dawn broke, I told Bharadwaj to fill a thermos flask with enough tea for two. When the flask arrived, I left once more for the Haldar mansion.

No one was about. Should I call out to Anath Babu, or should I go straight up to the west room? As I stood debating, a voice said 'Here—this way!'

Anath Babu was coming out of the little jungle of wild plants from the eastern side of the house, a neem twig in his hand. He certainly did not look like a man who might have had an unnatural or horrific experience the night before.

He grinned broadly as he came closer.

'I had to search for about half an hour before I could find a neem tree. I prefer this to a toothbrush, you see.'

I felt hesitant to ask him about the previous night.

'I brought some tea,' I said instead, 'would you like some here, or would you rather go home?'

'Oh, come along. Let's sit by that fountain.'

Anath Babu took a long sip of his tea and said, 'Aaah!' with great relish. Then he turned to me and said with a twinkle in his eye, 'You're dying to know what happened, aren't you?'

'Yes, I mean . . . yes, a little . . . .'

'All right. I promise to tell all. But let me tell you one thing right away—the whole expedition was highly successful!'

He poured himself a second mug of tea and began his tale:

'It was 5 p.m. when you left me here. I looked around for a bit before going into the house. One has to be careful, you know. There are times when animals and other living beings can cause more harm that ghosts. But I didn't find anything dangerous.

'Then I went in and looked into the rooms in the ground floor that were open. None had any furniture left. All I could find was some old rubbish in one and a few bats hanging from the ceiling in another. They didn't budge as I went in, so I came out again without disturbing them.

'I went upstairs at around 6.30 p.m. and began making preparations for the night. I had taken a duster with me. The first thing I did was to dust that easy chair. Heaven knows how long it had lain there.

'The room felt stuffy, so I opened the window. The door to the passage was also left open, just in case Mr Ghost wished to make his entry through it. Then I placed the flask and the torch on the floor and lay down on the easy chair. It was quite uncomfortable but, having spent many a night before under far more weird circumstances, I did not mind.

'The sun had set at 5.30. It grew dark quite soon. And that smell grew stronger. I don't usually get worked up, but I must admit last night I felt a strange excitement.

'Gradually, the jackals in the distance stopped their chorus, and the crickets fell silent. I cannot tell when I fell asleep.

'I was awoken by a noise. It was the noise of a clock striking midnight. A deep, yet melodious chime came from the passage.

'Now, fully awake, I noticed two other things—first, I was lying quite comfortably in the easy chair. The torn portion wasn't torn any more, and someone had tucked in a cushion behind my back. Secondly, a brand new fan hung over my head; a long rope from it went out to the passage and an unseen hand was pulling it gently.

'I was staring at these things and enjoying them thoroughly, when I realized from somewhere in the moonless night that a full moon had appeared. The room was flooded with bright moonlight. Then the aroma of something totally unexpected hit my nostrils. I turned and found a hookah by my side, the rich smell of the best quality tobacco filling the room.'

Anath Babu stopped. Then he smiled and said, 'Quite a pleasant situation, wouldn't you agree?'

I said, 'Yes, indeed. So you spent the rest of the night pretty comfortably, did you?'

At this, Anath Babu suddenly grew grave and sunk into a deep silence. I waited for him to resume speaking, but when he didn't I turned impatient. 'Do you mean to say,' I asked, 'that you really didn't have any reason to feel frightened? You didn't see a ghost, after all?'

Anath Babu looked at me. But there was not even the slightest trace of a smile on his lips. His voice sounded hoarse as he asked, 'When you went into the room the day before yesterday, did you happen to look carefully at the ceiling?'

'No, I don't think I did. Why?'

'There is something rather special about it. I cannot tell you the rest of my story without showing it to you. Come, let's go in.'

We began climbing the dark staircase again. On our way to the first floor, Anath Babu said only one thing: 'I will not have to chase ghosts again, Sitesh Babu. Never. I have finished with them.'

I looked at the grandfather clock in the passage. It stood just as it had done two days ago.

We stopped in front of the west room. 'Go in,' said Anath Babu. The door was closed. I pushed it open and went in. Then my eyes fell on the floor, and a wave of horror swept over me.

Who was lying on the floor, heavy boots on his feet? And whose laughter was that, loud and raucous, coming from the passage outside, echoing through every corner of the Haldar mansion?

Drowning me in it, paralyzing my senses, my mind . . .? Could it be . . . ?

I could think no more.

*

When I opened my eyes, I found Bharadwaj standing at the foot of my bed, and Bhabatosh Majumdar fanning me furiously. 'Oh, thank goodness you've come round!' he exclaimed, 'if Sidhucharan hadn't seen you go into that house, heaven knows what might have happened. Why on earth did you go there, anyway?'

I could only mutter faintly, 'Last night, Anath Babu . . . .'

Bhabatosh Babu cut me short, 'Anath Babu! It's too late now to do anything about him. Obviously, he didn't believe a word of what I said the other day. Thank God you didn't go with him to spend the night in that room. You saw what happened to him, didn't you? Exactly the same thing happened to Haladhar Datta all those years ago. Lying on the floor, cold and stiff, the same look of horror in his open eyes, staring at the ceiling.'

I thought quietly to myself, 'No, he's not lying there cold and stiff. *I* known what's become of Anath Babu after his death. I might find him, even tomorrow morning, perhaps, if I bothered to go back. There he would be—wearing a black jacket and heavy boots, coming out of the jungle in the Haldar mansion, a neem twig in his hand, grinning from ear to ear.'

Ghost of Korya Khar*

R.V. Smith

The dirt-path was long and lonely and not a sound was to be heard save the distant howling of jackals. The numerous stars seemed like mute sentinels guarding the portals of paradise; but below, wintry night had enwrapped everything. It was in such a setting that I made my way through the Korya Khar (ravine of the lepers), a few miles from Agra; and the thought of being alone made me nervous. My bicycle was punctured and to seek help in the village could be inviting murder, for it was in the grip of dacoits. So, I tightened the muffler round my ears and clutching the rifle firmly, moved forward with courage and determination.

I had hardly gone a few paces when I kicked up the half-eaten body of a child who must have been buried just a foot or two below, for the bodies of children are not cremated. Consequently, the corpse had been unearthed by jackals. I walked more cautiously now, but stumbled all the same over a skull which seemed to stare at me in the starlight. The hollow sockets probably once contained the smiling eyes of a village belle. But strange are the ways of the world. It now sent a tremor down my spine.

More ghastly sights awaited me on all sides of the cremation ground. I later learnt that it had been brought back into use to cope with the small-pox epidemic which had caught the nearby villages in a death-trap, some forty-five years ago.

As I walked, the night grew more malevolent. At last my legs just refused to carry me and my heartbeats came like a clock gone

* As related by Cyril Thomas, the famous shikari.

crazy. I pushed the bicycle to a nearby tree and sat down with a thump on a platform. I was dog-tired, scared and hungry, and longed for the comfort of my bed and the dinner my mother must have prepared for me. 'She must be worried, poor thing,' I thought, for this was my first night out in the jungle.

I drank a little from my water bottle and munched what remained of the biscuits in my pocket. Slowly my mind became easier and I breathed more freely. I took out the blanket from the bicycle carrier and placing the rifle below my head, lay down on the platform to sleep. But on second thoughts, got up again, for the hindquarters of the wild boar I had shot in the evening still dangled from the bicycle and could have made a good meal for the jackals. So I slung them on the tree and then sleep overcame me.

It must have been midnight when I got up with a start. Someone was pulling the gun from under my head. At first I thought I was dreaming. Then the thought occurred to me that probably it was a dacoit. I stood up, sleepy as I was, trying to pick up the rifle with one hand. But what I saw made me panic. There, grinning at me in the now bright starlight, was a hideous form, half swine and half man. Sweat broke out from every pore of my body and stood in big beads on my forehead. My legs shook and I felt a strange numbness creeping over me. The form confronted me even more menacingly—its grin was now diabolic, while from its snout-shaped mouth gushed forth a bluish flame which scorched my body. I closed my eyes and then opened them again, thinking that the apparition would vanish like a nightmare. But it did not; on the contrary, I saw that it had taken on a more concrete shape. The flame became bluer and by its hellish light I noticed that the fiend's heart and liver hung suspended from his neck, while big red drops of blood dripped from them endlessly like the sands in an hour-glass.

I made as if to move forwards, but he had tightened his hold on the rifle. I tried to pull the gun as hard as I could, but felt it slipping from my grasp. Fear and the fact that the rifle belonged to my cousin, an army officer who had come to spend a few days with the family, lent me new strength and I tugged and pulled at the gun with all my might and clung to it like a man clings to the proverbial straw. I knew that if the gun was lost my cousin might well lose his job, for those were the days of the Second World War. Besides, I had a strong feeling that my life depended on the rifle remaining in my hand. So I struggled harder, for who would like to throw away his life like this? But it was all in vain. The gun seemed to melt in my hands. In desperation I tried to strike him with my left hand, while I clutched the rifle with my right; but my fingers turned painfully backwards every time I tried to hit him.

At last it seemed to me that the gun would be lost and my life in the bargain, for the fiend pulled the weapon so hard that he dragged me along several yards. But I still had two of my fingers on the butt, and just as it was about to slip out of my hand I gasped, 'Oh, God.' And lo, a miracle happened. The apparition was gone in a flash—vanished into the thin air from which it had appeared. But the gun was back in my hands, surprisingly hot to the touch, warmed by the blasts of hell which, it is said, accompany the damned wherever they go.

I stood up dazed, too shaken to do anything and as my senses came back I breathed a silent prayer for deliverance from the Blue Devil's clutches. I passed my hand several times over my hair and over the gun to convince myself that it was still there. I next looked down on the platform where I had lain down to sleep and noticed that it was a grave. Perhaps I had desecrated its occupant by tying the boar's hind-quarters above it. The fiend sprang out of it, I was sure. The thought lent me wings and I ran. This happened long ago: but I still give a wide berth to Korya Khar. It may spring up again, who knows!

The Yellow-Legged Man

Sudhir Thapliyal

It was one of those early spring days in the mountains—brilliant sunshine, blue skies, and the terraced fields golden with ripening mustard. A light wind rocked the wheat crop, and Bhawan Singh of the Garhwal Rifles knew he was home, far away from the battle-fields of France where the trenches stank of death and putrefaction and where the sun never came out of the fog of cordite and mustard gas.

The year was 1918. Garhwal, in the Central Himalayas was thousands of miles from France. But for Bhawan Singh it seemed as if he had left home only a few days ago. He had been gone more than three years and in those days news from home was scarce. Now as he strode along the winding, narrow path that was to take him to his village, all he could think of was home food. His mouth watered at the thought of eating his mother's brown millet rotis of mustard leaves cooked in rich dollops of home-made butter, and the halwa, fine flour fried in butter and sweetened with jaggery. And then to wash it all down, fresh buttermilk!

It had been a long trek from the railhead at Kotdwar. This was his second day on the road. He had hoped to make it to his village by sundown. But now he had to take shelter under a huge oak as a sudden storm darkened the skies and hail beat about him wildly. In his knapsack he had some tinned food but he'd had enough of it in the trenches.

So, while he waited out the storm, he kept thinking of his mother's cooking.

Bhawan Singh also thought about the war. The foolishness of it all. He had joined the army because it was supposed to be his duty and a matter of family honour. His father had served in the same regiment. When the war broke out, in some place he had never heard of, his father said he had to go and help his British masters. In his remote mountain village, Bhawan Singh had never seen a white man. But he got to know them quite well in the trenches. They were just like him. Cannon fodder, they used to call themselves.

The storm died down as suddenly as it had started. He heaved his pack on to his back and set off. Soon, the birds could be heard and the sound of the thrush brought a song to his lips. It had been a long time since he had sung and the first notes didn't ring true. And then, somewhere along the path, he realized that something was wrong; something was missing.

He stopped, looked around. He was a few minutes from his uncle's village. But there was no one bringing the cows and goats home for the night. No smoke from the fireplaces.

It was like approaching a village in Verdun destroyed and abandoned because of the war. The houses were there as he remembered them. But what surprised him was that the village dogs were not barking.

He walked into the silent, empty village, his boots dragging him to his uncle's house where the door stood ajar. He walked in, and everything looked as it always had, except that there was nobody about. Had the whole family gone to work in the fields? But that, he reminded himself, was not possible, as his grandfather never left the house. He was too old to work in the fields and all he could do was look after the babies. However, there were no babies and no grandpa.

What he didn't know was that a bigger scourge than war had swept the Garhwal Himalayas that year. And that was the Bubonic Plague. Village after village had been totally destroyed of all living things, and the green and yellow mustard fields he saw around him were there because they had been planted before the plague. They were now ready for harvesting but there was no one to do the work. Those who had survived had abandoned their mountain homes and fled to the plains. As night fell, he stood in the courtyard wondering what he should do. His own village was just beyond the ridge and he set off for it, hoping all would be well there. As he rounded the path on the ridge he looked down at his village and it seemed as empty and forlorn as his uncle's. There were no lights and no activity. As he remembered it, there should be the sounds of children laughing or crying, people calling in their cows to be locked up for the night, and the occasional barking of dogs as they settled down for their nightly vigil against marauding leopards.

Yet, there was no sound and no light. The wind had picked up a bit and as it raced down the mountainside it sighed and moaned. It was still early for the moon to come up and so it was totally dark as Bhawan Singh felt his way home. It was a path he had known ever since he could walk but even then it seemed a bit unfamiliar to him. On the outskirts was the home of Bethalu, the outcast. As was the custom in those days, all outcasts had to live a little distance away from the main village.

The main path passed above Bethalu's broken-down shack. In the rains the roof leaked because Bethalu never had any money for new slate tiles. In the winter the snow went right down and through the roof. And in the summers you couldn't sleep inside because of the flies and the heat. Looking down at it, Bhawan Singh saw a narrow crack of light. Aha, he said to himself, somebody is around. So he turned back and took the lower path leading to Bethalu's house.

The light was a beacon of hope, a sign of some kind of life.

As he stood before the low, narrow door leading to the shack, Bhawan Singh wondered who could be inside. He called out for Bethalu and a voice from inside asked him to enter. He had to take off his knapsack because the doorway was too narrow, and he left it outside. As he stooped and walked in, he could just make out the figure of a man sitting near a wick lamp. It gave out a faint, yellow light but after the darkness outside, it had a welcome warmth of its own.

There was a peculiar smell about the room but he didn't pay much attention to it. He wanted to know where his family and the other villagers had gone.

'Where have the people gone?' the soldier asked.

There was no reply from the figure crouched in the darkness. Bhawan Singh repeated himself, but again there was no reply.

'Who are you?' he pressed on.

The figure stirred slightly and then, like someone who has not spoken for a long time and is not used to speaking much, said, 'What! Is that you?'

It was a hacksaw of a voice and it set Bhawan Singh's teeth on edge. He felt a shiver run down his spine and the hair on his back stand up. And then he recognized the smell in the room. It was the smell of death and putrefaction.

'Speak up, man,' he shouted, less in anger than in panic.

'Don't be frightened,' the figure said.

'I'm not frightened,' retorted the soldier.

'Ah, yes, but you are,' the figure replied.

At this Bhawan Singh lunged at him. But all he grabbed was thin air. The figure had moved away. And suddenly from behind him he heard wild laughter that filled the room and the countryside. He spun around but there was nothing to see. The young soldier had known fear, but that was of a different kind. Now he went cold all over.

Then the lamp went out and the shack was plunged in darkness. The soldier felt rooted to the spot. He wanted to get out of the shack but his limbs wouldn't move. What finally got him out of his paralysis was the growing stench of death and decay. It filled the room and he could hardly breathe.

On leaden limbs he rose to his feet and, head bent low, moved to the door. He only had a few feet to go but it seemed as though he was running for miles. His breathing was laboured and hard, his chest felt as though it was going to burst.

A little later he found himself flat on his back. Above him the moon was rising over the ridge. He struggled to his feet and looked around. The shack stood there in silent testimony. His knapsack was leaning against the wall where he had left it. He went to it and took out his canteen of water. But there was not a drop in it. Strange, he thought. He had filled it at a spring just before reaching the village, and hadn't touched it after that.

'Thirsty, are you?' boomed a voice. His throat was so dry he couldn't say a word. Then suddenly from out of the darkness a hand reached out with a pitcher full of water. The moonlight bounced off the brass vessel and the soldier grabbed it greedily. He drank his fill. Then, he started to feel hungry.

'Hungry, are you?' boomed the voice again. And this time the soldier didn't say a word. He had got over the initial shock and fright. He was now wondering what was happening to him. He looked into the gloom and saw nothing. All he could hear was the sound of somebody breathing heavily.

Then the voice came again: 'Want your mother's cooking?'

Getting braver and bolder the soldier said: 'Who are you? And can you give me any food?'

And the voice said: 'Wait and see.'

In what seemed like a few minutes there were piping hot mustard leaves cooked in dollops of home-made butter, hot brown rotis of millet and halwa. And to wash it down, fresh buttermilk. The soldier looked at the feast spread before him and could not resist reaching out for it.

The voice said: 'Eat heartily, my boy, eat heartily. . . . '

The soldier sensed a kind of menace behind the offer. By then he had realized that something terrible, something wrong, was going on. He was no longer hungry. All he wanted was to get away from that frightening spot.

He was wondering what to do next when he felt a cold, clammy hand on the nape of his neck. And the voice was urging him to eat before the food got cold. That was more than he could bear, and he bolted like a runaway horse. Into the fields he ran, jumping from terrace to terrace, cutting a wild furrow through the knee-high mustard. And at his heels came the laboured breathing of a man in pursuit. Then the voice: 'You won't get far, my boy. I haven't eaten for days and I don't like my dinner running away from me.'

That spurred the soldier to run as fast as he could. Chest heaving, legs pumping madly, he ran through the mustard fields and from time to time leapt from one terrace to another. And all the time the voice followed him. The soldier was now running out of steam and as he ran he looked around for some place to hide. Then he remembered something his father had told him when he was a child.

'Remember, my son,' the old man had said, 'when you are being chased by an evil spirit, a ghost or a witch, run into the nearest cowshed and grab a cow round its neck. These foul things are mortally afraid of the holy cow. They can never harm you then.'

The soldier recollected that there was a cowshed not too far from where he was. He changed direction and charged towards the shed. As he dived into it he felt a steely grip on one ankle. With his last ounce of energy, and driven by a great fear, he jerked his foot free and fell on the neck of a cow. He hugged her with all his strength and prayed for deliverance from the evil outside.

He was at bay and he knew it. The cow was his only lifeline. Outside, he could hear the deep breathing of a man who has run far and hard. His own breathing was slowly returning to normal but his heart was in his mouth. He also remembered his father telling him that these evil spirits ruled only at night and that by dawn they were gone. He knew he had to hold on till daybreak.

Outside, the voice said: 'That cow won't live long, my son. And when it dies I'll come and eat you.'

The soldier felt for the thick vein running under the cow's neck. The pulse was irregular and faint. Come on, mother cow, he prayed. Don't let me down now. And he began massaging the animal in the hope that it might last out the night. Outside he could hear his pursuer pacing up and down like a soldier on sentry duty.

Bhawan Singh did not know what the time was. All he knew was that he had to keep the cow alive till dawn. If it died, then it was his turn to go. So he worked hard at keeping the cow warm. He rubbed her with wads of straw till his arms ached and he felt he couldn't go on any longer.

And then, in the faint light of dawn, he saw the gradually brightening outline of the door to the cowshed. Outside a howling arose that echoed from hill-top to hill-top. It was a chilling sound, piercing through the soldier's very soul. He clapped his hands to his ears to shut off the sound but he could feel it in his bones. Just like the times when he used to be under an artillery bombardment!

Quiet returned, so suddenly that it was almost painful. A crow cawed somewhere and the cow fell limp in his arms. She had died. He disentangled himself and crawled out into the open. Taking large gulps of the sweet mountain morning air, Bhawan Singh started to get his nerves and mind together. Was it a dream? A nightmare? No, it couldn't be. He looked at his puttees. They were stained yellow from running through the mustard fields.

To further confirm his experience he set off for Bethalu's shack. He stood by the doorway and saw that his pack was still leaning against the wall. He mustered all his courage and entered the dingy hut. Sunbeams streamed through the cracks in the roof. In one corner he saw something laid out, covered in a white sheet.

With the toe of his boot he lifted one corner of the sheet. It was a man. A dead man, and from the smell it seemed he had been dead for some time. He lifted the sheet further until he had uncovered the whole body.

It was totally naked. And the legs were stained yellow from running through the mustard fields.

Topaz

Ruskin Bond

It seemed strange to be listening to the strains of "The Blue Danube" while gazing out at the pine-clad slopes of the Himalayas, worlds apart. And yet the music of the waltz seemed singularly appropriate. A light breeze hummed through the pines, and the branches seemed to move in time to the music. The record-player was new, but the records were old, picked up in a junk-shop behind the Mall.

Below the pines there were oaks, and one oak tree in particular caught my eye. It was the biggest of the lot and stood by itself on a little knoll below the cottage. The breeze was not strong enough to lift its heavy old branches, but *something* was moving, swinging gently from the tree, keeping time to the music of the waltz, dancing . . . .

It was someone hanging from the tree.

A rope oscillated in the breeze, the body turned slowly, turned this way and that, and I saw the face of a girl, her hair hanging loose, her eyes sightless, hands and feet limp; just turning, turning, while the waltz played on.

I turned off the player and ran downstairs.

Down the path through the trees, and on to the grassy knoll where the big oak stood.

A long-tailed magpie took fright and flew out from the branches, swooping low across the ravine. In the tree there was no one, nothing. A great branch extended half-way across the knoll, and it was possible for me to reach up and touch it. A girl could not have reached it without climbing the tree.

As I stood there, gazing up into the branches, someone spoke behind me.

'What are you looking at?'

I swung round. A girl stood in the clearing, facing me. A girl of seventeen or eighteen; alive, healthy, with bright eyes and a tantalizing smile. She was lovely to look at. I hadn't seen such a pretty girl in years.

'You startled me,' I said. 'You came up so unexpectedly.'

'Did you see anything—in the tree?' she asked.

'I thought I saw someone from my window. That's why I came down. Did *you* see anything?'

'No.' She shook her head, the smile leaving her face for a moment. 'I don't see anything. But other people do—sometimes.'

'What do they see?'

'My sister.'

'Your *sister*?'

'Yes. She hanged herself from this tree. It was many years ago. But sometimes you can see her hanging there.'

She spoke matter-of-factly: whatever had happened seemed very remote to her.

We both moved some distance away from the tree. Above the knoll, on a disused private tennis-court (a relic from the hill-station's colonial past) was a small stone bench. She sat down on it: and, after a moment's hesitation, I sat down beside her.

'Do you live close by?' I asked.

'Further up the hill. My father has a small bakery.'

She told me her name—Hameeda. She had two younger brothers.

'You must have been quite small when your sister died.'

'Yes. But I remember her. She was pretty.'

'Like you.'

She laughed in disbelief. 'Oh, I am nothing to her. You should have seen my sister.'

'Why did she kill herself?'

'Because she did not want to live. That's the only reason, no? She was to have been married but she loved someone else, someone who was not of her own community. It's an old story and the end is always sad, isn't it?'

'Not always. But what happened to the boy—the one she loved? Did he kill himself too?'

'No, he took a job in some other place. Jobs are not easy to get, are they?'

'I don't know. I've never tried for one.'

'Then what do you do?'

'I write stories.'

'Do people *buy* stories?'

'Why not? If your father can sell bread, I can sell stories.'

'People must have bread. They can live without stories.'

'No, Hameeda, you're wrong. People can't live without stories.'

*

Hameeda! I couldn't help loving her. Just loving her. No fierce desire or passion had taken hold of me. It wasn't like that. I was happy just to look at her, watch her while she sat on the grass outside my cottage, her lips stained with the juice of wild bilberries. She chatted away—about her friends, her clothes, her favourite things.

'Won't your parents mind if you come here every day?' I asked.

'I have told them you are teaching me.'

'Teaching you what?'

'They, did not ask. You can tell me stories.'

So I told her stories.

It was midsummer.

The sun glinted on the ring she wore on her third finger: a translucent golden topaz, set in silver.

'That's a pretty ring,' I remarked.

'You wear it,' she said, impulsively removing it from her hand. 'It will give you good thoughts. It will help you to write better stories.'

She slipped it on to my little finger.

'I'll wear it for a few days,' I said. 'Then you must let me give it back to you.'

On a day that promised rain I took the path down to the stream at the bottom of the hill. There I found Hameeda gathering ferns from the shady places along the rocky ledges above the water.

'What will you do with them?' I asked.

'This is a special kind of fern. You can cook it as a vegetable.'

'It is tasty?'

'No, but it is good for rheumatism.'

'Do you suffer from rheumatism?'

'Of course not. They are for my grandmother, she is very old.'

'There are more ferns further upstream,' I said.' But we'll have to get into the water.'

We removed our shoes and began paddling upstream. The ravine became shadier and narrower, until the sun was almost completely shut out. The ferns grew right down to the water's edge. We bent to pick them but instead found ourselves in each other's arms; and sank slowly, as in a dream, into the soft bed of ferns, while overhead a whistling thrush burst out in dark sweet song.

'It isn't time that's passing by,' it seemed to say. 'It is you and I. It is you and I . . . . '

*

I waited for her the following day, but she did not come.

Several days passed without my seeing her.

Was she sick? Had she been kept at home? Had she been sent away? I did not even know where she lived, so I could not ask. And if I had been able to ask, what would I have said?

Then one day I saw a boy delivering bread and pastries at the little tea-shop about a mile down the road. From the upward slant of his eyes, I caught a slight resemblance to Hameeda. As he left the shop, I followed him up the hill. When I came abreast of him, I asked: 'Do you have your own bakery?'

He nodded cheerfully, 'Yes. Do you want anything—bread, biscuits, cakes? I can bring them to your house.'

'Of course. But don't you have a sister? A girl called Hameeda?'

His expression changed. He was no longer friendly. He looked puzzled and slightly apprehensive.

'Why do you want to know?'

'I haven't seen her for some time.'

'We have not seen her either.'

'Do you mean she has gone away?'

'Didn't you know? You must have been away a long time. It is many years since she died. She killed herself. You did not hear about it?'

'But wasn't that her sister—your other sister?'

'I had only one sister—Hameeda—and she died, when I was very young. It's an old story, ask someone else about it.'

He turned away and quickened his pace, and I was left standing in the middle of the road, my head full of questions that couldn't be answered.

That night there was a thunderstorm. My bedroom window kept banging in the wind. I got up to close it and, as I looked out, there was a flash of lightning and I saw that frail body again, swinging from the oak tree.

I tried a make out the features, but the head hung down and the hair was blowing in the wind.

Was it all a dream?

It was impossible to say. But the topaz on my hand glowed softly in the darkness. And a whisper from the forest seemed to say, 'It isn't time that's passing by, my friend. It is you and I . . . .'

Around a Temple

R.K. Narayan

The Talkative Man said:

'Some years ago we had a forestry officer in this town who scoffed at things. He was sent down by his department for some special work in Mempi Forest and he had his headquarters here. You know the kind of person. He had spent a couple of years abroad, and after returning home he was full of contempt for all our practices and institutions. He was strictly 'rational' by which he meant that he believed only in things he could touch, see, hear and smell. God didn't pass any of these tests, at any rate the God we believed in. Accordingly to most of us, God resides in the Anjaneya temple we see on the way.

'It is a very small temple, no doubt, but it is very ancient. It is right at the centre of the town, at the cutting of the two most important roads—Lawley Road running east and west and the Trunk Road running north and south; and any person going out anywhere, whether to the court or the college, the market or the Extension, has to pass the temple. And no one is so foolish as to ignore the God and carry on. He is very real and He can make His power felt. I do not say that He showers good fortune on those who bow to Him; I do not mean that at all. But I do mean that it is very simple to please a god. It costs about a quarter-of-an-anna a week and five minutes of prayer on a Saturday evening. Ninety-nine out of a hundred do it and are none the worse for it. On any Saturday evening you can see a thousand people at the temple, going round the image and burning camphor.

'I have said that the temple is at an important crossing and every time our friend passed up and down either to his office or club he had to pass it, and you may be sure, particularly on

Saturday evenings, the crowd around the temple caused dislocation of traffic. Lesser beings faced it cheerfully. But our friend was always annoyed. He would remark to his driver. "Run over the blasted crowd. Superstitious mugs. If this town had a sane municipality this temple would have been pulled down years ago . . . ."

'On a Sunday morning the driver asked: "May I have the afternoon off, sir?"

"Why?"

"When my child fell ill some days ago I vowed I would visit the crossroad shrine with my family . . . . "

"Today?"

"Yes, sir. On other days it is crowded."

"You can't go today."

"I have to, sir. It is a duty . . . . "

"You can't go. You can't have leave for all your superstitious humbugging." The driver was so insistent that the officer told him a few minutes later: "All right, go. Come on the first of next month and take your pay. You are dismissed."

'At five o'clock when he started for his club he felt irritated. He had no driver. "I will do without these fellows," he said to himself. "Why should I depend upon anyone?"

'The chief reason why he depended upon others was that he was too nervous to handle a car. His head was a whirl of confusion when he sat at the wheel. He had not driven more than fifty miles in all his life though he had a driving licence and renewed it punctually every year. Now as he thought of the race of chauffeurs he felt bitter. "I will teach these beggars a lesson. Drivers aren't heaven-born. Just ordinary fellows. It is all a question of practice; one has to make a beginning somewhere. I will teach these superstitious beggars a lesson. India will never become a first-rate nation as long as it worships traffic-obstructing gods, which any sensible municipality ought to remove."

'It was years since he had driven a car. With trepidation he opened the garage door and climbed in. At a speed of about twenty-five miles an hour his car shot out of the gate after it had finally emerged from the throes of gear-changing. It flew past the temple and presently our friend realized that somehow he could not turn to his left, as he must, if he wanted to reach his club. He could only steer to his right. Nor could he stop the car when he wanted. He felt that applying the brakes was an extraordinarily queer business. When he tried to stop he committed so many blunders that the car rocked, danced and threatened to burst. He felt it safest to go up the road till a favourable opportunity presented itself for him to turn right, and then again right, and about-turn. He whizzed past the temple back to his bungalow, where he could not stop, and so had to proceed again, turn right, go up to Trunk Road, turn right again, and come down the road past the temple.

'Half-an-hour later the dismissed driver arrived at the shrine with his family and was nearly run over. He stepped aside and had hardly recovered from the shock when the car reappeared. The driver put away his basket of offerings, took his family to a place of safety, and came out. When the car appeared again he asked, "What is the matter, sir?" His master looked at him pathetically and before he could answer the car came round again: "Can't stop."

"Use the hand-brake, sir, the foot-brake's rather loose."

"I can't," panted our friend.

'The driver realized that the only thing his master could do with a car was to turn its wheel right and blow the horn. He asked, "Have you put in any petrol, sir?"

"No."

"It had only one-and-a-half gallons; let it run it out." The driver went in, performed *puja*, sent away his family and attempted to jump on the footboard. He couldn't. He stood aside on a temple step with folded hands, patiently waiting for the car to exhaust its petrol.

'The car soon came to a stop. The gentleman gave a gasp and fainted on the steering-wheel. He was revived. When he came to, the priest of the temple held before him a plate and said, "Sir, you have circled the temple over five hundred times today. Ordinarily people go round only nine times, and on special occasions one hundred-and-eight times. I haven't closed the doors thinking you might like to offer coconut and camphor at the end of your rounds."

'The officer flung a coin on the tray.

'The driver asked, "Can I be of any service, sir?"

"Yes, drive the car home."

'He reinstated the driver, who demanded a raise a fortnight later. And whenever our friend passed the temple, he exercised great self-control and never let an impatient word cross his lips. I won't say that he became very devout all of a sudden, but he certainly checked his temper and tongue when he was in the vicinity of the temple. And wasn't it enough achievement for a god?'

A Shade Too Soon

Jug Suraiya

After dinner we talked about ghosts.

We were sitting in what had once been the library in the big rambling house. Sitting in that quietly smoking circle, surrounded by the heavy bookcases of law, literature and obscure Victorian memories, which in turn were enclosed, beyond the old walls, by the midnight jumble of north Calcutta, we felt secluded and yet protected. Like children wrapped in blankets and flanked by adults on cold and especially dark nights.

There had been a marriage in the big house, in some complicated off-shoot of the family tree, and Freddy had invited a few of us from the college, chiefly for the dinner which had indeed been fantastic. The flurry of more important guests long over, we sat and talked and smoked in the library.

Freddy, immaculate even now in his silk kurta and intricately pleated dhoti, presided over the conversation. We others, in mundane shirts and trousers, were a little awed of him on that evening of flowing *chadors*, sprinkled rose water and elegant ritual. We almost stopped calling him Freddy.

Relaxing now after the strain of the evening, he still had a quick edge which gleamed through in his punctiliousness, his minute attention to details of hospitality. He was pampering us, with an almost narcissistic delight in his own subtle grace and charm. In his dark hands he held one of the roses which the guests had been given. As he talked he twirled the silver-papered stem, traced the warm red contour of a petal with a fingertip, or dipped his head to the fleeting fragrance. He could easily have been sitting for one of the massive portraits which lined the high walls. There was an almost overpowering sense of dynasty.

Suddenly someone asked, as though on a cue whispered off-stage, 'How old is this house, Freddy?'

He smiled and the flower in his hand stilled.

'Pretty old. My great-grandfather. That one, there. He built it, about a hundred years ago.' He swivelled in his chair, his out-stretched arm with the flower at the end of it a ranging compass, 'All around this was open land and jungle.' Timeless night, fraught with menacing greenness, stole in. Had tigers walked between tapestries of lianas, a growling distance from these dusty panes, while heavy-lidded men drank tea from blue and gilt French china and the voices of women lilted from the inner rooms?

Someone laughed, a mere fraction of an octave too high. 'This place must be haunted.'

'Not,' said Freddy, and his voice was a shade gleeful, 'this particular room.'

We edged our chairs closer together, ostensibly to hear better the round of stories everyone knew was coming.

Dip, as usual, was the first to speak. He told us about an experience, allegedly terrifying, he'd once had while on a shoot in Bihar. It was a long anecdote, lugubrious in its repetition of details which seemed to get nowhere. It contained the standard quota of haunted dak bungalows (one), local people who warned the shikaris not to stay there (no less than three), and the inevitable eerie noises during the nocturnal hours (exact number fortunately unspecified). At the end of the whole thing I doubted whether Dip had been on a shoot in Bihar or anywhere else, let alone seen/heard a ghost there.

Freddy sat patiently through all this, even managing to look politely interested most of the time. Like a star musician in an orchestra who knows that it is his night and is waiting for the prelude to be done with, so that he can launch into his solo turn. And he was in no hurry to start. The conversational circle finally came to a halt in front of him and we all looked at him expectantly, somehow confident that he wouldn't let us down. But he just sat there, quietly smiling and playing with the flower until finally someone had to prompt him, 'How about you, Freddy? Aren't you going to tell us one?'

He looked down at his dark hands where the red flower bloomed and his voice was as smoothly modest as a rose petal.

'Well, I don't know. These murky, elemental goings-on all of you have been describing have no affinity for me. Perhaps it's just that I'm not psychic or something.'

He let the anticlimax sink in. And then, almost casually, 'My father though, you met him this evening, did have a rather odd experience in this house. Years ago, before I was born.'

Freddy's father, of course! We recalled the kindly-looking, quiet-spoken man we had met. His every casual word or gesture was avidly re-examined, loaded in retrospect with a powerful significance. Freddy's father. We should have known.

'What actually happened?' blurted Dip.

And we sat back in our chairs and waited for Freddy, grown suddenly serious, to tell his story.

'My family, as you know, has been living here for four generations. It's a joint family, always has been, and the house has always been full of people. Various aunts, uncles and cousins, their visitors, children, servants. A busy, brightly lit place. Expect during the war years, '39 to '45. And once again somewhat later.

'I think it was sometime in '42 that the Japanese dropped a few bombs on Kidderpore. Comparatively little damage was done, but there was panic in the city. The Burma campaign was going badly for the Allies and people in Calcutta half expected the armies of the Rising Sun to come marching in any day. The bombing was the cinder in the haystack. The trains were packed with people leaving for the safer hinterland. Property prices crashed and they say *paanwallahs* became real estate tycoons overnight.

'Well, my family didn't sell out, but it was decided by my grandfather that everyone should move to the country house, about fifty miles further west. The old man felt, quite rightly, that no one was going to blitz rural areas. So everyone was sent off. No arguments either. The old man, as you can see, was a bit of an autocrat.

'Shortly after the evacuation, my father decided that he had to come to town for a few days for some business. Though he's told me the story twice or thrice he's never told me exactly what business. I don't think there was any. He had been embarrassed at having to leave Calcutta and this was his way of reassuring himself and at the same time showing that the city was not anywhere near as unsafe as some people made it out to be.

'There was quite a ruckus, I believe, but my father had his way and came back to town.

'You should hear his descriptions of the city in those days. Blackouts, of course, and the big houses all deserted and shut up. American and British soldiers all over the place, getting into fights, lording it around. The spooky wail of sirens echoing in the night streets. The way my father tells it, he seems to have enjoyed every minute of it.

'He could have stayed with friends, but probably felt guilty about putting up with those who had remained behind. "Not deserted", as he put it. Anyway, one of the main ideas of coming back was to stay in his own house.

'One or two of the trusted servants had volunteered to stay behind, to look after the place, and they were very happy, though a little worried, to see my father.

'They opened up his room for him, brought him some hurriedly prepared dinner and then he sent them off to their quarters. Incidentally, my father's room is the one behind that door there.'

We turned to look at the door set into the wall at the farther end of the long room.

'Well, he soon settled down for the night. The room was a bit musty, having been shut up all those days, and though he had opened the windows there was hardly any breeze and the atmosphere was very close. He couldn't sleep, so he decided to read a little. But he had brought only a newspaper with him for the journey, and had already finished reading it. There were no books in his room, and this place was locked up. Anyway the reading light would have necessitated shutting the papered panes. So he sat by the darkened window to get what little fresh air there was. The street below was deserted.

'It was then that he heard the sounds. Of someone running, gasping for breath in the corridor just outside. At first he thought it was one of the servants, but no one came to the door. Just the quick, light steps and the snatching gasps, neither nearing nor seeming to retreat.

'The strangeness of it did not strike him even then. He was in his own room, in the house where he had lived all his life. He pulled the door open and stepped out into the unlighted corridor and turned on the light switch just beside the door. She was standing there in the corridor, a girl of about seventeen or eighteen, like a trapped animal twisting around to look at unseen pursuers.

'Even in that moment of shock he realized she was very beautiful. He was a young man then, of course.

'Then someone from the street shouted "Light" and the girl, ignoring my father, ran past him into his room. My father hesitated briefly, but there were no further sounds from the corridor and he switched off the light and turned back to the room.

'She was standing there staring at the door, but even in the pale moonglow he could make out she had not noticed him. In her hysteria of terror, he did not exist for her. And suddenly, as though by contagion, he felt the fear flowing like a cold blue current through his body. And the room was full of the smell of roses.'

Freddy paused, and bent his head to the flower in his hand and I felt the hair on my forearms begin to rise.

'The only sound in that room was the breathing of the girl, harsher and sharper as the panic within her contracted and squeezed. She was crouched forward, every sense, every quivering nerve transfixed by a wordless menace that pressed in closer.

'Then my father shouted. He says now that if he hadn't done that he would have lost his mind—literally. The smell of terror and roses. He doesn't remember the exact words, but it was probably something like "Who are you?" and as though in response the sleeping sirens of the city sprang into screaming life. It was an air-raid alarm.

'The sudden tug of noise jerked his head towards the window, and when he looked around again she was gone. Within a second, with no sound. And the smell of the flowers had gone too.

'He stood there in that empty room while the sirens wailed and fell and rose again. He says now that even if a bomber had scored a direct hit on the house he doubts if he could have registered the situation.

'Fortunately no bombs fell in Calcutta that night, hardly any ever did, you know. And the sirens lulled and then sang out again in the all-clear.

'Finally my father managed to grope his way to bed and sprawled across it, past questioning, past fear, in a state of numb exhaustion. But as I said he was a young man, and a very strong-minded one, and by morning he was as normal as he was going to be for a fairly long time to come. He didn't tell the servants anything except that he was going back earlier than expected. He stayed two or three days more with a friend and then returned to the country house.

'He didn't tell anyone of what he had experienced, even when it was time to return to the city and to his room. He says he slept with the lights on for the first few nights and then it was all right.

'The inexplicable episode, for all its horror, might even have been forgotten, put down as a bad dream induced by post-travel tension. But then in '46 the Hindu-Muslim riots broke out and once again the family was shipped off to the country.

'And that's when it happened. People had become beasts in those terrible days. You've heard about the murders, the atrocities. This area was a sort of no-man's land, bloodily contested by armed groups of both communities. Everyone lived at a taut pitch of suspicion. Every individual was either an ally or a mortal enemy.

'No one knows how or why the girl was in this area. She must have got separated from her family in the chaos of the streets.

'A mob, a Hindu one incidentally, not that it matters, spotted her and chased her. She ran into this house. Perhaps the gates were open or perhaps the old *durwan* opened them for her. They followed her, through the empty rooms and corridors, and they finally found her in the room that was my father's.

'They must have seen by now that she wasn't Muslim. She was not dressed like one and she had vermilion in the parting of her hair and wore a *mala* of lilies and roses. She must have been married a very short time. But they raped her and then they killed her, and when the others came later they said the room had smelled of flowers. Especially roses.'

Freddy paused and turned the flower very slowly, almost languidly, between his fingers. In a voice drained of all tonal colour he said finally, 'Not much of a ghost story, I'm afraid. Most of those have their punch lines in their pasts. This one had its in the future.'

The silence was a hush. Then Dip, the irredeemable, came in, 'But I don't understand it.'

Freddy replied softly, 'Understand? I don't think it is something which one could understand. Call it a particularly vivid premonition. Or a psychical chain-reaction set off by my father's overstrained nerves, and which had a tragic coincidence later. People talk of fields of psychic emanation. Why must these work unilaterally from the past forward? Why not the other way round as well? All I know is my father hasn't used that room since.'

It was very late, and we were all tired; the evening had come to its conclusion. With a rattle of chairs we got up to leave and I casually picked up the cloth-bound book lying on the table. The faded title on the spine said *An Anthology of the Supernatural and Strange.*

I wanted to borrow the book, but Freddy smiled apologetically and said he had borrowed it himself and promised to return it the following day. I smiled in return, but before putting the book down opened it at random. The dried petals had been pressed between the pages and as they scattered across the table left behind a faint but unmistakable fragrance of roses.

Red Hydrangeas

Victor Banerjee

1.00 PM

As Sheila lay in bed a single crystal on the chandelier above her trembled. The footsteps in the hall had stopped. The moon shone straight through the skylight. Its beams falling on the dresser and the lace doily that lay under her sister's photograph: Yes that would make a great story, but this time let me tell it as plainly as it really happened.

*

Ranjit, the erstwhile Abbey cook, lived in the Protestant graveyard. Nobody had the guts to take his place and so no one threw him out. He earned a daily wage whenever he wanted to, and spent the rest of his time stoned on *charas*. He had bitten off his wife's nose when she was unfaithful and, tired of sophistry, had wrapped the Bishop's banquet in its table cloth and flung it down the hill. He once went down to Woodstock school to deliver a package to my daughters and scared the living daylights out of every Christian missionary he passed. A legend in Landour. Ranjit is a self-proclaimed *sanyasi*.

Last autumn, on the 7th of October, it had drizzled all day. By the time evening came around, a sticky fog had descended into the oak forests around us.

I watched a chestnut leaf spiral down and settle on the ground just outside the boundary wall of the graveyard. I was alone, taking an evening stroll. It was half past seven. I remember the time because our dog, Badshah, had been barking into the fog when our little kitten knocked over the onyx timepiece on the dressing table.

I could hear Ranjit's laugh resounding through the deodars

and wondered what was amusing him. As I passed the cemetery gate and looked up a sudden chill wind twisted around the weepy sycamores with a groan. Something caught my sleeve. I turned. A large red tongue, and dirty spiky teeth grinned at me. I could have died, but it was only Ranjit. He was swirling his head and glaring at me through the long strands of matted hair that swished past his face. He stopped and stared deeper, into my guts.

'What's happened?' I asked sheepishly. He grabbed my arm and swung me through the cemetery gate, up to his hut, and set me down, rather unceremoniously, beside the cypress planted in 1870 by H.R.H. the Duke of Edinburgh. Outside his room, there was a fire burning in a hole in the ground. Near it, seated on a broken cane chair, was a young European. Although he looked pale, I could tell from his face, licked as it was by the leaping flames, that he had spent some weeks in our country. Another scholar from the Language school, I thought, arrived in Mussoorie ostensibly for a cultural awakening through Hindi grammar, a bit of 'grassy', and curious forays into the villages of India.

'That's not true,' he said, barely audible over the sizzle and crackle of wet oak. The wind had dropped and the fire burned the mist, its nimbus enveloping the three of us. 'What's not true?' I asked hesitantly.

'I have come here in search of my daughter.' He continued, 'Ranjit knows my little girl.' A sudden roar of laughter from Ranjit startled me. 'She left looking for red hydrangeas and hasn't come back. It's a rare flower, difficult to find, blood red. There used to be some growing here.'

I noticed he held a twisted length of iron railing in one hand.

'I wish the rain would let up. I can't stand the monsoons, the sodden earth makes me feel wet to the bones.' His ashen lips quivered with a soft chuckle. 'I'd love some tea, but can't swallow the stuff Ranjit makes,' I turned around, to find that Ranjit had disappeared.

A mocking laugh rang through the silence and came from far off. There was a sudden crash in the branches above. A dark silhouette scrambled wildly through the tops, and then, disappeared.

A faint whistle oozed from the bubbling sap of a burning log and I squirmed when the stranger casually began to whistle, the same aria. There was something spooky about all this, and I wasn't going to stay to find out what it was. I tried moving but my legs wouldn't respond. I tried to speak, but my tongue had begun to swell.

The ghostly duet grew louder; its pitch hurt my ears. Then the stranger stood up, slowly, and I could feel my heart throbbing behind my eyes, gradually pounding them out of their sockets. The log stopped whistling, but the stranger didn't. As he drew close to me, the sharp air from his pursed lips froze the pores of my skin. I got a cramp under my jaw that jarred my head back in horrific spasms. And then he stopped. The blood rushed back into my face, scalding the skin around my eyes. But I still could not move. Then—.

'Goodbye, Victor,' he said, with a warmth that miraculously soothed every nerve in my body. 'If you see Anna, tell her not to bother about the red hydrangeas.'

He walked away past fallen angels and crumbling urns, tapping the twisted rod against the riding boots I now noticed he was wearing. The mists took him in and then rested on the curling ivy that shone weakly under a vaporous moon.

A barking deer coughed somewhere in the valley. For a moment I wondered what it was that had disturbed the trees above us. I was sure it wasn't a langur but then, what was it? And how and where did it vanish so suddenly? It's a mystery I have never been able to solve. I stepped out of the cemetery and walked back home.

The next morning, Ruskin Bond, a cheerful author of several ghost stories, dropped in for breakfast. I told him about my weird encounter. He paled and grew terribly excited. We decided to go talk to Ranjit, it would only take a few minutes.

We hopped over the boundary wall of the graveyard and could see Ranjit pottering around outside his hut. He saw us coming and burst into peals of laughter, his face artistically covered with the ashes of yesterday's fire.

Suddenly, through a cluster of irises, a piece of twisted metal caught my eye. It had been stuck into a grave whose identical railings had nearly all been stolen and obviously sold for scrap.

'Look,' I said to Ruskin, 'that's it! That's what he was holding in his hand last night.'

The morning dew still sparkled spectrally in the grass and a little drop ran down the length of the metal rod and seeped quietly into the earth. Ruskin had meanwhile cleared the lichen from the headstone and we both stared with disbelief at the words engraved: 'Here lieth Richard Andrew Hughes, Leiut. Col. of the 61st Cavalry, a loving father. Died 7th October 1926. Erected by his loving wife, Mary Anne.' Ruskin gasped as he saw something behind me. I turned quickly, and fell over backwards on him. It was Ranjit, who had quietly crept up on us.

We both laughed uncontrollably, untangled ourselves with enormous relief while Ranjit just stood there, laughing at us. He was pointing a grimy finger at a little mound of grass nearby. I crawled over, still sniggering from the fright we had got and tried to read the broken lettering on the grave. 'In loving remembrance of Anna Marie, our beautiful daughter, aged 6. Died October 2nd 1926. She rests beside her father, who died heartbroken. Erected in deep sorrow by her mother, Mary Anne.' Strangely though, my story doesn't end here.

About a week later, to my utter astonishment, a blood red hydrangea bloomed in our front garden—a flower that exists nowhere else in Mussoorie. I had never spoken to my wife about the happenings of that night and so went straight to Ruskin to discuss the phenomenon. For days we debated whether I should plant cuttings of the red hydrangea near Richard Hughes' grave. Finally, we decided against it.

Is that what Richard would want? Would he not feel cheated to discover his daughter had not returned? Further, was my hydrangea a gift from Richard, or Anna, or both?

This year on the 7th of October, I shall summon up the courage to ask.

*

The chandelier, had begun to sway. Its prisms cast patterns across her sister's face so it seemed she was drowning, again. The tinkling crystals muffled the steps that were coming closer to the door. The moon dipped into a solitary cloud, and the room was drowned in black. Crystals quivered in the dark, but its little alarms could not be heard outside the room.

The handle turned, the door eased open, and the pale face of a little girl appeared around the door. Sheila who was peeping through her duvet with one eye, screamed, 'Get into bed, your brat!'

Anna crept gingerly towards her bed and when she got there, dived under the quilt. The moon reappeared. The little red hydrangeas patterned on Anna's patchwork quilt glowed, while she trembled inside it.

She wished Grandmother would never tell her that story about her times in India again. But she loved the part about Ranjit biting off this wife's nose. Little Anna would never know that her Grandmother, Mary Anne, seated in a cane chair next door, was crying.

Mixed Blood

Ravi Shankar

The moon tugged at his blood making Kuttan fret for Grandfather. He awoke smelling the moonlight in the wind, an abstract liquid smell, full of distant incense and frangipani. In the family temple behind the house, Grandfather was praying late into the night, and he could hear the sacred bells rise and fall in rapid rhythm. And, as always happened on moonlit nights, when he looked out of the window, he saw the woman sitting under the frangipani tree, combing her hair.

She sat looking towards the temple inside which Grandfather prayed, as if she was waiting for him to finish. The temple glowed with a golden smoke, and the living darkness around it seemed to ripple with Grandfather's chants. Outside his window, the countryside was silvery with the moon, but in the corner of the coconut grove where the temple stood, it was always dark.

The woman had hair which reached her feet, and she ran her comb through it in long, slow sweeps. Her ivory comb looked like polished bone in the moonlight. She had her ankles crossed, and her anklets glistened like mating golden snakes. Though he could not see her face, he knew she looked at him from time to time from the corners of her kohl dark eyes, through the fragrant cascade of her hair, and he knew that her smile would be moist and white against her betel red lips. Grandfather had finished his prayer. His body glistened with sacred oil, and his loincloth was red like blood. The woman shifted imperceptibly, it seemed to Kuttan that she was uncoiling herself. Kuttan saw that Grandfather was smiling, and as he passed her, he paused to pick something up from the ground. It was an ivory flower, which he placed among the black curls of her hair. She rested her cheek against Grandfather's palm, and her hair spilled over Grandfather's forearm on to the ground, swirling among the fallen frangipani flowers. He felt they were looking at him, Grandfather with his small and secret smile, she covertly from beneath the curtain of her hair. And that look reached out to him with a satin darkness, involving him in a complicity he felt but could not fully comprehend.

When Grandfather came to bed, he asked him about her. As he had asked him many times before.

'Is she a yakshi, Grandfather?'

'What do you know about yakshis, little one?'

'The servants talk about the yakshi under the frangipani tree, Grandfather. They say she'll get them if they go out in the dark. Does the yakshi live under the frangipani tree.'

Grandfather stroked his hair gently, making him feel sleepy. His fingers smelt of frangipani flower, and fragrant hair. Kuttan's blood stirred. Outside, the nightwind raised the ravens from their nests, sending them flying in disturbed, noisy circles, showering the waters of the village ponds with dead leaves, surging across the black palms which grew on the hillsides and among the paddy fields.

'The yakshis sleep on the black palm tops, Kuttan,' Grandfather's voice was a slow, fond whisper, 'and when the moon is full, they wait at the crossroads for travellers.

'They have eyes like the night, skin like moonlight, lips wet and red like clean blood. Their hair is like a waterfall at night.

'Watch their feet, Kuttan,' Grandfather said, 'they never touch the ground. And when the yakshi meets a traveller, she will ask him for betelnut and vettila. And he who gives is lost.'

'What happens to them, Grandfather?'

'They are borne aloft to her nest on the black palm. In the morning all that will be left will be hair and bones.'

'Will they feast on me too, Grandfather?'

Grandfather smiled his secret smile, the one that was always on his lips when he came away from the temple at night.

'You are my blood, Kuttan,' Grandfather said, 'you are family.'

Kuttan felt safe, snuggling up to Grandfather's chest, which smelt of sandalwood and holy ash mingling with Grandfather's odour which was musky and strong. The cicadas and nightbirds came to him in the nightwind, which had the crispness of the distant rain. He knew he would dream of her that night, as he did on most, under the frangipani tree, combing her hair, teasing him with the hidden look. He never mentioned his dream to Grandfather, but he could tell by Grandfather's secret smile that he knew about it.

Grandfather was very tall, and the hair on his chest was still black. Every evening, Grandfather would take him for a bath in the temple pond. They would walk through the road which lay across the lands they owned, and people they met on their way would step aside, avert their eyes, and cover their faces with their shouldercloth. It was forbidden to look on Grandfather's face, and Kuttan suspected it was more than the rules of caste which forced them to look on the ground. It was fear.

They would walk along the cinnabar road which ran like winding serpent through the emerald paddy and black palms. In the near distance bullock carts swam through the sunset, the lanterns in their underbellies swaying in the dusk. Night would gather slowly, darkening the stone steps which led from the temples into the water; in the gloaming the waters of the pond were black and cold, and the reflection of the banyan tree which grew above on the bank was like a Shaivite silhouette, the long roots swaying and curling in the wind. It was the cursed hour, the villagers said, and no one bathed when the three hours met upon the water.

'This is supposed to be the hour of the *brahmarakshas*,' Grandfather said to Kuttan one evening as they walked to the temple tarn for their bath. Kuttan shivered, for an angry wind had suddenly sprung up. It seemed to flow down from the banyan tree, which Grandfather said was the haunt of the *brahmarakshas*, the soul of the brahmin virgin who had died, unfulfilled. The wind licked at his bones and left him deathly cold. But now Grandfather frowned, and raised his hand, commanding the wind to be still. And Kuttan felt the wind leave him, and spread howling with helpless malice across the paddy and the bamboo groves like a cold scythe, bending the black palms, putting out the light in the villagers' huts, fanning the fires in the forests of the hills. Later that night, in his dreams, he saw the wind again, like a pale woman with streaming, translucent hair and eyes without pupils.

Dreaming on in restless sleep, other familiars from other nights came to visit: the dark stranger who always stood in the shadows among the lanes which were full of foliage and shade; the presence who stood on the veranda of a distant, dead house, looking out into the night, waiting for he did not know whom. And the most disquieting dream of all, in which his sleep was cradled in hair perfumed with ivory flowers, while he sucked on a cold, blue-veined teat which was full of warm rich blood. He came awake, as he always did when this dream enveloped him, but Grandfather was instantly by his side, patting him back to sleep: 'Rest, little one, it is not yet time to wake up.'

He knew it wasn't time. Meanwhile he would spend the days of his happy, though somewhat lonely, childhood with his grandfather, walking through coconut graves and paddy fields, running ahead of Grandfather, along the village roads edged with spell-bound people averting their faces, and holding their children closer. He wasn't unhappy, but sometimes Kuttan wished he could play with other children.

He wondered why they wouldn't let him. He wasn't all that different from them. So what if his feet did not touch the ground.

The Little Ones

O.V. Vijayan

The compound bounding our farmhouse was extensive. It sloped down to the south towards the paddy fields, and where it met cultivated land was a hedge full of fruit trees—citrus, pomegranate and guava. Near the hedge was the little hut where old Nagandi-appan, our farm manager, lived. We spoke of him as the manager merely from the persistence of memory, for he had long since ceased to manage the farm. Nagandi-appan's wife and son were dead, and the old man lived on in the farm as a part of its environment. We, the children, who had always seen him on the farm believed that he would be there for all time.

Every evening Nagandi-appan walked along the paddy ridges, as he had in the days when he tended the crops. But he no longer looked after stile or waterway, he carried neither spade nor lantern, he merely walked the ridges. During these journeys, he carried with him a small earthen pot full of palm brew left over from his sundown drinking. He paused every now and then to sprinkle this over the ridges. Neither my father nor mother took notice of this ritual of many years. As a matter of fact, no one in the farm took notice of anything, nor did anyone do anything to manage it, and this included my father; in this state of happy indifference the paddy and the orchard and the cattle grew in fullness and health.

Nagandi-appan was fond of us children. He procured for us forbidden sweets, crude sugar shaped into pencils and onions, peasant delicacies. We went to his hut when the lamps were lit, and sat before him to hear his stories. These, he reminded us, were true; poltergeists encountered in the fields, winged tortoises which dived in and out of streams and tiny serpents who mocked his faltering steps. My sister Ramani and I found these stories more real than our lessons in history.

'Nagandi-appan,' Ramani asked him once, 'what colour are these serpents?'

'Aw,' Nagandi-appan said, 'some are gold, some are silver, and others, turquoise.'

We sat lost in a festival of little snakes, magical and capricious. 'Nagandi-appan,' Ramani asked, 'will these serpents come out to play?'

'Of course, they will.'

'Then shall we call them?'

Nagandi-appan smiled sadly. He said, 'The time is not yet.'

There was no place in Nagandi-appan's story for why it was not yet time. There were no questions in our contented lives, nor in the story of how our farm prospered unmanaged and untended. We spent the greater part of the evening listening to Nagandi-appan and went back home reluctantly for supper. After this we were too tired to open our books. Thus was our education unmanaged and untended like the farm, with neither recitation nor revision.

'My children,' Nagandi-appan once said, 'you will become big and important people. I have done something to ensure that.'

'What, Nagandi-appan?'

'You don't have to pore over your books. They will come and teach you while you sleep.'

'Who?'

Again the quizzical smile, Nagandi-appan said, 'It is not yet time to tell you.'

We grew up. When Ramani came of age she no longer attended the charmed evenings and I went alone to Nagandi-appan's hut. Every night Ramani would have me repeat the stories to her. It was still the poltergeists and tortoises and snakes, but a more mysterious presence now lurked on the fringes of the narration as the days went by. But the time had not yet come for him to tell us what this was. All he did say was that he sprinkled the palm brew to propitiate this presence. Back home we discussed the presence and wondered.

'It must be some creature smaller than a snake,' Ramani said.

'A kind of pest perhaps,' mother said irreverently.

But it was no laughing matter for us children. 'How can it be a pest?' Ramani. 'Our crops are fine. If Nagandi-appan is feeding the palm brew to pests, how can the paddy grow so well?'

Mother put an end to the dispute. 'Why do you waste your time, my children? Let Nagandi-appan keep whatever little creatures he chooses to.

Now it came about that mother was stricken with a paralytic seizure. One leg grew limp. The *vaidyan* began his ministrations. One evening Nagandi-appan made a sacrificial offering of flower and fruit and palm sugar. I sat watching. After the offering he dipped his finger in the earthen pot and sprinkled the palm brew around the room.

'They will go now,' he said. 'They will go to mother and heal her.'

'Who, Nagandi-appan?' I asked, daring to venture into forbidden country. 'The little ones?'

Reluctantly Nagandi-appan conceded, 'Yes.'

That night I dreamt of Nagandi-appan's little ones, minute creatures, luminous and subtle bodies. I saw swarms of them descend on my mother and enwrap her leg like mist. The *vaidyan* had told us that it would take her three months to get well, but her leg was restored in ten days. Neither mother nor we spoke about the little ones. Nagandi-appan made no more offerings but took his earthen pot out to the fields and there propitiated the little ones with the brew.

There was yet another memorable incident. Ramani was seeking admission to the college of medicine. It was when they called her for the entrance examination that she broke down, she was unprepared.

'I won't make it,' she told me, sobbing. 'They will reject me.'

That evening I went to Nagandi-appan and suggested with a sense of absurdity, 'Nagandi-appan, can you send your little ones somewhere for me?'

'Where to?'

'To the medical college.'

'Of course, I could.'

He made the ritual offering of flower and fruit and palm sugar, then sprinkled the brew in the room. 'My little ones,' he spoke to his invisible host, 'go.'

Sobbing and unprepared, Ramani sat for the test and passed. She enrolled in the college of medicine and in five years was a doctor.

And I started working as a factory engineer. Both of us left the farm and went to faraway towns. Once she confided to me, 'When I make an incision, I don't see anything I learnt in the books of anatomy. Often I marvel how all that gets back into place once again, how it heals.'

'The work of nature, I suppose.'

'I don't know. But it keeps reminding me of Nagandi-appan's little creatures.'

In time our parents died, and there was no one left on the farm except Nagandi-appan who had become brittle with age. The farm looked after itself. On one of my visits home, I found Nagandi-appan bedridden. I sat by his bed and talked about the poltergeists and tortoises and snakes in nostalgia. 'But, Nagandi-appan,' I said, 'one thing remains.'

'What is it, my child?'

'You have not shown me the little ones.'

Nagandi-appan's eyes grew distracted, scanning the far spaces. He clenched his fist, and opening it again read the lines on his palm.

'You have come,' he said, 'at the right time. I shall now show you the little ones.'

'Really, Nagandi-appan?'

'Yes.'

'When, Nagandi-appan?'

He read his palm again, and concentrated.

'Tomorrow night,' he said.

I wondered what the old man had seen in his palm; I felt his forehead. 'Nagandi-appan,' I asked, 'are you very ill?'

Nagandi-appan looked at my face and smiled, contented.

'The breeze,' he said.

'What about the breeze, Nagandi-appan?'

'It blows over me. And it is full of the scent of the wild *tulasi*.'

It was a closed room, yet a subtle and aromatic wind, beyond my senses, blew in for Nagandi-appan. Sleep was coming over him, his eyes began to close.

'Rest, Nagandi-appan,' I said.

He looked at me again, intently, and said, 'Let your mind be pure tonight.'

*

In my dreams that night, I sat on a paddy ridge and felt the breeze of the sacred *tulasi*.

The next day, as the dusk darkened over the farm, I went to the hut. Nagandi-appan had grown even more feeble, he struggled to breathe. 'It is time, my child.'

I gazed on the old face in the silent enquiry. Speaking each word with visible effort, he said, 'Go into the compound at the west end and watch the sky.'

I caressed the fevered forehead, and walked out into the compound. I looked to the west. It was a moonless night, and the stars were large and bright. I sent up a childhood prayer, *Little ones, oh my little ones!* Only the stars shone.

Then, slowly, in the far segments of the sky appeared gentle luminescences, soft green and red, glimmering like stardust. They came from the caverns of space rising in infinite multitudes, flying from *mandala* to *mandala* to fulfil the last wish of their high priest. Now they were a deluge, refulgent, dense, another milky way.

'God,' I said, *'Nagandi-appan's little ones!'* I raced back to the hut.

'Nagandi-appan,' I cried out as I ran, 'I saw them!'

I entered the hut breathlessly.

'Nagandi-appan, I saw them!'

But the bed was empty.

The Loving Soul-Atmah

Jaishankar Kala

They were shaking and lurching in a rickety bus on their way to a Yatra of the ancient temples situated in the Himalayas. The bus had just stopped at Haridwar, and they had lunch. Most of the passengers, or pilgrims, were divided out into two buses, about thirty in each. Haridwar is a holy city and through the bus window, a young pilgrim, Sunil, could see hundreds of people bathing in the sacred Ganga. An old bearded Sadhu was singing hymns from the Rig Veda.

When they were about an hour's drive from Deo Prayag, at about 8 p.m., those in the front of the bus suddenly saw and heard in simultaneity, headlights plumetting precipitously down, crashing sounds, human voices wailing. The bus behind them had left the road and plunged down the precipice. It was pitch dark. Himalayan roads, mere winding threads, poorly metalled, have no lights. The ill-fated bus had broken up, strewing its passengers. Most fell right below into the fierce Ganga river; but a few had spilled out, quite close to the road. Some of them clung to trees and shrubs and their cries were heart-rending. The men of Sunil's bus managed to rescue a few. None of them even had a torch. But the bus driver, the only smoker among them, distributed cigarettes, and to their glows they managed to clamber down with the help of a rope and rescue five people. Sunil brought up a girl of fifteen, who died in his arms.

*

Savitri had been fast asleep, head nestled against her elderly aunt. She felt suddenly the untowardness of something that was happening, the feeling instantly accompanied with being tossed out into the dark, straight into a leafy shrub to which her snatching arms clung. In simultaneity to her ejection, and merger with this precipitious shrub, echoes of successive smashing noises, wails and screams, squelched out of the bloated doomed plunging bus, growing progressively fainter. Suddenly the steep hillside sprouted pain. Savitri's limbs and face were gashed, and if she hadn't been entangled in the shrub's branches, she would have slipped and fallen. A sprouting foliage of incredibly wild screams very near her suddenly withered and died. Another, a prolonged scream, as a man fell down the steep hill. The strangest flower, violently erupting, and then its colours all fading. From Savitri who was silent crept out an almost inaudible moan.

After what seemed like a long time a dark form had dangled down hundreds of feet. Drawn by her whimpers. Suddenly the dark blob was upon her, amalgamated with the bush and her limbs. Her life was ebbing. 'Put your arms around my neck,' he murmured. 'Don't let go—you're going to be all right.' Then he jerked his head up and howled 'Pull, Pull!' Her frail arms were entwined chokingly round his neck. They pulled from above, the rope made of shirts, pajamas, sheets, towels, turbans, even the driver's tough army surplus stockings. The shrub now accustomed to her soft suffering body wasn't going to let go of her. He had to tear off the terrible prickly rough branches that held her. They slowly ascended, buffeted in jagged tearing rocks, a bundle swinging on a rope. She was half dead. They brushed the steep hillside, and a huge shape, a dark sweep of erratic eerie flaps dived with deafening cries, deserting a bouquet of pitiful tiny cries. He said: 'Little birds, if you knew how timid and frightened we are, you wouldn't be frightened of us.' She was aware at last of the clamour of voices on top, and she died looking at Sunil's face, for so long just darkness, lit up now by the bus's headlights.

*

Every insect, plant sap, flower, the very stones, let alone humans, were they to pray with a sort of sudden vehemence of urgent desperate yearning to Shiva to spare them, to feel love a while longer, Shiva would, even while caught up in the frenzy of eternal creation through love's ecstasy, fling a scrap of longevity to the insect, to the plant's sap, to a flower, managing not to omit even the pebbles. So declaims a Sanskrit chant. How could Shiva ignore this blood-soaked girl's soul's plea, not to forget her love for her rescuer, and let her linger on a bit. After the pilgrim's bus with the injured had arrived at Deo Prayag, the wounded dropped at the local hospital, Sunil sat on the bed of the rest-house, the hardness of the millimetre-thick mattress assailing his buttocks.

Mr Rajneesh Patel, who had sat next to him in the bus, and now shared the dingy room with dirty walls, was sixty-two, with a winning boyish smile. Savitri's Soul-Atmah, a dab of smokiness stuck in a shape bearing a frayed likeness to herself, invisible to all but a colleague soul, had crept close to Sunil, its head pressed to an arm. Preserving a sort of modesty of undressing, Mr Patel in pursuit of wearing his night clothes had wrapped his towel around his trousers, and was easing the trousers below to the floor. Then he squirmed his pajamas up. Mr Patel was sharing his supper, packed by his daughter-in-law, with him. One bed was vacant. The yellow blankets and sheets, were filthy. The window was wide open, the light of one bulb dim. Sunil, whose arm and head was bandaged, munched, but barely even tasted the food. He was far away. In retrospect it seemed daft to have put oneself at such risk. Yet when puffing away to create a bit of light, all they could risk in lieu of the petrol-soaked hillside, his own life had receded in import. All that mattered was to reach the source of the whimper.

*

The dim bulb laboured, about to be defeated, dimming further. The mosquitoes came, the fan revolved at low voltage, providing them with little inhibition in torturing them. Mr Patel was poor of seeing and hearing. Sunil had washed, changed into his pajamas, and interchanged with Mr Patel a word about the mechanics of waking up early next morning.

'Will you rouse us early?' Sunil howled at Mr Patel, who lay one leg hoisted and crossed on a raised knee.

'What?' he lowered his leg, and his head loomed towards Sunil's mouth that howled a repetition.

'Yes,' Mr Patel broke into a boyish smile. 'But the birds will wake us with their chatter.'

'The only alarm is . . . a natural one . . . of chirping birds,' Savitri thought. She could still think.

Mr Patel gave a loud belch, turned to the wall and started to snore.

No one bothered to turn off the dim light.

From his lying posture Sunil sprang up. He went up to the chair and lifted his coat slung on the wooden back. Out of one of its pockets he took out a tiny box that once contained gramophone needles and was now used for keeping supari. However its present contents bore no resemblance to the crushed fragmented nut. Through the box's dark lips opened a tiny bit, a sort of blackish thread had already squirmed out as if asking for help. Opening the tiny box fully, both hands clawed out, hooked out, this mass of a sort of tiny demented thinly frayed dark fish-like creature. That nestled to his mouth like a warm kiss. And the disaster earlier on, came back, in a sudden flutter and flapping all over his face, like those frightened birds.

Sunil had sat on the long back seat that spanned the whole width, to peer at the silent bundle, between him and the conductor. And even in the dim light of the bus, crawling at tortoise-pace after the accident towards Deo Prayag, his fingers kept coming across long meanders of wiry hair on his pullover. As if the threads were looking for him. Endless dark twinings on his revolving finger, the threads enjoying endless cartwheels, covered in her gore. And the net result of drawing so many tiny circles, he buried in his handkerchief. The hair was transferred into the empty supari box later on.

It was a little after 2 a.m. that Sunil put away the box, and crept under the yellow blanket. But Savitri could feel the liquefying eyes of her rescuer. The hot sensation of his tears meeting hers, wet her cheek. How little her feeling had been tampered with. Yet when she tried to say 'I love you, Sunil,' it wasn't possible. She moved her lips to no sound.

She had snuggled so close to him that his breathing fanned her face. Night was punctuated with Mr Patel breaking wind several times during the night. And there were some obvious advantages in not being full-fledgedly alive. The spirit was spared Sunil's orgy of scratching, his body restless all night owing to the lice in the sheets.

In the whole of the rest-house, not one mirror. There was no question of being able to procure hot water for shaving in the morning. And a flock of lather-covered cheeks, including Sunil's vied for a glimpse of the bus's huge external mirror. This amused the Soul-Atmah.

After his ablutions, Sunil ate his breakfast. Savitri wound an arm round his, as he stared endlessly, leaning on the fence of the gravel and plant-covered courtyard, in front of the rest-house, at the mingling of the two rivers far down below. The Bhagirathi is so effeminate, frolicsome and slender, and the Alaknanda so thunderously forceful and fierce. The poor transparently blue frightened thing merges into union with this grey pitiless roaring mass.

*

The time allowed to Savitri's Soul to linger with her beloved Sunil, was fast getting spent. The pilgrims reached Kedarnath, after a couple of days of rickety bus rides and trekking. It was 5 a.m., bitterly cold, and Savitri had crept into Sunil's haversack. Sunil had just stepped out of the ancient temple built by the Pandavas of the *Mahabharata*. Suddenly Savitri stretched out her hand to touch Sunil's face, as pulling away overtook her. An irresistible pull soared her away—a beggar without legs sang an exquisite hymn, plucking at a one-stringed instrument. It faded for Savitri. All around, watching with intense curiosity, were the snow covered Himalayas. And the distant echo of the Ganga flowing right below mingled with all. Sunil gave the beggar a rupee. Confronting, Shiva's Linga had been a stunning spiritual experience for him. He lingered at the entrance, from where the posterior view of the golden bull's titanic balls assailed him. But it was in the adjoining room, that the greasy-with-oil, huge, mountainous Linga flowered, as if boring through the crux of the universe, to create the sobs and gasps of union, oneness, love, art, death and tumultous life. All the privation he had encountered was forgotten. A strange tearful emotion gripped him. All around him were crowds of pilgrims.

Savitri overtook her colleagues. Soul-Atmahs teeming everywhere. Like a flock of phlegm-coloured flowers. Some were like a badly rubbed blackboard, all but a faded vestige rubbed off. This herd of pales and greys, scattered in abundance like a Pointicist's speckled picture, were suddenly on the move, *en masse*. Shimmering in tremulous motion. One among them still pulsed with the memory of a man she loved.

lingered at the entrance, from where the panoramic view of the golden bull's titanic bulk assailed him. But it was in the adjoining room that the fantasy with all huge monuments [illegible] as a corridor through the [illegible] of the universe, to [illegible] the [illegible] and gasps of union, endless love, art, death and tumultuous life. All the irritation he had encountered was forgotten. A strange powerful emotion gripped him. All around him were crowds of pilgrims.

Soviet [illegible] took their colleagues, [illegible] everywhere like a flock of phlegm-coloured flowers. Some were like a badly rubbed blackboard, all but a faded residue rubbed off. This herd of pales and greys, scattered in abundance like a Pointillist's speckled picture, were suddenly on the move, [illegible] shimmering in tremulous motion. One among them still pulsed with the memory of [illegible] the [illegible]